THE **EX** WHO **CAME** **BACK**

BOOKS BY DANIEL HURST

The Holiday Home
The Couple's Revenge
The Family Trip
The Husband
The Baby Swap
The Couple Before Us

THE PERFECT NURSE SERIES
The Perfect Nurse
The Nurse's Lie
The Nurse's Mistake

THE DOCTOR'S WIFE SERIES
The Doctor's Wife
The Doctor's Widow
The Doctor's Mistress
The Doctor's Child

THE EX WHO CAME BACK

DANIEL HURST

bookouture

Published by Bookouture in 2025

An imprint of Storyfire Ltd.
Carmelite House
50 Victoria Embankment
London EC4Y 0DZ

www.bookouture.com

The authorised representative in the EEA is Hachette Ireland
8 Castlecourt Centre
Dublin 15 D15 XTP3
Ireland
(email: info@hbgi.ie)

ISBN: 978-1-80550-324-8
eBook ISBN: 978-1-80550-323-1

PROLOGUE

I'm in what should be my safe place, yet I've never felt more afraid.

This bedroom, the one that is littered with so many familiar items, should be where I am most comfortable. But as I look at my pale reflection in the mirror, I fail to recognise myself almost as much as I'm failing to recognise this room.

Everything has changed for me.

But things might be about to get even worse.

As I glance at my marital bed, where I have spent so many nights lying beside the man I love, I can't help but fear that soon my husband might be sleeping alone. It makes me feel sad, just as sad as when I think about what might happen to the little boy who sleeps in the bedroom just down the hallway from this one.

My precious son.

What will become of him if I'm no longer here for him?

As my panic rises, I think how not so long ago I had everything. The perfect family: married to the man I love, with a handsome, cheeky four-year-old son. I don't need anything more. I already have it all.

But I'm terrified it's all going to be taken away from me. And I worry that my family is in danger.

I should go downstairs and join them in the kitchen. It's breakfast time and there is a busy day ahead. My To-Do list is: Packed lunches. Emptying the dishwasher. School run. Work commute. *Kill a man.*

It's that last item that is causing me to feel like a stranger in my home. That's because, as I stand here, looking at all my possessions, from clothes to cosmetics to a framed family photo, my eyes ultimately land on the one thing that doesn't belong here.

I pick it up and feel the weight of it, but it still seems so unnatural. I want to throw it away. I want to go back to my life of ordinary domestic bliss. But I can't. I have no alternative. I know my only chance of keeping my family is to use the item in my hand.

Without giving it another second's thought, I hide the knife in my handbag so it won't be seen again until I brandish it. Then I go downstairs to join my family, reminding myself that they can never know what I am about to do.

What I am about to do to save them.

BEFORE

ONE

'We're going to be late.'

I stop what I'm doing and look back at my husband. He is standing at the bottom of the stairs with the car keys in his hand, checking the time on his wristwatch. He's put a coat over his smart shirt, and he has his smart shoes on, so he looks ready to leave the house. I am ready too, wearing a jacket over the pretty dress I've picked out for this afternoon, and the laces on my shoes are fastened into neat little bows.

If it was just the two of us, then we'd already be in the car on the way to the restaurant. But it's not. There's a third person in this house.

And that person is never ready on time.

'Could you help me instead of just standing over there and stating the obvious?' I ask Seth, my clock-watching partner, and thankfully, he comes to provide some assistance. I need all the help I can get. That's because it's time to try and get our four-year-old son to put his shoes on, and seriously, it feels like it would be easier to design a shoe than to get him to wear one.

'Freddie, please. Just stop messing around and let's go,' I say, wishing we could just leave home without a challenge like this on every day of the week.

'Listen to your mother,' Seth adds, showing solidarity, though when have two parents against one child ever been enough?

Freddie stops spinning around and, for a second, I think he might be about to do as we wish. Then I see the familiar cheeky grin spreading across his face and, another second later, he runs off into the kitchen.

'I'll get him,' Seth says, trying his best not to be amused by our child's never-ending energy, and as he goes into the kitchen too, I let out a deep sigh before checking my appearance in the hallway mirror.

I look okay, not my best, but four years of parenting will take its toll on anybody. I love Freddie more than anything in this world and I'd lay down my life for him if I ever had to. But at this moment, I'd lay down my life to get him to put his shoes on and get in the car.

Like Seth, I check the clock. We're going to struggle to make it to the restaurant on time. Everybody else will be on their way there now, but they don't have to get a child into their car, so they are free to go at their own pace.

My parents are meeting us at the restaurant. Bless them, they are through their child-rearing days and know what this is like. When we eventually get there and explain why we are late, they will be sympathetic to my plight. I'm sure they'll also be quick to remind me that I was a handful as a youngster and my mischievous ways were the reason they were late for many a social occasion in the past. My sister, Georgia, will be there too, but she doesn't have kids yet, so she's got absolutely no idea how the simplest of tasks can turn into the biggest chore of the day when little ones are involved. But maybe she will find out sooner than I think, as we're all getting together this afternoon to meet her new man. It will be the first time we've ever met anyone she has been dating. One, because she's quite private, and two, because she doesn't really date, or at least not to the point where the relationship goes beyond the bedroom.

I have always presumed Georgia would stay free and single forever, mainly because she has made it to thirty-six without getting close to putting a ring on her finger. I would love to be a bridesmaid for her one day, like she was for me. More than that, I would love for her to find somebody she truly loves, the type of man who fills her heart like Seth fills mine. Despite my sister's freedom, I wouldn't swap marriage and parenting for anything. And as we have each moved into our late thirties, albeit with her a couple of years behind me, it seemed she was happy with single life and wasn't going to settle down. That's because my sister has never had a long-term relationship. Just one example of how siblings really can be the complete opposite of one another.

As I wait for Seth to hopefully return from the kitchen with our son in tow, I think about how we recently celebrated our three-year wedding anniversary. It was the perfect date night, an early evening meal followed by tickets to see a show at the theatre and rounded off with a nightcap in a cosy cocktail bar. My parents had Freddie for the night, so it was a reminder of our life before our son. We were together for three years before we married, so in total, I've spent the last six years in a committed relationship with Seth.

Well, most of those six years.

As my panic builds, reminding me of the one mistake in my past – the worst thing I've done to Seth, and the thing I regret more than anything else in my life – I act fast to push the memory away quickly, the way I have trained myself to do over the years. Then I decide that we really cannot afford to be any later than we already are, so I grab Freddie's shoes and head into the kitchen with a strong sense of determination.

I find my son being chased around the kitchen table by my

husband. There is another table we really need to be at in the restaurant. But that table will have three unoccupied seats if we aren't there to join my family soon.

'Freddie, please. We need to go. Put your shoes on and get in the car. I won't ask again.'

My desperate parenting prayers are answered when Freddie inexplicably stops playing around and does as he is told, and as Seth and I share a surprised look, our son skips away to the front door, seemingly finally ready to leave. We know better than to tempt fate by not seizing this opportunity when we have it, so we quickly get out of the house and get Freddie into the car and suddenly, we're making progress.

'I'm hungry,' Freddie says from the backseat as I reverse away from our house and steer us onto the road and in the direction of the restaurant. I offered to take driving duties today so that Seth can have a couple of drinks at the meal. We usually take it in turns. Anyway, I'm happy to stay sober this afternoon as it's a Sunday and nearing forty feels like being too old to be starting the week with a fuzzy head.

'Yeah, I'm hungry too,' Seth replies from the passenger seat beside me. 'But we'll be there soon.'

He is right. As we get nearer, his thoughts turn to the person we are about to meet for the first time.

'I hope he likes football,' he says, referring to my sister's mystery new man. 'Or at least some kind of sport. That will make the conversation easier.'

'For you, maybe,' I reply. 'But we don't all like discussing eleven men trying to put a ball in the back of a net.'

Seth laughs. 'Seriously, do you know if he likes football?'

'I'm sure he does,' I reply, although I have absolutely nothing to base that idea on. That's because Georgia has not told us anything about this new guy. All we know is what she wrote in the text message to our family group chat last week.

Can we do a late lunch at Giancarlos next Sunday? There's somebody I'd like you all to meet xx

No sooner had we received that message on our phones than we were all excitedly trying to prise more information out of my sister. We wanted a name. A physical description. A story of how they met. Anything to sink our teeth into. But Georgia kept quiet. That didn't quench our thirst for more information, and while I sent a few teasing remarks to try and tempt my sibling into offering us more info, it was my dad's response that was the funniest. He sent a GIF of a father walking his daughter down the aisle on her wedding day, a joke clearly designed to tease Georgia about the fact that very soon they might be doing it for real. Eventually, the joking stopped, and we all said we would be at the meal and here we are, on our way, ready to meet this potential new addition to our family.

I hope I like him. I'm sure I will. Even if not, the main thing is that my sister is happy, and I guess she must be if she is willing to introduce him to us, a gigantic step for her based on past performance. As the restaurant comes into view, I prepare to walk in and make the best first impression I can. I know Seth will be aiming to do the same. As for Freddie, I'm not sure he's as anxious as we are, but that's just the beauty of being a little kid without a single care in the world.

I find a parking place beside what I recognise is my father's car, and I figure my parents are already inside. Then, as we make our way in, I spot my sister's car too, so I guess she and her new partner are here as well. Unsurprisingly, thanks to Freddie's theatrics back at the house, we're the last to arrive, but we're only five minutes late so it could have been worse.

Seth opens the restaurant door for us and stands aside to let Freddie and me in first, and I smile at my man because he really is a gentleman. Then I look around the busy restaurant to try and spot my family.

There they are. At the big round table over by the window. I see Dad first, which is normal because he's over six feet tall, so his head is always rising above a crowd, even when he's seated. He's wearing his familiar stripey shirt, the one he wears for special occasions. Then there's Mum beside him, looking resplendent in a cream blouse that looks like it might be new. Then I catch a glimpse of my sister, her blonde hair is always capable of turning heads as well as the bright red lipstick that she is well known for always sporting. So that just leaves the other person at the table, although I can't get a proper look at him yet because he is seated with his back to us.

As we approach the table, the only thing I can tell is that he has short, dark hair and looks to be in good physical shape judging by his broad shoulders and the way his shirt fits his physique. If I'd ever had to predict who my sister would eventually partner up with, I suppose I would have picked the traditional type of handsome guy for her – tall, dark and athletic. Maybe they met at the gym. I guess I'll get the full story in just a few short seconds.

'We're here!' Freddie cries as he races up to the table before leaping into his grandmother's arms. As my family members spot us and get up from their seats to welcome us, I put a big smile on my face and prepare to meet this new man.

'Hey sis, thanks for coming,' Georgia says rather formally as we hug. Then we separate and I turn to meet the person she is about to introduce me to.

'This is my sister, Corinne,' she says, introducing me before I'm given the name of the person I'm meeting. 'And this is Mateo.'

The name jars with me as soon as I hear it, but that's not all it does. As I look into the eyes of my sister's new man, I feel my world is about to come crashing down around me. Everything

I've worked hard to build could be gone in the next few minutes.

I have met this man before.

He's the reason I still panic about the one mistake I made in my past.

That's because he *was* my mistake.

He's the man who turned my head, and made me do the one thing I never thought I would.

He made me do something I didn't consider myself capable of doing.

TWO

'Pleasure to meet you,' Mateo says as he leans in to give me a hug.

I feel weak and powerless as he gives me a squeeze before he steps back but maintains strong eye contact. 'That's a lovely name you have. *Corinne.* Am I right in saying it has Greek origins?'

'Erm,' I stumble, lost for words although it has nothing to do with not knowing enough about my name. Instead, it has everything to do with the fact that I am face to face with the one man I hoped I would never see again.

'Yes, it did originate in Greece,' my father chirps up, seemingly pleased that the name he and my mother chose for me as a child is being well received. It usually is. People love my name. I love my name. But I don't love that he is saying my name again. Or that he has found a way into my family and is making out like everything is okay.

'And Seth. It's a pleasure to meet you, buddy,' Mateo says, turning and giving my husband a strong handshake.

As I watch the pair of them interact, I feel like the room is starting to spin all around me. I have to reach out and put a hand on the back of my sister's chair to stop myself from falling over, but thankfully, nobody seems to notice. Certainly not Seth because he is still too busy greeting Mateo. This is bad. Very bad. But things get even worse when Mateo sets his sights on my son.

'Hey, champ. Can I get a hi-five?' he asks Freddie, who is standing a little shyly and staring at this new person.

'Say hello,' Seth tells him, giving Freddie a nudge, and he eventually steps forward and gives Mateo a hi-five.

I want to grab my son and get him out of here. I want to take Seth too. I need this meal to be over before it's even begun. I want to go home and pretend this was all a bad dream and when I wake up tomorrow, I want to shake my head and make the memory of it disappear.

But it's no dream. This is as real as it gets. And the nightmare is only just beginning.

'Can I get you all a few drinks?' an eager waiter pops up and asks us, and as I watch everybody else take a seat at the table, I'm left standing. I still want to leave.

Dad orders some wine, while Georgia opts for a cocktail. Then Mateo asks Seth what beer he recommends here.

As I watch my husband converse with the man I now hate, I realise I can't do this. I have to get away from this table.

'Corinne? What are you having?'

Georgia's question hangs in the air and causes everyone to look at me because I'm now the only one who hasn't given the waiter my order. But I can't even think about a drink. I'm too busy just trying to breathe.

'Erm, I'll just get some water,' I say before looking around for the toilets and spotting them in the far corner of the restaurant. 'I need to go to the ladies' room. Please could you all keep an eye on Freddie while I'm gone. Excuse me.'

I hurry away from the table, passing several other diners, all of whom look happy to be here and are enjoying tucking into their meals on this relaxing Sunday afternoon. But not me. What should have been a nice few hours out of the house has suddenly taken a very sinister turn. Instead of making polite conversation and consuming calories, I'm simply trying to get into the bathroom without having a full-blown panic attack.

I burst into the ladies' toilets and find myself a vacant cubicle before slamming the door shut behind myself and locking it quickly. I press my back against it, as if worried that somebody might try and break in and force me out of here. But I don't hear anybody else enter the bathroom after me. Not my husband or my son or my sister or my parents.

And not Mateo.

But he's still out there. Sitting at that table with my loved ones like he belongs there. Pretending like everything is okay. But that is all he is doing. Pretending. He has to have recognised me. There's no way he can have failed to remember who I am.

I guess he's got more composure than I have.

Or he was expecting to see me?

That thought is a horrible one, but what if it isn't just bad luck that we have crossed paths again? What if this was intentional on Mateo's part?

Has he purposely got with my sister to get closer to me again?

It's taking all my strength not to start hyperventilating in this claustrophobic cubicle, but I'm well aware that I can't stay in here much longer. I need to go back to the table before anybody suspects something is wrong and before Mateo might say anything. A short toilet break is not noteworthy, but a long one invites concern and questions and the last thing I need now is anybody asking me if I'm okay.

At this moment, I'm as far away from okay as can possibly be.

Closing the toilet lid before taking a seat on it, I give myself a pep talk, whispering under my breath and looking for the right combination of words that will allow me to be confident enough to stand up and walk out of here in a minute's time.

No, Mateo did not do this on purpose. It's just sheer bad luck, but right now, the situation is not irretrievable. Nobody suspects a thing. Seth doesn't know what I did.

My secret is still safe.

'Keep it together, Corinne,' I say to myself as I stand up and unlock the cubicle door.

I remind myself that I'm not a bad person and I do not deserve this. It happened in the early stages of my relationship with Seth, before we married, before I knew I wanted to be with him forever. The mistake I made with Mateo was a terrible, out-of-character one, though it made me appreciate what I had with Seth even more and realise he was the one for me.

One mistake shouldn't ruin a life, *should it?*

As I go to leave, I see another woman enter the bathroom, though thankfully, she's not known to me. She gives me a smile before making some harmless comment about how I should absolutely try the prawns because they are delicious. How nice it must be to be able to just sit and enjoy a lovely meal on this fine Sunday afternoon. Instead, I feel nauseous and doubt I'll be able to stomach a single bite of anything.

But for Georgia's sake, I have to try.

I leave the bathroom and slowly start making my way back to my family. But all the way there, *I see him.* Mateo looks like he is already comfortable with my family, holding court, regaling them all with some story. What is he talking about? What is he telling them? I dread to think. But he wouldn't be so stupid as to tell them that he has met me before. He wouldn't blow up whatever he has got going on with Georgia. Would he?

Make no mistake, I need their relationship to end as soon as possible. Because despite how happy my sister might be with him, and as much as I want her to experience love, their relationship is only going to end in tears. But their break-up needs to be for any other reason than because what we did together in the past is exposed. Nobody can know. It will be a disaster if they find out.

Georgia will be heartbroken. My parents will be mortified. Freddie will be confused because he's too young to understand. But Seth is the one I care about the most. If he finds out what happened with Mateo, my marriage is over.

Just before I reach the table, a fleeting but optimistic thought occurs to me.

Based on the fact that Georgia has never been one to settle down and get embroiled in long-term relationships, the odds are that this won't last. Even if Mateo doesn't do the right thing and end things with my sister himself, things will surely fizzle out between them and come to a natural conclusion very soon. I'll just have to bide my time until that happens, if I can't warn Mateo off before then, that is.

'There you are! I was just about to come and check on you,' Georgia says with a smile, and I see that she already has the cocktail she ordered. 'Everything all right, sis?'

'Yeah, fine,' I mumble back as I take my seat and do everything I can to avoid making eye contact with Mateo, who is sitting a couple of places to my left. It's a little easier to do that when Freddie goes to get out of his seat, telling me he wants to go for a walk around the restaurant, but I manage to convince him to stay seated and give Seth a nudge to grab the crayons and colouring book from our bag. But that brief distraction only delays what's next.

'I was waiting for you to get back before I gave you all the news,' Georgia goes on, and I hold my breath as I realise there is some big announcement to be made that I'm probably not going to like.

'Mateo is going to be moving in with me next weekend,' she says proudly, as if this is excellent news that deserves celebrating. But it's not. It's awful news, the worst kind I could have heard.

I was obviously wrong about this relationship being a brief thing.

It's far from over.

Instead, it sounds like it's moving forward faster by the second.

THREE

'That's wonderful news, darling,' Mum says, raising her glass of red wine, and Dad quickly follows suit.

'Well, you certainly both seem happy, so why not?' my father says with a big smile, and I can see how pleased my parents are that Georgia seems to have found somebody she can settle down with. They've both expressed some sadness to me in recent years that I might be the only one of their children to marry and give them a grandchild, so this is all music to their ears. Meanwhile, it's like pure horror to mine.

As much as I am afraid to, I turn to look at Mateo and when I do, I see that he is beaming widely. I keep watching as he reaches out and takes my sister's hand and gives it a squeeze.

What the hell is he doing? Is he toying with her? Using her like a pawn in a chess match, ultimately planning to sacrifice her for some bigger gain? Messing with my little sister's heart whilst simultaneously messing with my head? That's not a game I want anyone to play with my sibling, yet here we are.

'You're moving in together?' I ask, finding my voice through the fear that is threatening to suffocate me. 'Isn't it a bit quick?'

'We're ready,' Georgia replies calmly.

'Yeah, I'd say so too,' Mateo adds.

'How long have you been together?' I have to know.

'A couple of months,' Georgia replies with a shrug.

Mateo grins. 'It's been a whirlwind romance,' he says, still smiling.

'I can't believe you kept it so quiet,' Mum says then with a chuckle. 'It's not like you to be quiet about things, Georgey.'

'I wanted it to be a surprise,' my sister replies.

It's certainly that.

'Plus I wanted to see if it was the real thing,' she adds, turning to look into Mateo's eyes and looking like she could lose herself in there for days. The sight of the pair of them gushing over each other makes me feel sick, but before I can figure out a way to get my family out of here quickly, a waiter appears to take our food order.

As everybody places their request, I glance over at Mateo. And I find he is looking at me too. I quickly avert my gaze, but I can still sense him watching me.

'Corinne?'

'Huh?'

I turn to see Seth staring at me. Then I notice everyone else is looking my way too, including the waiter.

'What are you having to eat?' Seth asks before laughing as if I've suddenly forgotten how a restaurant works. But of course, I haven't. If anything, I'm fully aware of the need to exit this restaurant before tying myself down here anymore. Ordering food would only do that, which is why I don't even look at the menu and instead, turn to look at the door.

'I'm not actually feeling very well,' I say, starting the process of extracting myself from this delicate situation. 'I don't think I should eat anything.'

'What's wrong?' Seth asks me, genuine concern in his voice, which only makes me feel worse. My husband cares so much about me and it's another reminder of how bad he would feel if he knew what I did with Mateo.

'I'm not sure. I think it might be a stomach bug,' I reply, and then I put a hand over my stomach as if to try and add some truth to my lie. I feel like a schoolkid trying all the tricks they can to get out of going to school. I'm sure Freddie can see through my feeble attempts at feigning illness because he's certainly tried all the tricks himself recently, but everybody else around the table seems to buy it. Everybody, that is, except Mateo. He knows why I do not want to prolong this meal any longer than it has to be. But he doesn't say anything, simply sits and watches on with a calm expression on his face.

'You were okay in the car,' Seth comments, which is true, but it's not helpful – he inadvertently casts doubt on what I'm saying.

'It's come on very suddenly,' I try before grimacing slightly. 'I'm really sorry, but I think we're going to have to leave.'

'Oh, that's a shame,' Dad says, disappointed because he's on his first glass of red wine and he'll certainly want more than that.

'You guys stay and enjoy yourselves,' I tell him, realising I don't want them all to leave the table with me. 'But please can you cancel our orders for us? We need to go home right now.'

I turn to Seth as I say that last part, so he is aware that he and Freddie are to come back with me, and fortunately, he doesn't try and change my mind. I rarely get ill so he must be taking this very seriously.

I stand up then and Seth follows, but Freddie stays in his seat.

'I don't want to go home,' he whines. 'I want to stay with Grandma and Grandad.'

'No, we're going home. Come on,' I say, not in any mood for another delay. Every second in Mateo's presence is making me feel worse.

'Can I stay? Pleeeeease,' Freddie tries again. 'I want my pizza.'

'We could bring him home after,' Mum suggests. 'I won't have any more wine, so I can drive.'

That sounds reasonable and Freddie likes the idea of it, but I do not want my son staying here.

'Thank you, but we're all going back together,' I say firmly. 'Freddie. Come on.'

Georgia stands up to give me a hug before we leave, but I don't have time for any of this because Mateo's eyes are still on me. As Freddie continues to stall, I lose my temper with him.

'Stand up now and get in the car!' I shout, hating having to raise my voice to him and it's something I rarely ever do, but I just cannot help it.

The volume of my command causes everyone in the restaurant to go deathly quiet, and now it's not just Mateo who is looking at me but every single person in here.

When I look at Seth, I can see he is shocked at my outburst, just like Freddie is. My little boy is looking very sullen in his seat. But then he gets up and does what I asked him to.

I say sorry one more time to everyone before turning and walking out. As I go, I hear Seth making a few apologies on my behalf. Then I hear him address Mateo.

'It was a pleasure to meet you, mate. Hopefully we get to chat more next time and at least finish our first beer.'

If it's galling to hear my husband talk to him in such friendly terms, the response that comes back is even worse.

'I'm sure there will be plenty of opportunities for us to get to know each other,' Mateo replies.

When I glance back, I see him shaking Seth's hand before slapping him heartily on the back.

How can he do that? How can he be so false? But then I remember that he was always better at that than I was. While I was being torn up by my stupid mistake all those years ago, he was acting as if I had nothing to worry about. I realise then that nothing has changed about Mateo.

As Seth and Freddie finish saying their goodbyes, I leave the restaurant and the fresh air that greets me in the car park is the only thing that stops me from bursting into tears. I just need to hold things together long enough for us to get home. Once we are there, I can tell Seth that I need to go for a lie down on the bed and then, when I'm finally alone, I can cry into my pillow all I want.

Once I've got all those tears out of my system, I can start to make a plan.

My plan will have one simple objective:

To get my sister's new boyfriend out of our lives as quickly as possible.

FOUR

I didn't say much in the car on the way home, under the guise of still struggling with my sudden 'illness'. I hate having to lie and be fake to my family, the people I love the most in this whole world, but I didn't start the lies and the fakery. Mateo has done that, so anything I do from here on out is simply about me trying to figure out Mateo's motive and de-escalate the situation before anybody I care about gets hurt. Seth was mostly quiet too, though he did have to speak a couple of times to get Freddie to stop moaning from the backseat. I feel bad for dragging my son away from the meal because it would have been quality time for him to spend with the rest of his family members beyond his parents. He's also hungry and I've just delayed him getting some food. But I had no choice. I couldn't have spent another second in that restaurant. Mercifully, I made it out of there and all the way home without my secret being spilt.

Now I'm back in our house, I have spent the last couple of hours trying to think of a way that our lives aren't in total disarray. But so far, I've not been able to find a compelling argument against that.

The knock on the bedroom door forces me to stop wallowing and roll over on the bed. Then I hear a tentative voice from the other side of it.

'Are you okay?'

It's Seth, my doting partner, coming to check on my welfare. As the door opens, I see that is not all he has done. He has also brought me a hot water bottle and some pills, as well as another glass of water to go with the one he poured for me just before I came up here.

I rub my eyes and sit up a little on the bed, feeling fortunate that I stopped crying just long enough ago for my eyes to no longer be bloodshot. That would have been a big giveaway that something was seriously wrong because most people don't cry over stomach bugs. Therefore, Seth would have got a clue that there was something else troubling me, something much worse, and I would have hated to have to try and make up another lie.

'I'm feeling a little bit better,' I say meekly as Seth takes a seat on the bed beside me and puts down all the items in the care package he has just brought for me. He notices that I didn't drink the water, but I have taken the first batch of pills he gave me to keep up the appearance of being sick.

I accept the hot water bottle and place it on my stomach before smiling.

'Thank you,' I say, though as I do, tears well up in my eyes because I'm feeling so guilty about having the best man in the world and not deserving him. I'd give anything to go back and change what I did, but I can't, a constant thought that always makes me feel sad.

Seth suddenly notices my tears and looks instantly concerned.

'Hey, there's no need to get upset,' he says as he moves in for a hug to comfort me, and I bury my face in his shoulder because I don't know what else to do.

'I'm sorry,' I say, and I am, although he can't know why I feel that way.

'What are you sorry about?' Seth asks me, and I'm not sure what to say, so he has a guess and fortunately for me, he's wrong.

'Don't worry about the meal, your family will understand,' Seth goes on. 'And Freddie is fine too. He's in his bedroom and he's had a sandwich now, so he's not hungry anymore. And I'm fine, so don't worry about anybody else but yourself, okay?'

I nod my head and wipe my eyes before taking a deep breath and trying to get this wave of emotion to pass. As it does, Seth sits patiently beside me, still the perfect partner and, therefore, still making me feel bad.

'You need cheering up,' Seth decides then with a mischievous grin on his face. 'How about we talk about something fun? Tell me what you think about Mateo.'

'What?' I reply, terrified of the question.

'I'm dying to know your opinion on him. Do you like him? Do you think your parents like him? I mean, he seems nice but what do I know? He likes beer and football, so he's a winner for me. But what about you? Do you approve?'

Seth is blind to the true reason for my anguish and is busy rabbiting on about the very cause of it. He wants me to talk about Mateo. How can I do that openly and honestly without him suspecting something?

'I'm not really sure what to think,' is the best I can come up with.

'I suppose we weren't really around him long enough to get a true gauge of his personality,' Seth says then with a shrug. 'But you must have got a first impression of him? So, what's your view?'

'I don't know,' is my lame response before I realise I need to add something more. 'I don't think it really matters. He probably won't be around for long.'

Seth frowns then.

'Why do you say that?'

'This is my sister we are talking about. Her track record suggests she'll be single again soon. She's just not the long-term relationship type.'

'But he's moving in with her next week,' Seth reminds me, which I don't need him to. 'That tells me it's very serious. And Georgia seems very happy.'

I wish he would stop talking. I don't need an analysis of what I witnessed back in that restaurant because I'm not blind. Yes, my sister is happy and yes, it appears like Mateo is here for the long haul. But just because it's true, it doesn't mean I want to accept it.

'You're happy for your sister, aren't you?' Seth asks me suddenly.

'What?'

'It's just that you don't seem pleased for her, which is weird because you guys are so close, I thought you'd be delighted for her.'

'I'm ill,' I reply tamely, hoping that garners me some sympathy and stops him pestering me over this.

'Yeah, I get that and I'm sorry. But there's something else, isn't there? Something bothering you.'

Oh my god, what is he going to say next? Could he possibly be about to guess my secret? Does he know?

'There isn't anything,' I try, fear rising up inside me as I say it, but Seth shakes his head and I'm still imagining the worst. Then he fixes me with a serious stare and asks me a direct question.

'Do you have a crush on him?' he asks, and the hot water bottle resting on my stomach suddenly feels like it has got a hundred degrees hotter.

'What? No!' I cry, hopeful that Seth will believe me.

Then he bursts out laughing.

'I'm only teasing you,' he says with a grin. 'Don't take everything so seriously.'

He is still laughing but I'm not, although I force myself to smile so he thinks I'm actually okay. Except I'm really not and I need to be on my own again as soon as possible.

'I might try and get some sleep,' I say and, thankfully, Seth takes the hint.

'I'll sleep in the spare bedroom tonight. Give you some space,' he says.

'You don't have to do that.'

'It's fine. I want you to get a good night's rest. I love you.'

Seth leans in and gives me a kiss then and as he continues to be perfect, I continue to hate myself more and more by the second.

As Seth leaves the room and closes the door behind himself, I feel like crying again. But before any more tears are shed, I hear my phone vibrate on the bedside table. When I pick it up, I see that I have a new message from Georgia.

Hey sis. Are you OK? It sucks that you had to leave so quickly. I hope you're feeling a bit better now. Let me know how you are. Love you xx

No sooner have I read that message than another one immediately follows it.

And let me know what you think of Mateo. I'm dying to hear your opinion! Xx

Instead of replying to that last message, I want to throw my phone across the room and pretend like this is still not happening. But this is not going away. Even if I toss my phone to the floor, Georgia will still be waiting to hear my thoughts on her new boyfriend, and if she hasn't heard them by tomorrow, I imagine she will phone me or call around to see me in person.

I get it. She's excited and she wants me to be excited for her too. But I can't be.

Why did it have to be him? Any other man on this planet would have been fine. Just not him.

The phone is still in my hand, but I wish I'd thrown it away when I receive another message. This one is not from my sister. It's from a number I don't have saved in my phone. A number I don't recognise. Although when I read what the message says, I know exactly who has sent it.

Great to see you again after all these years. You haven't changed one bit.

It's from him. I don't know how he has got my number, but he has just made contact with me. And it isn't good.

I presume Mateo secretly got my number from Georgia's phone when she was away from it. That would explain how he was able to get in touch with me. But what is not yet explained is why he would want to make contact. And why does he seem to be flirting with me?

I could just block his number. But while that might stop him texting me, it doesn't get rid of him from my life. He's still with my sister, so blocking him will only mean I have one less way to try to get out of this mess and, right now, I need as many opportunities as possible.

I had been hoping that the brief meeting between us at the restaurant was at least as awkward for him as it was for me. That way, I hoped, he'd maybe break up with my sister and go back to leaving me alone. But he doesn't seem bothered by this at all, which keeps my biggest fear alive.

This was no accident.

Now I decide to throw my phone to the floor, and as I watch

it bounce across the carpet, I think about how I never want to pick it up and look at it again. That's because if I do, I might see another message from Mateo on there.

Another reminder of him.

Another reminder of what we did together.

Another reminder of the biggest mistake of my life.

FIVE

FIVE YEARS AGO

As I notice the wedding ring on the hand of the woman stretching on the ground beside me, I contemplate asking for her experiences of marriage. It would be in the hopes that it might help me decide if I'm ready for it myself. But I've never met this woman before, so it would be quite a bizarre thing to try and break the ice with. In the end, I hesitate for too long and lose my chance, as the exercise class I'm a part of suddenly gets started. Now, I'm jogging along with everybody else.

The woman with the wedding ring seems to be finding this exertion easier than me, as she eases ahead, while I quickly start to fall towards the back of the pack. There are twelve of us in this outdoor gym class being run on a weekday summer's night, twelve people trying to improve their health or, as I fear, twelve fools who should know better than to think that this class is going to be anything but hell.

I'm already regretting my place here as I push myself to keep jogging. I only joined the gym a few weeks ago and, after years of inactivity, I'm not ready to be put through my paces so vigorously by some energetic, youthful instructor. Yet here I am, trying, because that's what people should do, isn't it? Get off the sofa and give things a go? Prioritise health and wellbeing over TV and snacks? That's what I'm attempting to do, but as my heart rate increases, my breath gets shallower and my legs already start to burn, I fear I have bitten off more than I can chew.

'Don't worry. We only have to run for one more minute and then we move on to something else,' says the male voice to my right.

I turn to see a tall, toned man in a black Nike vest jogging alongside me, and while I feel like a fish out of water here, he looks like he actually belongs in this strenuous environment.

'However, the thing we move on to might be worse than this,' he adds with a knowing smile. 'Kettlebell swings. Over there.'

He points to where I see twelve kettlebells laid out on the grass, and I realise that is probably the next part of this circuit class, assuming I survive long enough to get to that part.

'First time?' the man asks me as we both continue to jog at the rear of the group.

'Yeah, and I'm regretting it,' I breathlessly reply.

'Just take each step at a time and don't try to go as fast as everybody else. You're here for yourself, so don't worry what other people are doing. You got this. I believe in you.'

Such a motivational pep talk might be out of place in almost any other setting, especially between two people who have never met before, but in this exhausting moment, it's exactly what I need to hear. I appreciate the man's encouragement, although I don't have much chance to thank him or even say anything because, as he rightly predicted, we move on to the kettlebells next.

Suddenly, I've gone from running around to swinging a heavy gym item up and down between my legs, and I'm still wondering how I'm ever going to get through all of this class. Maybe I should have listened to Seth, my boyfriend, who is currently back at the apartment we rent together, on the sofa eating ice cream and watching his favourite TV show. I could be sitting right alongside him, yet here I am, doing this nonsense instead.

'Why do you want to go and do that?' he asked me when I suggested that the pair of us attend this fitness class tonight.

'Because it might be fun,' I'd naively replied. 'Plus, it would be good to do something active together. We can't just come home from work and watch TV every night of the week. The only exercise we get is walking to the bar when we go out drinking with our friends at the weekend. We're in our thirties now, we need to form a few healthy habits.'

'I like my life as it is,' Seth had casually replied then from his place on the sofa, and it was obvious to me that he had no intention of moving.

I had thought about just giving in and sitting down beside him, but something else drove me to come here to this fitness class instead. I'd like to say it was just a simple desire to get healthier like I told Seth it was, but deep down, I know there is another reason I really wanted to break our routine and do something different.

It's because I'm becoming bored in our relationship.

More than that, I'm starting to wonder if Seth is the right guy for me.

As I keep swinging the kettlebell with every ounce of determination I've got, I think about how we have been together for just over a year. At first, everything was fun and great, and I loved being Seth's girlfriend. He's a good guy, he's honest and sweet, which is about all one can ask for. Hanging out together used to be fun. We could always be found in restaurants or bars or coffee shops or even the local library, chatting, laughing, sharing the same interests. But recently, he seems to have stopped making as much effort as I do in the relationship. Date nights have become less common, simple but romantic spontaneous surprises have already dried up, and most nights, he spends more time looking at his phone than he does looking at me. I know it takes two to tango, and I can be guilty of being a little lazy myself sometimes. I've certainly felt tired enough after work to prefer to scroll mindlessly through social media rather than sit down for a candlelit conversation over dinner. But the thing is, I have realised that our relationship seems to have stagnated a little and we are possibly already drifting apart.

If we are, which I believe is the case, I need to figure out what I want to do.

I tried to broach this subject with Seth a couple of times, eager, curious, and a little afraid, to see if he felt the same way. But both times, he was distracted and dismissive, seemingly unable or unwilling to open up and have a considered adult conversation. Of course, that only reinforced my fears. But my biggest fear?

Time.

I'm thirty-three now and I am aware of the ticking clock that hangs over my life. I want to marry and become a mother one day, but those dreams take time to accomplish and, as each year goes by, they can get harder to obtain. My forties are a while away, but time has a nasty habit of going by quicker than you thought it would. That's why I need to know if Seth is the one for me, sooner rather than later. If not, I need to move on and find the right person, the one who may be the father of my future children. Otherwise, I could leave it too late and end up in either an unhappy marriage or a life where I'm totally alone and never get the opportunity to walk down the aisle or hold a baby of my own.

'Ten push-ups!' comes the cry from the instructor, and as everybody drops down to the floor to follow the command, I am thinking I'm ready to quit. That's when I hear the voice again.

'You can do this. Just take it one at a time,' my motivational classmate says to me, and I see that he is still beside me and clearly still trying to help me.

I start doing push-ups, which is not a pretty sight because I don't think I've ever done a push-up in my life until today, but before I can succumb to embarrassment or weakness, I'm asked a question.

'What's your name?' the motivated man doing push-ups beside me asks.

'Corinne,' I somehow manage to get out as my face gets closer to the ground before I push up and it rises again.

'Pleasure to meet you, Corinne. I'm Mateo, and yes, life is probably too short to be doing press-ups on a Wednesday evening, yet here we are.'

I can't help but laugh at the unexpected comment, and my giggles cause me to lose my rhythm and the press-ups cease as I collapse onto the ground before rolling onto my bag and trying to get my breath under control. I notice the instructor doesn't seem impressed by the sound of laughter or the fact that I've stopped exercising, but I don't care because that moment of levity was what I needed to get through the next few seconds of this class.

As we all move on to the next exercise, Mateo continues to make me chuckle with a few witty lines about exercise, life and our instructor's stern personality, and before I know it, the class is coming to an end.

I did it. I somehow survived. I'm still alive.

'Thank you,' I say to Mateo as my heart rate eventually comes down and my breathing returns to something more manageable. 'That was hell, but you helped me through it.'

'No problem at all. I remember how hard my first class was. This was your first class, right?'

'Yeah. That obvious?'

'I just knew I hadn't seen you here before. I'd have remembered if I had.'

Suddenly, Mateo is not just motivating me. I think he is flirting with me.

I see his warm smile and feel a fuzzy feeling inside, though I quickly catch myself as I remember I'm not just some single girl who can get picked up by a handsome guy at a gym class. I have Seth. But still, it's nice to get a little harmless attention.

'I'm going to grab a drink in the café,' Mateo says as he rests his hands on his sturdy hips. 'Would you like to join me? I promise I won't make you do any push-ups.'

I laugh again and almost say yes before I think about getting back home to Seth.

'I need to go. But thank you,' I say.

Mateo looks a little disappointed, but shrugs it off with another smile and then he turns to walk away.

'Hopefully see you at next week's class!' he calls out to me cheerfully as he leaves, and while I don't confirm my attendance with him right now, I realise that I would actually quite like to see him again.

As I make my way back to my car on weary legs, I know there is no way I would willingly choose to go back to that class again. It was too hard for my beginner level of fitness. But as I start to drive away, I realise that if I do go back, it will not be for health reasons.

It will be to see Mateo again.

I instantly tell myself it's silly. How predictable of me to have a crush on some hot guy at the gym. I bet every woman has the same. It doesn't mean she does anything about it. It just means it's a silly fantasy to entertain for ten seconds before going back to real life. I've never cheated before and have no intention of ever starting.

Seth is my real life. I should focus on him. Especially when I feel like we are going through a difficult spell.

But by the time I've driven home, I have more questions on my mind than I left with.

Initially, my only question was: is Seth the right guy for me? But now, another question has joined it.

If it's not Seth, could it be Mateo?

SIX

PRESENT DAY

A sleepless night is no way to start a week, but that's how my Monday begins because I got no rest last night.

As I get dressed for work alongside my husband, while listening to my son running around in his bedroom, I know today is going to be hard to get through due to the lack of sleep. I also know that the reason for my unrest still looms large and remains unresolved, despite spending all night worrying about it.

'Are you sure you're okay to go to work?' Seth asks me, placing a concerned hand on my shoulder. 'You look tired. You're probably not over whatever made you ill yesterday. Why not have a day off?'

I look at my husband standing beside me in his shirt and tie and he looks smart. Handsome. A respectable man on his way to earn money to provide for his family. He must have a lot on his own mind, perhaps pondering all the things he needs to do when he gets to the office. Deadlines. Schedules. Meetings. I know he is busy. Yet he still has time to stop and make sure that I'm okay.

'I'm fine,' I lie because that seems better than being honest and saying that the reason for my lack of sleep was not illness but fear. 'There's a lot I need to do at work today, so I better go in. I'm sure I'll feel better when I get there.'

'Okay, but if you don't feel better then I want you to come straight home and get back in bed. You need to get yourself well again,' Seth advises before giving me a kiss and finishing getting dressed.

Despite my exhaustion and the fearful thoughts clawing at me continuously, I somehow make it through the testing time of the day that involves getting Freddie ready for school and in the car on the way to that school. Seth is in his own car and already across town from us now, so at least I don't have to try and put on a brave face around him anymore. Then finally, when I drop Freddie at the school gates, I am alone and can take a deep breath because I know I've got several hours before I am around my family again. That gives me some time to figure out what I am going to do about the Mateo problem.

While I'll be at work all day, processing insurance claims for people who have been in car accidents, I am not planning on doing anything productive for my boss. Instead, I will be wracking my brains to try and think of a way that I can do the most productive thing for my personal life, and that would be to figure out how to get Mateo away from my sister and me and return things to their safe normalcy.

But after parking my car and just before I can enter my office, I hear my phone ringing and the sound of it causes me to freeze.

What if it is him calling me?

I deleted the messages that Mateo sent me last night, afraid that Seth might somehow see them even though I've never known my husband to check my phone before. I deleted them instead of replying to them and that was the tactic I decided upon, at least for the time being until I think of a better one. But I've still not blocked his number because as the old adage goes:

keep your friends close and your enemies closer. As I check the caller ID, I am expecting it will be him.

But it's not Mateo who is calling me. It's my sister.

'Hi,' I say as I hit connect, figuring it might seem suspicious of me to ignore my sibling. I'm aware that I haven't replied to the messages she sent last night. We usually message every day, if not every other day, so radio silence for too long on my part will only signal to her that something is wrong with me.

'Hey sis. Are you okay? I was worried about you,' Georgia says, sounding sincere, which only makes me feel worse. 'You didn't text me back last night. Are you still ill?'

'Sorry, I was asleep,' I reply as I see one of my colleagues approach the office and smile at me as if everything is okay in the world.

'Are you feeling better?' Georgia asks me next, sounding very much like Seth. It's lovely to have people who care about me, but it's not so lovely to know that those same people would be hurt if they knew what I'd done in the past.

'Yeah, a little better, thanks.'

'Great. So, I'm dying to know. What did you think of Mateo?'

My sister's innocent question hangs in the phone line between us, and unlike the same question that she asked over text message last night, I can't just easily ignore this one. But I can try.

'Sorry, I've just got to work,' I say, doing my best to sound busy. 'I'm going to have to go.'

'Wait!' Georgia cries.

And so I have to do as she asks because I'm afraid of what she might say next. Is she going to guess that I have history with Mateo and that explains my avoidance strategies ever since he appeared yesterday? If so, what will I say to that?

'Please, I'd really value your opinion on him, sis,' Georgia says next. 'You know it means a lot to me.'

Why does my sister have to be tugging at my heartstrings? Doesn't she realise this is only making things harder for me? Of course she doesn't. Why would she? She has no idea about my inner turmoil and instead, is living in a blissful bubble, the kind that comes when you're in love and want the whole world to know. Is it really going to come down to this? Am I going to have to choose between my sibling and my husband and child? I really can't see a way how I can keep everyone happy in this situation. That doesn't mean I can't try though.

'He seems nice,' is the best thing I can come up with under the circumstances.

'Come on, I know you have more of an opinion than that,' Georgia replies with a little laugh. 'You've never been one to be shy, so come on, sis. Spill the beans. What do you really think about him?'

'Well, I hardly got to talk to him, so it's impossible for me to say,' I try next, flailing around looking for some words that will get her to stop asking me to talk about him.

'What do you think of his appearance?'

'What?'

'How he looks? Do you think he's cute? Handsome? Hot?'

Oh God, I really need to end this call. Could I get away with just hanging up?

'Like I said, he seems nice,' is my response again.

'What's wrong with you?' Georgia asks me, and I detect a shift in her tone of voice, as if she is suddenly not happy. 'Why aren't you excited about this? You always used to tell me how much you couldn't wait for me to find someone. Even when I said I would never settle down with a guy, you used to tease me and tell me I'd change my mind. Now that I have, why aren't you happy for me?'

My sister is right. I am acting very out of character here considering how eager I have been for her to meet her dream man. The problem is, he is my nightmare man. I wish I could be happy for her, I'd love nothing more than to be, but I can't feel happy when I'm pretty sure Mateo is only using her to get closer to me.

'Are you sure about him?' I ask then, taking a risk because I know I might upset her. 'I mean, is moving in together the right thing to do? Should you not take things slower?'

'What?' Georgia cries, sounding very annoyed.

'I just don't want you to rush into things and get hurt,' I say, a statement that does a better job of making me sound more caring than callous.

'I'm not rushing into anything,' Georgia protests fiercely. 'Like I said at the meal, I have been seeing him for months. We've been on loads of dates. He's stayed over at my place several times. Hell, we've slept together so many times that I've lost count!'

This is way too much information.

'I'm just saying, I want you to be careful,' I try next. 'You're my little sis. I don't want a guy to break your heart.'

'He's not going to break my heart,' Georgia tells me as if she has any idea of the man she is dealing with. But I can't argue this point anymore without giving myself away, so I'm left with no option but to stop protesting.

'Okay, then go for it, sis,' I say, defeated.

'Thank you. And it's a shame you didn't get to hang out with him more at the meal, so we'll all have to get together soon, and you can get to know him a lot better then. When you do, I'm confident that you'll see why I like him so much.'

'Sure,' I reply quietly, figuring our conversation is finally about to be over. But unfortunately for me, my sister adds one more thing, a sentence that is going to haunt me for the rest of the day.

'He may even be marriage material,' Georgia says happily, proving just how confident she is that she has found the perfect guy for her.

Those words rattle around in my head before Georgia says she will let me get to work, and with that, she says her goodbyes and hangs up.

As I lower my phone, I actually consider throwing it in the bin that is outside my office. Anything to stop this device delivering me any more bad news. But such an act would be stupid because like most adults in this day and age, I can't live without a phone. I need it in case my husband calls or my son's school tries to urgently contact me, so I have to keep it on me. That means I'm susceptible to seeing more messages from Mateo, and as I look at my screen to see any notifications that have popped up during my call with Georgia, my heart sinks.

He has messaged again.

As I read Mateo's latest text, I manage to feel even worse than I did after my sister mentioned the possibility of marriage with him.

You haven't replied to my last message. You wouldn't be trying to ignore me, would you? If so, it's impossible. We're practically family now.

I reread the words several times, but they only get worse with each pass.

Mateo is calling himself *family.*

I feel sick.

But what truly makes me sick is that I know that my current despair is all my fault.

SEVEN

FIVE YEARS AGO

I never thought I'd be back here again. The last time I was, I nearly died, or at least it felt that way, so the idea of returning was not one I thought I'd act on.

Yet here I am.

Back for another fitness class.

I'm nervous and daunted by how much physical exertion is ahead of me over the next half an hour. But that's not all I'm feeling as I stand here warming up with the other attendees while the instructor sets out the equipment.

I'm also feeling disappointed.

That's because I can't see Mateo anywhere.

As much as I'd like to tell myself that I came back to do this class again because I need the exercise or that I'm trying to be healthy, the truth is I left home this evening and drove down here because I was excited at the prospect of seeing him again. Mateo, the guy who motivated me to not give up when things got hard. The guy who made me laugh while I was struggling. The guy who gave me attention. The guy who possibly even flirted with me.

He is why I am back here tonight, even though I shouldn't be.

I should be at home sitting on the sofa with Seth.

Why am I more excited about seeing a guy I've met once than my current boyfriend of over a year?

It was a silly, foolish thing to do, to come here because... what exactly? I want to be made to laugh again? Want some attention? Want to be flirted with one more time? This is so out of character for me. I have no idea why I have suddenly started acting like a teenager rather than the grown woman I am, but as I can't see Mateo anywhere, it seems my foolishness has been served right. I'm now going to have to go all the way through this class and that is my punishment for being a fool.

The class begins and I immediately start struggling, which is no surprise because why would I fare any better than I did last week? I don't have my motivational help this time, so the whole thing is even more of a slog than it was before, and I genuinely consider quitting and walking away several times as the exercises go on. But something keeps me going. Is it personal pride? Or is it that I think Mateo would be disappointed in me if he knew I gave up when he wasn't around?

It could be either of those or it could simply be that my wobbling, lactic-acid-laden legs simply don't possess the strength to allow me to walk away now. Whatever it is, I somehow complete the class, although I am left lying on the ground huffing and puffing as a result. By the time I get back up, the other attendees have left and the instructor has put away most of the equipment she just used to destroy me.

I start in the direction of my car but realise my water bottle is empty – and I really need to take on more liquids before the drive home – so I divert towards the café for refreshments. Once in there, I pluck a bottle of water from the refrigerated shelf, grateful that it's not any heavier than it is because I really am running on fumes here. Then I pay the friendly woman behind the checkout before preparing to leave...

'Hey, Corinne.'

I look to my left, towards where I just heard my name being called, and when I do, I see Mateo sitting at a table. He has a laptop open in front of him and a cappuccino sitting beside it, and instead of the gym attire I saw him in last week, he is wearing corporate clothing.

'Oh, hey!' I say, trying not to sound as surprised as I am to see him.

'Did you just take the fitness class again?' he asks, looking impressed.

'I did.'

'And you survived! Well done!'

I laugh. 'Barely. It was awful. I'm pretty sure I passed out at one point.'

Now it's Mateo's turn to laugh.

'I'm sure it wasn't that bad.'

'Are you kidding? I must have looked awful, trying to get through all my push-ups.'

'I seriously doubt that,' Mateo replies calmly, and there it is again. Another hint of flirting from him. I brush it off quickly.

'Why weren't you at the class?' I ask, hoping that I sound slightly inquisitive rather than desperate to know.

'Unfortunately, I have an injury,' Mateo replies, and he gently rubs his right shoulder. 'I was playing squash last night and think I overdid it. I woke up this morning and could barely move my arm.'

'Oh no. I hope you feel better soon,' I say as he continues to rub his muscular shoulder.

'As long as I'm fit enough to type then at least my job is safe,' he says as he nods towards his laptop, making me assume that he is working now.

'Well, you didn't miss much at the fitness class,' I say, trying to make him feel better.

'I almost missed seeing you,' he replies, catching me off guard.

'I'm sorry?' I ask naively.

'Well, if I had gone to the class tonight, it wouldn't have been for the exercise,' Mateo says suggestively. 'It would have been to see you.'

I almost try and pretend like I didn't hear that because what else am I supposed to do? In the end, I just laugh nervously and almost drop my water bottle. But Mateo doesn't do anything awkward. He just sits there looking calm and composed.

'Well, I better get home,' I say before adding something that I feel is necessary to mention at this point. 'My boyfriend will be wondering where I am.'

If I had hoped the mention of my partner would put Mateo off, I am wrong.

'I'm not sure if my shoulder will be better for next week's class,' Mateo says as he reaches into his shirt pocket before pulling out a pen. 'So could I get your number?'

'What do you need that for?' I ask, surprised at how bold he is being.

'Why else does a person need somebody's number?' Mateo asks rhetorically. 'So I can speak to you, of course.'

I am flattered, but this has gone far enough. I realise he is not getting the hint, and I also realise that I need to nip this in the bud right now before it goes any further. It's one thing to have an innocent gym crush, but it's another thing to start swapping numbers with them.

'I have a boyfriend,' I reiterate, figuring I wasn't clear enough the first time I mentioned it.

'So...' Mateo says leadingly.

'So, I don't just give my number out to guys who ask for it. Because I'm not single. You understand?'

I feel like I've done a pretty good job of making myself clear, and I'm about to leave when I notice Mateo start to write something down on the napkin beside his coffee. Then he holds out the napkin for me to take.

Perhaps foolishly, I do take it and when I look down, I don't need to ask him what it is that he has written for me. Eleven digits.

He's given me his number.

'Send me a message if you ever want to chat. Otherwise, we'll have to rely on bumping into each other here,' Mateo says with a smile.

I stare at the number then at him without saying a word. I then consider throwing the napkin back down on the table and walking away. Eventually, I start walking and figure I'll toss the napkin in the bin on my way out to the car park. Whatever I do, I'll get rid of this at the next opportunity.

But something goes wrong with that plan.

I still have the napkin when I get to my car. It sits on the passenger seat beside me as I drive home.

And despite doing my best to focus on the road ahead, I cannot stop looking at it.

That tells me that I am seriously entertaining the idea of calling Mateo. But if I'm going to do that, I should end things with Seth first. I have no intention of cheating on him, so if I am to do anything with this number, I need to end it with Seth first.

No wonder it's so hard to concentrate on driving.

How can I with all this going on in my head?

EIGHT

PRESENT DAY

Phone numbers. Why are they capable of causing so much trouble?

As I think about the time Mateo gave me his number, his digits scrawled across a napkin that made it into my car and, eventually, my home, I wish mobile phones had never been invented. Sure, I love the fact that I can call family and friends at any time from anywhere in the world and yes, I absolutely adore the fact that I have thousands of images on my mobile documenting the four years of my beautiful son's life. But right now, I wish I could erase the whole invention from human history, because if I could do that, it would not be possible for Mateo to be sending me messages. Of course, the option to block his number is still available to me, but then my paranoia will run rampant as I think about Mateo trying to call me only for him to figure out he's been blocked. How much might that anger him? Then what might he do without being able to communicate via the phone? Turn up at my house unannounced and speak to Seth? That would be way worse than a text message or missed call that only I have to see.

I reread his last text for the umpteenth time, the one I just received after getting off the phone with my sister.

You haven't replied to my last message. You wouldn't be trying to ignore me, would you? If so, it's impossible. We're practically family now.

One thing is for sure, I don't feel any better no matter how many times I read it. I need to get to work. I'm going to be late. But I also know that I need to do something else.

I can't ignore Mateo.

I need to text him back.

I think what the best thing to say to him would be. Should I threaten him? Warn him to stay away from me? Tell him to leave my sister and go before he makes anything worse? I seriously consider it, but decide against it when I realise I first need more information about Mateo's motives and his state of mind.

What about begging? I could send him a pleading message, urging him not to do anything stupid, not to do anything that could hurt anybody and ruin people's lives. That might work, but then again, it puts me in a position of weakness instantly and I don't want to hand over all my power to him, even if I am very much in the compromised position here.

Then I decide what I am going to do.

I'm going to ask him a question.

My fingers type quickly until I press send before I can chicken out. Once that is done, I wait impatiently for a response. I'm so impatient that I start pacing around, my feet wearing out a small patch of concrete outside my office as I keep staring at my phone and waiting for Mateo to reply. It shouldn't take him long because it was a very simple question.

Did you know Georgia was my sister when you got with her?

I anxiously await his answer, assuming it will be prompt and fearing it will confirm what I'm most afraid of – that he got with her to get nearer to me. But bizarrely, considering I have just given him what he wants, which is attention, Mateo does not reply. I linger outside my office for a few more minutes, waiting to see a text arrive on my phone, but in the end, aware of how late I am, I have to give up waiting and go inside to my desk.

As I settle down at my workstation and hear a few of my colleagues wishing me a good morning, I keep checking my phone but it's still radio silence from Mateo. Is this part of his game? Get me on the hook and then leave me hanging? If he is toying with me, he has picked the wrong person because I am not going to stand for this. I almost feel like sending him another message, a firmer, more direct one, in which I make it clear that whatever he is doing, it is not going to work. Before I can do that, my work friend at the desk beside me arrives and starts chatting.

'How was your weekend, Corinne?' she asks me as she drops her handbag on her desk before taking a seat. 'Was it as wild as mine?'

I turn to Janet, my colleague and nine-to-five companion for the past seven years, and try to make out like I didn't just have the weekend from hell. It won't be easy though, because when I left the office on Friday, I couldn't have predicted a worse set of events to occur before Monday rolled around again.

'It was okay. Pretty quiet,' I reply before checking my phone again and seeing that Mateo has still not replied.

'Didn't you say you were meeting your sister's new guy?' Janet recalls annoyingly, making me curse the fact that I told her my weekend plans before they occurred. But of course I did because I tell Janet everything. Well, almost everything. Just like everybody else in my life, the only thing they don't know about me is what happened with Mateo.

'Oh right, yeah,' I say, awkwardly.

'So, did you meet him?'

'Yeah.'

'And...' Janet coaxes, her eyes widening as she eagerly waits for my juicy piece of gossip.

'He's okay,' I say with a shrug.

'Give me details. What's his name? What does he look like? Is he hot? Does he have a good job? What did he talk about? Did he get on well with Seth?'

The more Janet fires questions at me, the more I cannot sit here and listen to them.

'Sorry, I've just got a lot of emails to catch up on. Can we talk about this later?' I try. She looks surprised – because I never put work before chitter-chatter – and reluctantly agrees.

We start working in silence then, which is an alien concept for us, because by now, we're usually on our first cup of tea, our second chocolate biscuit and our third piece of gossip. But I appreciate the peace, and I certainly need it. In order to keep up appearances with Janet, I do as I told her and get to work on my emails, although I stop to make several cursory glances at my phone throughout. But still no word from Mateo.

Eventually, Janet cannot take the silence between us anymore and wheels her chair closer to my desk while looking concerned.

'Is everything okay at home? Is it Seth or Freddie? Is something wrong with them?' she asks, worried, and I know she would be because as a loyal friend she only wants everything to be well in my world.

'Everything is fine,' I say, which is the truth, although only for the time being. Things certainly won't be that way if it gets worse with Mateo, who is still ignoring me and causing my imagination to run wild with fearful thoughts about what he might be doing instead of texting me back.

'Are you sure? You're very quiet and you look very pale. I know the only time you ever get like this is if Freddie is ill or if

Seth is having a hard time at work. So I'm just checking your boys are okay?'

I really appreciate my dear friend's concern, but it also highlights something I am well aware of. If I am ever acting like this – quiet and withdrawn – it's because I am worrying about my family. My boys, as Janet calls them. Seth and Freddie. *My world*. Like Janet says, usually it's illness or work stresses on their part that cause my worry, and I really wish that's all it was now. I can't explain to Janet that it is something deeper than those things, something that threatens the very existence of the family she is showing such concern for.

'They're okay,' I say meekly before adding something stronger. 'We're okay.'

Janet still looks unsure, so I grab my phone and offer to make her a cup of tea. When she accepts, I have my excuse to get away from my desk and away from her and her prying questions. As I reach the kitchen, I take a deep breath before checking my phone once more, but Mateo is still tormenting me with his lack of a response, so I get out two cups and fill the kettle.

As the kettle boils, seemingly mirroring my stress levels, Mateo responds.

I asked him if he knew that Georgia was my sister when he got with her, and he has just given me his answer.

What if I did?

That's pretty clear-cut and as the kettle gets louder, I send him my reply.

Why are you with her?

He's much quicker to reply this time.

To get closer to you, of course.

Another colleague enters the kitchen and says something to me, but I don't hear it because I'm too busy typing.

What do you think is going to happen?

I ask anxiously, desperate to know what is going on in Mateo's head.

Whatever I want to happen.

My colleague says something else to me then, but I just abandon the boiling kettle and leave the kitchen as my heart pounds and my breathing intensifies.

You're deluded if you think you can break up my family

I respond, wondering what effect that statement will have on my foe. But it does not stop him in his tracks, though his response certainly stops me in mine.

You're deluded if you think I can't.

NINE

FIVE YEARS AGO

I feel like this is going to be a make-or-break weekend for me and Seth. After harbouring doubts about the future of our relationship, as well as having my head turned slightly by Mateo at the gym, I've decided that I am giving myself the next two days to figure out what I am going to do with my love life. I thought I loved Seth, and I thought he was the only one for me. But lately, his behaviour has been making me think that he doesn't feel the same way, and if he continues to not show me any attention and affection, surely I am within my rights to reconsider things between us. But I want to give him one more chance.

'Let's do something fun today,' I say as I enter the bedroom of the apartment we rent together to find my boyfriend rubbing his eyes and looking like he could have done with more sleep. But it's nearly 9 a.m. and while I sneaked out of bed earlier to allow him to have more rest, I don't want him to sleep the entire weekend away.

'What shall we do?' I ask as I sit on the edge of the bed beside him. 'Catch a movie? Picnic in the park? Fancy restaurant for lunch or drink cocktails all afternoon and regret it tomorrow morning?'

I'm throwing around a few fun ideas and really, I'll be happy to do any of them or be keen to do something else that Seth might suggest. The main purpose of today is to remind myself that we are great as a couple, although I'm not letting Seth know that because this is somewhat of a test too.

Sadly, Seth fails it in the first minute.

'I have to work today,' he says as he wearily gets out of bed and starts getting dressed.

'What? But it's the weekend!'

'I know that,' Seth says, seeming slightly irritated as if he didn't need telling what day of the week it is. But if he's irritated, so am I.

'You never work on the weekend. What's going on?' I cry, wondering why my boyfriend's Monday-to-Friday, nine-to-five tax advisory job has suddenly seeped into the weekends.

'Nothing is going on other than the fact that I have extra work to do, so I better go and do it,' he replies with a sigh. 'I'll be back early evening, unless it drags on, which it might because it's been a tough quarter and there's a lot to sort through. But you can have a good day without me. Just relax. Or maybe call a friend. You'll be all right, won't you?'

Seth disappears into the bathroom, leaving me on the bed with a whole day to fill by myself. It could also be a whole day of wondering if he is really going to work or if he is going to see somebody else. Why wouldn't he tell me about this extra work sooner? Is he hiding something?

I consider following him into the bathroom and expressing my unhappiness about this, or my anxiety surrounding if he is telling the truth. I could even wait for him to return before telling him that I'm not sure we are working anymore. Sure, sometimes, work gets in the way of weekends and things don't always go to plan. That's just life. But what if there's more to it than that? Or what if it is just work, but if so, it's not just today.

Seth has been distant and dismissive of me for a while now. I genuinely can't remember the last time we did something fun together. Seth might not realise it but today was about so much more than just going for a picnic or a couple of cocktails. It was about having fun as a couple again and, most importantly, making sure we are still a couple. That's because right now, I feel we are like a pair of flatmates, cohabitating and making small talk whenever we pass each other before leaving separately and spending days in different places. In the end, though, I say nothing as Seth finishes getting ready and leaves the apartment.

Frustrated and forlorn, I think about what Seth suggested I do in his absence. He suggested I relax, but that seems unlikely given the thoughts I am wrestling with about the two of us. He also suggested that I call a friend.

That's when I think about the napkin I was given the other day at the gym.

When my boyfriend suggested calling a friend, he would surely have meant for me to call one of my female friends. Not another guy and certainly not a guy I've just met at the gym. But it is Mateo I'm thinking about as I go into the kitchen and stare at the bin. I'm staring at it because inside that bin is the napkin. I threw it in there the other night after deciding that I didn't need it in my possession.

So why am I now rummaging around in the bin to take it back out again?

I find the napkin and despite where it has been lying for a couple of days, it's mostly clean and the number written on it is still very much decipherable. But just because it is, it doesn't mean I should use it.

Instead of texting Mateo, I need to sort things with Seth, so even though my boyfriend has left, I decide to call him. I'm going to say that we need to talk and maybe he will come back to the apartment to do that. If not, we can have the conversation on the phone and maybe, if it doesn't go well, it will be one of the last conversations we will have.

I call Seth and wait for him to answer. He'll be walking because his workplace is only ten minutes away and he likes the fresh air. However, though he isn't driving, he does not answer my call.

Feeling even more frustrated than I was five minutes ago, I consider storming out of the apartment, finding Seth on the street and asking him if he loves me anymore. It would be very dramatic, and probably a little foolish, but I'm feeling so fed up that I don't know what else to do.

Then I end up texting Mateo.

I did it to cheer myself up, to get some attention, to see if he will answer me when my own boyfriend did not. My message is a short and simple one.

Hi. Are you going to the gym today?

I don't feel too guilty about sending it because it's just a simple question to a friend I met at the gym. If the recipient was female, I wouldn't think twice about this, but just because the recipient is male, it doesn't mean I can't make conversation with them.

Good morning, Corinne. No, I'm not going to the gym today.

Mateo's response is quick and polite. But also disappointing. He won't be at the gym. I was thinking I could go down there, get a workout in and maybe make some small talk with him if I happened to see him in the café. It would have killed some time for me on this lonely Saturday and probably made me feel a little bit better about myself. But alas, it doesn't seem like Mateo will be there. Then he messages me again.

I'm having breakfast at Angelos right now. Would you like to join me? The eggs are to die for.

The invitation to meet him for breakfast is unexpected, but tempting. I am hungry. I do like eggs. And our fridge is pretty much empty. But should I go?

Thinking about how easily Seth left this apartment not so long ago, without so much as a kiss on the cheek for me, I decide to leave just as easily and now I'm on my way to Angelos. I know the place, although I've never actually eaten there. But I'm going to change that fact today.

When I arrive at the busy café, it takes me a few moments to spot Mateo among the sea of diners. Then I spot him at a table at the back and he spots me too. He gives me a casual wave as I approach before he gets up out of his seat to welcome me.

He opens his arms for a hug and I'm not sure what to do, so I kind of just go with it before sitting down awkwardly and feeling like I shouldn't have come here.

'What would you like?' Mateo asks me as he hands me a menu. 'I'm buying.'

'Oh no, you don't need to do that. I can get my own breakfast,' I say as I look at all the food options, but Mateo insists.

A friendly woman in an apron comes around to take my order, which is for eggs Benedict and a pot of tea, before Mateo and I are alone again.

'So, why did you message me this morning?' Mateo asks with an interested smile.

'Erm...' I say, unsure how to answer that one.

'I'm glad you did,' Mateo says, filling the silence. 'I was hoping you would.'

I've only been at this table for a few minutes and already I feel the tension building between us, so I change the subject and bring up something that one friend would ask another.

'What do you do for work?' I enquire.

'Is that really what you want to know?' Mateo says, looking amused. 'Or would you like to know something a little more interesting about me? Like whether or not I am single.'

I don't know what to say to that, so Mateo carries on the conversation for the both of us.

'I already know that you have a boyfriend. What is he doing today? Why are you not having breakfast with him on this fine Saturday morning?'

'He's working,' I reply quietly as my pot of tea arrives.

'So you were bored and contacted me,' Mateo says, filling in the blanks, not that I confirm that for him.

'Is everything okay between you and your boyfriend, or are you having a few issues?' Mateo asks then.

'I'm not sure that's any of your business.'

'Perhaps not. But I am interested.'

'Why?'

'Why do you think?'

I'm starting to blush and as my skin grows hotter, I realise that taking a sip of hot tea is not going to help me cool down. The best thing to do would be to leave this warm café and get back outside into the cool air, away from the food and the drink and Mateo and the heavy air of anticipation that hangs between us.

'I shouldn't have come here,' I say as I go to get out of my seat. 'I'm sorry.'

I try to leave the table but just before I can, Mateo places a hand on my arm.

'Don't feel bad for doing something you wanted to do,' he says, looking into my eyes. 'I am glad I got to see you today. But even if I hadn't, I was going to be thinking about you all weekend.'

Mateo could leave it there, but his hand remains on my arm. Then he adds one more thing.

'And I'm pretty sure you were going to be thinking about me too.'

I wish he wasn't right. But he is and now I don't know what to think because if he is a mind reader, I better be careful. But I'm also being careful because I'm conflicted.

I know I shouldn't be here.

Yet I still am.

TEN

PRESENT DAY

I burst out of my office feeling as confused as I did on the day I burst out of Angelos after Mateo had told me he couldn't stop thinking about me. But my reason for leaving where I was today is slightly different to the reason I left that café five years ago. This time, I'm not going outside because I need to get away from a man that is seriously tempting me to do something I shouldn't. Instead, I am going outside because I need to call that same man and order him to leave me alone.

I am calling Mateo now after deciding that the pair of us texting each other was not getting me anywhere. His last text, the one in which he said that I was deluded if I didn't think he was capable of breaking up my family, is the reason for my sudden desire to speak to him.

This needs to be sorted out right now, before it gets any worse.

'Pick up the damn phone,' I say out loud as I wait for Mateo to answer. He should do because after texting me so much this morning, I know he is holding his phone and apparently is free enough to communicate, so why isn't he answering? But the call rings out and I get his voicemail. I decide not to leave a message that might be heard by the wrong person at a later date. I'm not giving up. Not yet.

I start texting Mateo, telling him to answer his phone, and as my fingers fly furiously across my screen, I suddenly see an incoming call. I answer it so quickly that I don't even check the caller ID but I assume it is him, so I get straight to the point.

'You leave me and my family alone, I am warning you!' I cry into the phone, hoping I come across as more threatening than desperate.

'Corinne? What's wrong? What's happened?'

I freeze when I realise the voice at the other end of the line is not Mateo's, but Seth's.

Oh my god, how do I explain my outburst?

'Oh, Seth? Hi. Sorry, I thought you were someone else,' I say, which should be obvious but hasn't helped me explain this any better.

'Who did you think I was?' is the obvious question I get asked by my startled husband.

'Erm...' I say, stalling and searching for a good answer. Then I get one. 'There's a sales number that has been calling me for the last few days, pestering me and trying to sell me something. I told them I wasn't interested but they keep calling, so I thought it was them again. But it was you.'

Will that work? As excuses go, it doesn't feel like the worst one in the world. But will Seth buy it?

When I hear him start laughing, I'm still unsure.

'Wow, I guess that sales company really picked the wrong person to mess with,' he says, still chuckling. 'I wish it was them who were calling you now because you really would have given it to them.'

I realise Seth has believed me and breathe a sigh of relief. The fact he seems impressed by how I would handle a sales call is just another sign of how much he loves me. He's on my side, batting for me, and it has been that way for a long time now, showing how much he has grown and how stronger we are for it. The sound of his laughter always makes me smile, like I've achieved something by getting to hear it, and I've always felt that way. I remember the first time I made him laugh. It was during our first date and I mispronounced the word 'empanada'. So much for showing off my Spanish skills. He still teases me about that to this day.

'What were they trying to sell you?' he asks me, still amused.

'Oh, erm, just some insurance thing,' I answer, completing the lie.

'Well, if they do call you again, I'm pretty sure that they'll get the message if you talk to them like you just did to me,' Seth chuckles.

I'm relieved that I seem to have got out of this unfortunate situation, but I still have the problem of Mateo to deal with and being on the phone with my husband unfortunately isn't going to help me there.

'I need to get back to work,' I tell him, needing to keep the line clear.

'Wait. I was just calling because I've had an idea,' Seth says. 'I was thinking about how it was a shame that our lunch with your sister got cut short yesterday, and we never really got to talk properly with her or get to know Mateo better. So how about we invite them around for dinner at ours one evening this week?'

'What?' I cry, thinking that such a thing sounds like the absolute worst idea in the world. But of course, in Seth's world, he thinks he's come up with something great.

'We could get Freddie to bed early and then the four of us could sit down and have a nice meal. Your sister and Mateo are obviously a serious couple, so it would be good to get to know him more, and hopefully, it can be the first double date of many between us.'

I don't know what to say to that, although I know what I want to say. I want to dismiss the idea and tell Seth to never suggest it again. But I can't.

'You were always talking about how you wished your sister had a boyfriend so the four of us could do things together,' Seth goes on. 'So now is our chance. What do you think?'

'Erm, I'm really busy at the moment,' I reply, which isn't actually a lie. 'I've got a lot of work to do. Can we discuss this later?'

'Oh, okay. I thought you'd be excited at the idea.'

'Like I said, I'm really busy. I have to go. Sorry. Bye.'

I hang up then before my husband can give me any more of his bright ideas, although I know he will just want to pick up this conversation when I get home this evening. At least I have delayed it for a few more hours, which is the best I can do in the circumstances.

I consider trying to call Mateo again, but I've been away from my desk for a while now, and if my boss has noticed, she might want answers. I've done enough lying already today so I turn to go back inside my office, figuring I'll have to wait until lunchtime before trying to deal with Mateo again. But I'm wrong. I see who has appeared behind me while I was on the phone to Seth.

It's him.

He's here, at my place of work, in broad daylight, where anybody could see us together.

It's Mateo.

ELEVEN

'What the hell are you doing here?'

The question leaves my mouth in a burst of both shock and disgust. No sooner have I fired it at Mateo than I am nervously looking around to make sure none of my colleagues are out here to see me talking with him. The last thing I need is Janet seeing this because as much as she is my friend and loves me, she loves to gossip too, and this is one thing I do not want to be gossiped about.

'It's nice to see you too,' Mateo replies with a confident smirk. 'I'm glad you didn't greet me like that at the family meal yesterday. That would have been very awkward if you had. Very awkward indeed.'

'It was awkward enough,' I retort. 'You need to leave right now. I don't want to be seen with you.'

'I'm afraid it's a bit late for that,' Mateo replies. 'And it's not as if we aren't going to be seeing a lot more of each other in the future. Not now I'm dating your sister. Or had you forgotten about that?'

'How did you know where I work?' I ask anxiously, recalling that I never told him that back when I was making my stupid mistake. 'How did you find me here? Have you been following me?'

'You're always asking me questions,' Mateo replies, rolling his eyes as if I'm some minor irritant that he hasn't irritated. 'You want to know how I found you, as well as why I'm with your sister. What it all means for you. You can be very selfish at times, Corinne, although it doesn't put me off. Quite the opposite in fact.'

The way Mateo is looking at me is turning my blood cold. Right now, he looks nothing like the man who charmed me when I first met him at the gym. Sure, the imposing physical appearance is the same, but I can see beneath the surface and what his eyes are saying belies a change in character. He's gone from being someone I liked to someone I detest, though he seems to be finding that the villain role suits him well.

'You can't be here. This is my workplace. You need to leave,' I try, not that Mateo budges an inch from where he confidently stands.

'I thought it would be better to carry on our conversation face to face rather than over the phone,' Mateo tells me. 'Not that I minded using the phone to communicate with you. It reminded me of when we first met. You do remember that, don't you, Corinne? How you messaged me first? How you agreed to meet me for breakfast at Angelos?'

'It was five years ago,' I spit back. 'It's in the past.'

'Except it's not. Not really. Not when it still has so much to do with the present,' Mateo goes on, not backing down in the face of my anger towards him. 'I do assume Seth still doesn't know about us. Am I right?'

I don't need to dignify that with an answer.

'Therefore, what we did five years ago is still very much relevant today,' Mateo says to follow on. 'So you can't ignore me, Corinne. Not when so much is at stake for you. Unless of course you aren't worried about Seth leaving you and taking Freddie with him. Not to mention your sister hating you and probably your parents too for good measure.'

I suddenly feel like rushing towards Mateo and hitting him in the face. I've never punched anybody before, but I've seen plenty of people do it on television and it doesn't look that hard. Just aim and swing. I don't know if I possess enough power to truly hurt Mateo, but I'd love to find out. But something stops me from trying. Maybe it's that I lose my nerve at the last second and realise there's probably more chance of me hurting myself than hurting him, and any injury I sustain would have to be explained to my husband. Or perhaps it's because I'm afraid Janet or anyone else I work with could look out of an office window and see me assaulting Mateo – that would be just as bad as me hurting myself.

So I do nothing. *For now.*

'What do you want?' I ask, drained from this brief exchange already.

'I want you, of course.'

'You can't have me. I'm with Seth.'

'That was never an issue before.'

'It was a long time ago!' I try again, but I know I'm wasting my breath. 'I love Seth, and I don't want to hurt him. I don't want anybody to get hurt. Not him, or my sister, or my parents and certainly not my son. So just leave us all alone, please, I'm begging you.'

'You can beg all you like, but I'm not going anywhere. Not until I get what I want.'

That hot and handsome look Mateo had five years ago? Long gone. Now he just looks mean and menacing. That makes me fear for my sister. She has no idea how close she is to this danger. Would he hurt her? I mean physically, on top of emotionally? I have to hope he wouldn't go that far, but I also have to resolve this before there is a chance to find out.

'And what is it that you want exactly?' I desperately

demand to know. 'You want me? You want us to run away together? Live happily ever after? You're crazy if you think that is going to happen; you're certainly crazy if you have been waiting five years to try and get me back.'

'What you call craziness, I call patience,' Mateo says chillingly.

'Have you been planning this all this time?' I ask then, very afraid of what the answer might be. 'Have you been looking for a way back into my life ever since I told you I didn't want to see you again?'

'There you go with more questions,' Mateo replies with a laugh. 'Can't you just stop asking and start answering?'

'What do you want me to answer?'

'Do you still think about me?' Mateo fires back instantly, and it seems like he has been waiting for the opportunity to ask me that.

I don't even know what to say. I shouldn't have to answer it because it should be obvious. It's absurd if he thinks I have been pining for him for five years. Yet he waits for me to respond.

'No, absolutely not,' I say firmly. 'I have not been thinking about you, and I was glad that I would never see you again. That's why I'm so angry and upset now. I thought you were out of my life forever. But you've tricked me, and you've tricked my sister too. You don't love her, do you? She's just a pawn in whatever game this is.'

Mateo doesn't argue with any of that, so I keep going.

'Maybe I tell her that you are hiding something and get her to leave you. That would ruin your game then, wouldn't it? You wouldn't be able to get close to me then.'

'Fine, give her a call and tell her,' Mateo says, holding out his phone towards me, instantly calling my bluff. But he knows I won't do that, so he slowly lowers the phone and puts it back into his pocket.

'That's right,' he says with a satisfied smile. 'You won't tell her about me and you, just like you won't tell Seth or anybody else you know. It's because you, the perfect Corinne, are not so perfect, after all. You just don't want anybody to know it.'

I'm starting to contemplate punching him again, but before those thoughts can be put into action, Mateo takes a step towards me, and I sense his mood for debating this is over. As his face gets dangerously close to mine, the closest it has been in the last five years, I get a flashback, one that isn't welcome yet it crosses through my mind anyway.

Me and him, our faces moving together until our lips meet.

We kiss and it's electric.

We keep kissing until I pull back.

As the flashback ends, Mateo gets closer to my face, though there is no danger of me kissing him this time. I just dread what he might be about to say.

I was right to be afraid.

'You have until Saturday night to tell Seth about us or I will do it for you,' Mateo whispers, as if we are the only two people in the world right now. 'Saturday night. That's when everybody finds out about us, including your sister. So it's up to you. You tell your husband about what we did. Or I do it for you.'

With that, Mateo steps back before walking away, leaving me staring at him, dumbfounded.

I try to call after him because I need to beg him not to do this, or at least beg him to give me more time.

But when I open my mouth, I can't speak.

TWELVE

'Corinne? Are you okay?'

I turn around to see Janet approaching me, concern etched on her face, but rather than feel reassured that my friend is coming to check on me, I'm now worried she just witnessed my interaction with Mateo. He's walking away, but Janet must have seen that I was talking to him if she's here now.

So how much of that conversation did she hear?

'What are you doing down here?' I cry, which isn't the friendliest way to greet my co-worker, but I need to know why she is not still at her desk.

'I was worried about you. I could sense something was wrong, so I came looking for you. I couldn't find you upstairs but when I looked out of the window, I saw you down here talking to that guy. Who was he?'

Oh no. She has seen me with Mateo. Suddenly, the man I have tried to keep secret from everyone in my personal life is starting to infiltrate it. I feel like I'm unravelling.

Thankfully, Mateo has gone now, although I didn't see him get into a car. He just disappeared around a corner. Maybe he left on foot. I don't know. He's like a mystery to me, and while that mystery was once a part of what attracted me to him, now it just means I cannot guess what he might do next and there's simply too much at stake for me not to know that.

'He's nobody,' I reply to Janet's question about Mateo's identity. But I quickly realise I need a better answer than that. 'He was just asking for directions.'

'Directions? Where to?'

'Somewhere I've never heard of, so I couldn't help him,' I say, maintaining the feeble lie.

Janet looks sceptical, and as she should, because she's a smart woman, not a stupid one, so I doubt she believes me.

'What were you doing out here?' she asks me then.

'I just needed some fresh air,' I reply. 'I wasn't feeling well.'

Janet still looks unsure, but I realise that just like yesterday with my husband, feigning illness is my best way of excusing my unusual behaviour.

'I started to feel unwell yesterday afternoon,' I go on, which is technically true if I can count seeing Mateo for the first time again as a reason for feeling sick. 'I went to bed early last night, and I thought I was feeling better today, but I guess not.'

Suddenly, Janet looks sympathetic.

'Oh, you poor thing. Do you need to sit down? Or do you need to go home?'

I wish I could go home, but what will I do there? I'll only worry. At least if I stay here at work, I might be able to forget about the terrifying ultimatum Mateo just gave me, for a couple of seconds at least.

'I'll be okay,' I say, heading for the office entrance, and Janet quickly follows alongside me, asking me more questions about my health and what I think might be causing my illness. I can't listen to her babbling on at me all day, so I have to make a polite request.

'I'm sorry. I have a bit of a headache and probably need to

just be quiet for a while, so I won't be very chatty today. Is that okay?'

Janet, my well-meaning motor-mouth friend, takes the hint and stops talking. She silently accompanies me back to my desk before getting me a glass of water. I smile at her before returning to my work, or at least making it appear like I'm working. But while I am staring at my computer screen and looking like I'm deep in thought about work matters, behind my eyes, all I can see is Mateo and the expression on his face when he told me what he wanted me to do.

'You have until Saturday night to tell Seth about us or I will do it for you.'

That dreadful deadline might be six days away, but just because it's only Monday, it doesn't mean I can take my time to think about this. Even if Mateo had given me six months to tell Seth, I still wouldn't want to. There is no timeframe in which I want to tell my husband that I cheated on him five years ago. We were still boyfriend and girlfriend at the time and, if my mistake had been exposed, Seth might never have decided to marry me.

I know that Seth will be heartbroken if he finds out and he'll most likely hate me too. He'll hate me because he'll probably feel like he has wasted the last five years of his life and could have been spending them with somebody else if I hadn't misled him into thinking I was the perfect partner. At best, I will break his heart and cause him to look at me with something other than love. He'll look at me with pain and I cannot bear the thought of that. While I might deserve it, Seth does not. He is a good man. A loyal man. I might not have been sure about him at one point in time, but he has proven himself to be a perfect partner, one I'd never recover from losing. If I crush him and he then decides to leave me, there will have to be a reason given for that and that reason will be heard by all my family members and friends. My parents will be dismayed and disappointed. My sister will be shocked, and no doubt hate me too for what I did with the man she now clearly loves. And while that would all be awful, the worst thing would be when Freddie learns that his parents are separating.

He'll know it's all his mummy's fault.

As everybody else in the office works diligently around me, living in their blissful state where all they have to worry about are irritating emails and what to have for lunch, I am drowning in my sea of despair. So much so that I feel like crying, but desperate not to do that here, in such a public place, I force myself to find a reason why this might not be as bad as I fear it is.

What if Seth could forgive me? What if he says five years was a long time ago and he doesn't care about something that happened in the past? What if this doesn't have to spell the end of my marriage?

It might be wishful thinking but, right now, it's all I've got. I desperately cling on to this thread of optimism for as long as it will hold. But it's a painfully thin thread and it easily snaps when I quickly come back to the realisation that this won't go away as easily as I want it to. Knowing Seth as well as I do, knowing exactly how much he dotes on me and worships the ground that I walk on, it will devastate him to find out that I did something behind his back. Not only that, but to have kept it a secret for five long years will make him think that I have been deceiving him all this time. He might believe I've been playing him for a fool, and I really don't want him to think it's like that because it's really not the case.

The truth is, there isn't a day that has gone by in these five years where I haven't thought about what I did and hated myself for it and, sometimes, I even have nightmares. I've suffered depression, anxiety and sleep deprivation since my Mateo mistake, but I was always able to either hide it from my husband or disguise it as being pregnancy symptoms or postnatal problems after childbirth or life as a new parent to a demanding toddler. In reality, all the mental anguish I have suffered was not down to Freddie giving me sleepless nights but because my own actions have caused me to lose sleep. The problem is, while that is the truth, it would be impossible to convince Seth of that because he'll no longer be looking at me as an honest woman. He'll be looking at me as a liar and therefore, anything I say after that point will be wasted.

I'm now imagining the worst-case scenario, which is that Seth decides to leave me, but he also fights for full custody of Freddie. If he wins, I barely get to see my son, reduced to weekends or whatever time a court might decide is fair. Our terrific trio will be halved, sliced right down the middle, a family cut in two, and while the impact of that on me would be devastating, I hate to think what it might do to Freddie's development too. It could completely change the person he one day becomes.

I don't know how long I spend staring at my screen. I don't know what time it is or how long is left until I get to go home. I don't even know that Janet has brought me another glass of water because I'm too lost in my own thoughts about losing everything I love.

All I do know is that this is all my fault.

Then it's back to what I don't know.

How can I stop Mateo acting on his threat?

How can I save my perfect family?

THIRTEEN

FIVE YEARS AGO

I left Mateo at Angelos, finishing his breakfast alone. But what he said to me just before I went is true.

He told me that he bet I wouldn't be able to stop thinking about him.

And he is right.

I'm back home in the apartment now, the one I share with Seth, but he is nowhere to be seen. He's still at work, not that he has given me any update. But surely he will be finishing soon. It's six o'clock and it's going dark outside. It's almost dinner time, and with that in mind, I have decided to cook us a lovely evening meal. There is a lasagne in the oven and the table is set with plates, knives and forks, a couple of wine glasses and a candle ready to be lit. This is my attempt at being romantic, although, if I'm really honest, it's my attempt at keeping myself busy so I stop thinking about Mateo. But no matter how much I cook, or set the table, or spend time picking which bottle of red wine to open, I cannot stop thinking about how he grabbed my arm and looked into my eyes before telling me that I had been on his mind all the time. It was a powerful moment and it's been replaying in my mind ever since.

No matter what I do, I can't seem to make it stop.

Maybe opening a bottle of wine will help instead of waiting for Seth to come home and share it with me, so I get to work on that. Pouring myself a big glass, I gulp down some of the refreshing liquid before letting out a satisfied sigh. I just need to let the alcohol take effect and soon I'll forget all about Mateo and can focus on having a nice evening with my boyfriend.

Half a glass later, and with some music playing in the apartment, I am feeling a little bit better. So, when I receive a text message on my phone, I pick it up excitedly, presuming that it's Seth telling me he has finished work and is on his way back. That should give me just enough time to slip into something a little sexier, so that by the time he walks through the door, he will realise he is the luckiest guy in the world to have a girlfriend like me. I think he needs a reminder of that. Then I read Seth's message and my plans for the evening disappear as quickly as the wine in my glass.

Sorry, there's still lots to do at work. I'm not going to be back for a while. Get yourself a takeaway and I'll see you later xx

I actually laugh when I read it. That's because I'm genuinely thinking that this has to be a joke. If not, I'm going to be furious. Despite waiting for Seth to send another message telling me that he was only joking and is on his way home, I receive nothing, so I realise that this is really it. I'm home alone on Saturday night and the romantic evening I have planned is left in ruins. I could say it was my fault for not telling Seth that I was preparing us a candlelit dinner. If I had told him, maybe he wouldn't have put work ahead of me. But deep down, I feel like it wouldn't have made a difference. When it comes to work, Seth can be very focused, to the detriment of all else. I didn't realise it was possible to be so passionate about tax, but he takes his job very seriously and has told me before that without people like him looking out for his clients' best interests, they could be losing money that could otherwise be going to their families.

I put my phone down and finish my glass of wine before pouring another one, and as I do, I feel like this is it. The end. Not only am I unhappy in this relationship now, but I also fear that if one day Seth and I were to have a child together, there might be a little boy or girl who is unhappy too. That would be the case if their daddy disappointed them by working on the weekends instead of spending quality time with them. I'd hoped to start a family with him one day, but now I just feel sad that things don't seem to be progressing that way for us. Sure, I've had my head turned but that's only because I was burying it in the sand before that, trying to tell myself that everything was still perfect with Seth when it wasn't.

Now I'm thinking about the logistics of our break-up if it goes ahead. We pay equal rent on this apartment, but neither one of us could afford it on our own, so I guess we'd have to notify the landlord and then start preparing to move. It's depressing to think about because I always thought the next time I moved, it would be when Seth and I bought a house together. But I guess not.

Should I make a start on the packing tonight? It seems a bit hasty, especially when I haven't told Seth that I want to split up yet, so I'll have to delay my next move until he gets home, whenever that may be. But it sounds like it will be a while before he's back, so what am I going to do to kill time until then?

When my phone beeps again, I wonder if Seth has somehow been able to read my mind and is urgently getting back in touch to try and persuade me that staying together is the best thing for us both after all. But it's not a message from my boyfriend. It's a message from Mateo.

Hey, I'm having a drink at Pablo's this evening and despite being on my second glass of wine, I still can't stop thinking about you. I think you should join me. In fact, I insist.

I wish I had never received this message. If I hadn't, I would have spent the rest of the evening sitting on the sofa, eating the lasagne I made and quaffing what's left of the wine I opened earlier. But now I feel a strong pull, almost a magnetic one, and it's a pull towards the door of my apartment. Pablo's is not far from where I am, a fact Mateo surely can't have known. Unless I did slip where I lived to him before and he's purposely chosen to be somewhere nearby, knowing that it will increase the chances of me agreeing to meet him. If so, he's right.

I do want to go out.

I do want to see Mateo.

I do want to be wanted.

It's a basic human desire to feel appreciated and valued by another human being, so we're all entitled to run towards it when it's offered. The problem is, as humans, we tend to over-complicate things and that's why my situation is complicated now. I'm in a relationship where I don't feel wanted and I don't want to feel like this anymore. I seem to have the solution to my problem, yet my relationship is still active, which explains the guilt and shame I currently feel.

Maybe more wine will help.

After pouring myself a second glass, I go into the bedroom to get changed. I slip on a dress I haven't worn in a while before applying some make-up. Then I gulp down my glass, telling myself that consuming it will mean that I've now drunk the same as the man I'm on my way to meet.

After leaving my apartment, I make the short walk to Pablo's, the trendy wine bar that I've been in a couple of times before, although it was years ago, when I was in my twenties, and I bet it's changed a lot since then. The whole way there, I tell myself that I am just going to meet a friend for a drink, no different to what countless other people are also doing at this time of the week. But deep down, I know it is more than that. As I enter the bar and see Mateo sitting at a table in a dark suit that makes him look extremely distinguished, I know I am powerless to prevent what happens next.

I approach the table nervously, but unlike with Seth, I don't have to wonder what might happen next or run the risk of being disappointed. It's because I know exactly what Mateo will do when he sees me and, sure enough, he does.

He breaks into a big grin before complimenting my appearance and telling me that I look beautiful. Then he beckons for a waiter to approach us, and once I have ordered my drink, Mateo asks me why I came to join him. But the devilish smile on his face seems to suggest he knows he had tipped the odds in his favour by picking this venue rather than one all the way across town. By doing so, he put me under more pressure to say no. Did I simply succumb to that pressure? Is he playing me? Or is it still fifty/fifty?

'I don't know,' I reply, which is mostly the truth. I made the decision to come here so quickly that there wasn't really time to truly explore my motives. Then I ask a question of my own.

'Why did you invite me here?'

'You know why,' Mateo replies. 'I told you why. Because I can't stop thinking about you.'

This bar is busy, but it feels as if we are the only ones in here. As Mateo and I look into each other's eyes, I feel that strange but captivating magnetic pull towards him that I felt back in my apartment when he first messaged me. Then he leans in closer to me, showing that he feels it too. We're interrupted by the waiter bringing me my drink, and I quickly take a glug of wine, feeling my face flush, though I doubt it's only from the alcohol.

'I think you should leave your boyfriend and be with me,' Mateo says, the words just slipping out of his mouth as easily as the red wine he drank must have been slipping down. But he's not the only one who has loosened his tongue with a little alcohol this evening, which is why my reply slips effortlessly out too.

'I think you're right,' I say, my mind seemingly made up as easily now that I'm here and Mateo is giving me the attention that Seth hasn't. There is a voice at the back of my mind that is asking me what I am doing, but we just keep looking at one another, our faces getting closer by the second.

Then we kiss and the magnetic feeling consumes my entire body.

That was the moment I was in too deep.

That was the moment my troubles really started.

FOURTEEN
PRESENT DAY

I'm driving home after what was a very exhausting day in the office. It's been a few hours since Mateo surprised me outside my workplace and told me that I had until Saturday night to tell Seth about what happened between us in the past. I've spent all that time trying to figure out how my life isn't going to be totally ruined by it. I've also spent a lot of time trying to decipher why Mateo gave me the deadline of Saturday night to tell Seth. What's so special about that particular time of the week? I'm not sure, but does it really matter? I've been given a deadline and if I miss it, it's not going to end well for me.

As I continue making my way to my house through rush-hour traffic, I think about how Seth will already be at home now. Mondays are his day to finish work a little earlier and collect Freddie from school, so I know the pair of them will be safely and comfortably in our living room with the TV on and various toys scattered on the carpet around them.

I feel a sting of pain in my heart then because, while driving home to my family would usually fill me with happiness, now it is just a reminder of what I stand to lose. If Mateo has his way and exposes what I did with him, and if Seth then leaves me and takes Freddie with him, this time next week, I could be driving home to an empty house.

Seth putting family before finances and finishing work early to collect Freddie from school at certain times of the week is just one example of how he has shifted his priorities away from his career throughout our relationship. He is nowhere near as focused on his work duties as he was when I met him, and while he is still driven and an excellent tax advisor by all accounts, it is more time with me and Freddie that really motivates him these days. He really has changed since that time I thought he valued work over me. Maybe all this would have been easier if he was a workaholic who didn't prioritise parenting or relationship romance, but the longer we've been together, the more of a perfect partner Seth has become. I should be thrilled about that, but in my situation, it only makes what I stand to lose even greater.

As I park outside my home, I still have to decide what I'm going to do about Mateo's ultimatum; however, I plan on doing my best to get through this evening as normally as possible. I'll do some household chores, I'll get Freddie's things ready for school tomorrow and, of course, I'll play with my son before his bedtime, and I'll ask Seth all about his day. With a bit of luck, neither of them will detect that I am carrying the weight of the world on my shoulders at this moment in time. But as I open the front door and step inside my house, I know it's not going to be easy. Things only get more difficult when I walk into the living room and see who is sitting with my husband and son.

It's Mateo.

He's in my house.

And he looks like he's made himself at home.

'Hello, Corinne,' Mateo says with his hands resting on the arms of the chair he is sitting in. He doesn't quite have his feet up on the coffee table yet, but he looks like he's so comfortable that it might be his next move.

I am frozen with fear and find myself looking to Seth to tell me what is going on here. Am I already too late? Has Mateo told him about us? Has he decided that he can't wait until Saturday after all and has come here to blow up my life sooner?

Although if he has, why is my husband looking so happy?

'Hey, honey,' Seth says, getting up and walking over to me. I remain frozen to the spot as my husband leans in and gives me a kiss on the top of my head, which is his customary welcome for me when we are reunited after a day at work. I suppose that is a good sign that everything is still normal, but then the fact that Mateo is still sitting here, only a few feet away from my husband, is proof that nothing is normal at all. He's close to my son and I look down at Freddie who is sitting on the carpet playing with one of his toy cars. He looks happy enough too, which is good to see, so I guess I'm the only one with something to worry about here. Looking back at Mateo, it seems like he is very much enjoying that fact.

'Mateo just got here and says he has something to tell us, but he wanted to wait until you got home,' Seth explains. 'I just got him a drink and he's been telling us all about some of the big football games he has been to over the years. Freddie has been enjoying hearing about them, haven't you, son?'

'Yes!' Freddie chirps up, and I guess he would have enjoyed hearing about football, because he loves the sport, as does my husband. It seems Mateo found a conversation topic that would ingratiate himself with them both, which makes me think he really has been doing his research on us. But of course he has because a man like Mateo is always one step ahead.

'I said how it was a shame we didn't get to speak properly at the meal yesterday, but it's been great to start making up for that now,' Seth goes on. I can tell that he really likes Mateo, which is even more galling.

'Are you feeling any better?' Mateo asks me then, an expression of worry across his face as if he really cares. But I know he's faking.

'What?' I reply, still shocked at his presence here.

'You weren't feeling well yesterday,' Mateo goes on. 'You left the meal early. I do hope you are feeling a little bit better now?'

The cheek of him. He knows exactly why I left that meal early and it had nothing to do with me being ill. He's playing along with that façade, and no doubt getting great amusement out of it at the same time. Unfortunately for me, with my husband and son so close to us, I have no choice but keep up that façade too.

'I am a bit better, yes,' I reply quietly, an answer which keeps me safe, but for how much longer? According to my husband, Mateo came here to tell us all something. So what is it?

'I'm sure you've all had a busy day, so I'll get straight to the point as I don't want to waste any more of your evening,' Mateo says, standing up out of the chair, and as he rises to his full height, I feel my stomach sinking all the way to the floor.

Is he really about to do this? Is he really about to stand here in my house and break Seth's heart, confuse poor Freddie and at the same time, paint me as the villain?

'Wait,' I say, the word just leaving my mouth before I have a chance to think it through, and Seth turns to me to see why I stopped Mateo from saying anything more.

'What's wrong?' my husband asks me, but I have no good answer for that one and Mateo knows it too, so he carries on.

'Georgia and I are throwing a party, and we'd like you all to be there,' Mateo says.

I slowly start to exhale when I realise he hasn't said what I thought he was going to say.

'A party? That sounds good,' Seth replies before looking at

me with a dopey grin on his face, because if anybody enjoys a party, it is my husband.

'I hope so,' Mateo goes on, smiling too. 'As you know, Georgia and I are moving in together, and she wanted to have a housewarming meal, just the two of us, to celebrate. But I've decided to make it a bigger event, so we're throwing a party, and we're asking her family and friends to be there. Sound good?'

'I think it's a great idea,' Seth says. 'Don't you, Corinne?'

I actually think it sounds awful, not to mention unnecessary. If Mateo is planning on exposing what we did and hurting my family as well as shocking my sister, why does he feel the need to throw a party for her?

Then I get the answer.

'The party will be this Saturday night,' Mateo says next and suddenly, it all falls into place. This is why he gave me the deadline of Saturday night to tell Seth about us. It's because if I haven't done it by then, he is going to do it for me and worse, it will happen in front of all our family and friends.

'Saturday night? I think we're free,' Seth says before I've even had a chance to think of an excuse as to why we can't be there, and now my husband is asking if there is anything we can bring to the party to help.

'Just bring yourselves,' Mateo replies. 'Your presence is our present.'

Seth loves that cheesy line. Mateo is loving it as well and as he looks at me, his look of happiness only expands. But I'm reeling here, unable and incapable of doing anything to stop this trainwreck occurring right before my eyes.

The party is going to be where my life falls apart, unless it hasn't done so before then, and I haven't failed to see the irony in this. That's because it was another party that got me into this mess in the first place...

FIFTEEN

FIVE YEARS AGO

I stumble out of Mateo's apartment and make my way down the stairs to the ground to find my taxi to take me home. I'm leaving by myself as Mateo is still in the apartment behind me, lying naked in the bed, only a crisp linen sheet covering his modesty. He tried to get me to stay in bed with him for the rest of the night, but I told him I had to go back to my own apartment. I'm not wrong because when I get there, I'm hoping I have beaten Seth home. It's ten o'clock in the evening and if I have got back before him, he won't ask where I've been. That will save me having to either lie or upset him with the truth, which is that I've just slept with another man. That will then give me a slightly easier transition into doing what I need to do next, which is going to be to break up with Seth.

It's time. I know it now and while I regret not doing it before I was intimate with Mateo, I'm better off doing it before I get any more involved with him. I need to do the right thing. I need to let Seth go so I can be free to move on with Mateo.

I step outside into the cold evening air, and I see the taxi I ordered on my phone waiting for me. I get into the backseat and confirm the address for my apartment, and once we are moving,

I check the time on my phone. It's only ten, so there is a chance Seth could still be working. It's unlikely, but the fact I don't have any messages or missed calls from him suggests he is not home yet and wondering where I am. But as I look at my phone again, I see somebody has made contact with me.

That was fun xx

It's Mateo and he's just very succinctly summarised what the pair of us did in his bedroom. We ended up in there after things got a little hot and steamy between us in the wine bar. I could blame it on all the wine I drank during the ninety minutes we were in that bar, and how I wanted things to continue between us beyond kissing at our table in the corner. That's why, when Mateo suggested we go back to his place nearby, I didn't disagree.

As much as I am a grown woman and can make grown-up decisions, I am now starting to feel shame as the taxi makes its way back to my apartment. It's the shame that comes with knowing that I have done something that a woman in my position should not have. I have cheated on Seth. Even though I have already decided to end things with him, I haven't actually done it yet. We are still a couple and, as such, I should be acting like I am still part of a couple. Usually, I hold myself to a higher standard than what I just did, yet I did it anyway. I never thought I'd be capable of such a thing, but then I hadn't met a man like Mateo before. I lost control of myself and while I could blame it on my sadness over Seth and me drifting apart, all the wine I have drunk tonight or that irresistible magnetic feeling I get whenever I'm around Mateo, really, I know it comes down to one thing.

I made a decision and now I'm going to have to live with it.

As the taxi arrives outside my apartment, I take a deep breath, pay my fare and then step outside, feeling like a lot has changed since I left this place earlier in the evening. If Seth hadn't been working late then the pair of us would have enjoyed dinner together and who knows, maybe the evening would have been good enough to save us. But he left me alone, for one time too many, and look what has happened now.

I enter the apartment but quickly realise Seth is not home, so I take off my dress and get in the shower. Once in my pyjamas, I slump down onto the sofa and wait for him to get back. While it might not be the best idea to break up with him while I'm drunk, at least I'll have more courage to blurt the words out than I will when I am sober. Now I just have to wait for him to walk through the door.

'Corinne, honey. It's time to wake up.'

I slowly open my eyes. Seth is looking down at me with a sweet smile. Then I see that I am in the lounge area of our apartment before noticing that I am lying on the sofa.

Wait, what happened?

'I almost woke you when I got home last night, but you looked so peaceful, so I didn't want to disturb you,' Seth says as I slowly sit up and rub my face. 'Looks like you had a couple of glasses of wine and fell asleep. It's my fault, I should have come home sooner and I'm sorry. But at least you got plenty of rest. Do you know what time it is?'

I have absolutely no idea of the time, just like I had no idea I'd fallen asleep on the sofa until I was just woken up.

'It's eleven o'clock,' Seth informs me, sitting beside me on the sofa I seem to have called a bed. 'It's quite the lie-in, but you obviously needed it and it is a Sunday, I suppose. How much wine did you have last night exactly? I found a half-open bottle and an empty glass. Did you have any more than that?'

I remember that I had a lot more than that, just like I remember who I had most of it with. I also remember what I ended up doing with that person in their apartment. Last but not least, I remember that I was waiting for Seth to come home so I could end our relationship. But stupidly, drunken me fell asleep before I could do it.

'I need to talk to you,' I say as I rub my eyes and realise it's hard to get my words out with such a dry throat.

'And I need to show you something, so get yourself ready and let's go,' Seth says, suddenly springing up off the sofa.

Though I try to get him to slow down and listen to what I have to say, he puts on his coat and shoes, looking like he is ready to go out.

'What is it?' I ask, but Seth won't say; he insists I put on something more appropriate than pyjamas, so I do that, throwing on a blouse and a pair of jeans before putting on my own coat and shoes, and once I have, we leave the apartment.

As we step out on the street, I wince at the bright sunlight and my head is pounding. This threatens to be a bad hangover and it's only going to get worse if I have to break up with Seth while feeling like this. Why couldn't I have just stayed awake last night? I would have done it already and the awkward conversation we need to have would already be in the past. Instead, it's still ahead of me, but I can't even seem to get the opportunity to talk to Seth because he's really keen on showing me something.

'Are you hungry? I'm starving,' he says as he leads me down the street. 'We've missed breakfast but it's almost lunchtime, so let's get something to eat. I know just the place. They do a great roast dinner at the cricket club, so let's go there.'

'Wait,' I say, slowing down slightly, but Seth is in such an eager mood that he keeps me moving, and I realise that even if I had the chance, the street is no place to end a relationship. We should have this conversation somewhere private, not out in public, so I won't do it here. But I do need to do it soon.

However, we seem to be going for lunch at the cricket club, which is no better place to break up with him.

'I can't wait for some good food,' Seth goes on, blissfully unaware that this is anything but a peaceful Sunday. 'It'll be nice just to chill out together. It's what weekends are made for.'

I am hungry and I desperately need some water, so a good meal would help. But it would do nothing to remedy the difficult conversation ahead of me, so I should stop walking. But how can I break Seth's stride when he is so happy? Maybe I'll just have lunch with him and then, when we return home, I can have the difficult conversation away from anybody else. Would a full stomach help heal his broken heart quicker? I don't know, but hopefully it can't hurt.

But as we reach the cricket club and walk through the front doors, I realise that I made one of the biggest mistakes of my life last night and it wasn't only what I did with Mateo. It was actually falling asleep before I could break up with Seth. That's because, as we walk in, I instantly see dozens of my closest loved ones, from family to friends, and they all shout 'SURPRISE' before rushing towards me to welcome us in.

'What's going on?' I mumble to Seth as my parents and sister give me a hug and I notice that he is smiling widely beside me.

'It's an early birthday party,' he replies, seemingly proud of how he has been able to organise all of this without me knowing. 'I have a confession to make. I wasn't at work yesterday. I was actually here helping get this place ready. I was blowing up balloons and helping prepare the food. That's why I was so late. I'm sorry, but I hope it was worth it?'

Seth looks to me for my approval, no doubt expecting me to laugh before giving him a hug and thanking him for going to all this trouble for me. But all I can do is cry. Everyone mistakenly thinks I am sobbing out of a mixture of shock and happiness, but the truth is that my tears are flowing because I know I'm too late.

I'm too late to end things with Seth because I can't do it here, in front of everyone, and not after what he has done for me. And I'm also too late because I can't take back what I did with Mateo last night in his apartment.

I've just cheated on the man who clearly loves me enough to give me a surprise party. I was too foolish, or too anxiety-ridden, to consider that Seth not spending time with me on a Saturday could be in my best interests after all. Not everything he does has to be selfish, and he has just proven that with this party. The fact I was so quick to doubt him only adds to the overwhelming sense of guilt I feel.

I don't know how it can get any worse.

Then I get my answer.

That's because, a second later, I see Seth is down on one knee. Then a ring appears from his pocket and, as the room falls quiet, I see my boyfriend's mouth moving.

I can't hear the words though, due to the rush of blood in my head, but I don't need to.

He is proposing to me.

SIXTEEN

PRESENT DAY

Another sleepless night sees me awake at dawn and fully aware that I am now one day closer to the deadline Mateo has given me to tell Seth about us.

All through the darkest hours of the day, as well as lying beside my husband and listening to him sleeping easily, I tried to figure out Mateo's plan in all of this. I mean, he has to know that if he exposes what he and I did, my sister will leave him. Why would she want to stay with the guy who has already been with her sister? Of course, Mateo has made it clear that he doesn't care much for Georgia and only got with her to get closer to me, so I would love nothing more than to get her away from him so she can meet a man worthy of her love. But how do I do that without blowing up my own relationship with her? As for Mateo, as much as things will get awkward for me when the truth comes out, they won't be easy for him either. My parents will be angry at him, especially if they see that he has been playing a game with Georgia's feelings this whole time. What does Mateo expect is going to happen? That he can just drop a bombshell and then walk away without suffering some of the consequences of his actions? My father might be angry and want to throw a punch in his direction, certainly if he sees both his daughters in tears. And the threat of physical violence might not end there, not if Seth loses control of his actions too and decides to take out his shock and anger on the man who has just revealed he slept with his wife years ago.

Mateo might think he is in control and immune to the problems I am facing, but he is wrong. As Seth continues to sleep, I decide to remind my tormentor of that. I send him a text message in which I clearly lay out that if he goes ahead with his awful and unnecessary plan, he stands to lose as much as I do, if not more.

You're crazy if you don't think that you're in danger if you tell everyone what happened. People are going to be angry and upset and you can't predict how they might behave after that. You need to reconsider this. It's not too late to change your mind and just leave.

I press send, feeling it was a good attempt at getting Mateo to have second thoughts, though I have no idea when he will read it. For all I know, he could have slept wonderfully last night and still be snoozing now. It's galling to think that he might be achieving perfect rest while I'm growing more sleep-deprived by the day, but I wouldn't put it past him to be getting eight hours of shut-eye a night while I slip further and further away from that recommended target.

Checking the time and seeing that it is still too early to get out of bed without risking waking Seth or Freddie and starting the day badly for them, I am forced to continue lying in my bedroom that is quickly beginning to feel like a prison cell. Since Mateo's return, I've spent a lot of time in here, either feigning illness or failing to sleep, and it's really starting to get on top of me now. I need to make a plan, a proper one, something that can end this waking nightmare for me, so I open the

Notes app on my phone and start typing. Initially, I'm trying to come up with a solution to my problem, but very quickly, I just end up typing out my thoughts and feelings.

I'm so scared. I don't know what to do. I can't lose my husband. I love Seth so much.

Then my thoughts turn darker.

I hate Mateo so much. I hate myself so much. Why did I make such a stupid mistake?

As I stop typing and reread a few of the things I have written about myself, I realise it has been a long time since I did this. But it's not unusual for me to be exploring my feelings through writing. This is how I tried to process the regret and shame I felt after I did what I did with Mateo five years ago, the night before Seth threw me the surprise party and showed me just how much he actually loved me. Back then, weeks after that party, instead of using the Notes app on my phone, I wrote down my feelings, furiously scribbling all sorts of stressed sentences across several sheets of paper and, at the time, I felt I was doing it as a form of confession. I would write what I did with Mateo in the naïve belief that one day I would give the confessions to Seth, and he would see what I had done. That's because I'd quickly realised that I didn't have the guts to tell him face to face, unable and unwilling to break his heart that way, so I took to writing it all down instead. However, the fact that he remains sleeping in the same bed as me all these years later, and with two wedding rings and one child between us, shows I did not ever get around to giving him those pieces of paper. Things only got better between us after he threw that surprise party for me, so not only did I not want to ruin things, but I also couldn't bear to hurt him and the longer it went on, the more it made my task of telling him the truth harder.

I decide to stop writing on my phone, but it's not making me feel any better, nor is it helping me come up with a plan of how to deal with Mateo. Even if I had come up with a plan though, it doesn't mean it would have worked. That's because I already thought I had dealt with him five years ago, just after Seth had thrown me the surprise party and precisely when I had realised that I didn't actually want to throw away what the pair of us had for some exciting but potentially doomed fling with the hot new guy I'd met at the gym.

I once figured I had the solution to my Mateo problem, and I thought it had worked. But if I was wrong to spend the night with him in the first place, I was certainly wrong to think I could end it so easily.

SEVENTEEN

FIVE YEARS AGO

I can feel the eyes of all my family and friends on me. But it's the eyes of the man who wants to become my fiancé that I feel the most. As I look down at him on bended knee, I know I need to give him an answer quickly.

He just asked me if I would marry him and I haven't replied yet.

I feel tears welling in my eyes. This should be a special moment, the perfect proposal, one that is the culmination of Seth's love up to this point. All I have to do is say 'yes' and the atmosphere at this party will only improve, as everybody will rush forward to congratulate us and eagerly start preparing for our upcoming wedding day. I can see my parents standing to the left of us, watching on eagerly, my mother no doubt already planning what colour dress she will wear, while my dad will be looking forward to putting on a smart suit and walking me down the aisle. I can see my sister too, the shocked look on her face because she can't believe this is happening here. Although she looks excited and is simply waiting for me to say yes before she rushes forward and gives me a hug. She'll expect to be chief bridesmaid, of course, and plan my hen party, and come with me to dress fittings, and oh my god, I still haven't answered Seth yet.

'Corinne?' he repeats as he starts to look less hopeful romantic and more jilted lover. Another couple of seconds tick by and now the heavy silence in the room feels less filled with anticipation and more with nervous tension. Is everybody starting to think that I might say no?

I feel like I have to. I should. How can I accept this marriage proposal without telling Seth what happened between me and Mateo last night? But then again, how can I break his heart right here in front of all these people we know? This marriage proposal, complete with a beautiful sparkly diamond ring, proves exactly how much he loves me, as if this surprise party didn't do that enough. I have misread the situation so badly. He wasn't neglecting me at all. He was planning the rest of our lives together.

'Yes,' I say when I realise I can't say the alternative. I love Seth, I do, and I want to marry him, I really do. Then, as he gets to his feet and wraps his arms around me while everyone cheers, I realise that is what is going to happen.

We'll get married.

The only thing that could ruin that now is if I confess to my one-night stand.

'What was it that you wanted to talk about?' Seth asks me as we make our way home from the surprise party he just threw for me, the party that had the mother of all surprises when the engagement ring came out. Now we're not just boyfriend and girlfriend, but husband and wife to be. How crazy is that? It's been a long afternoon of socialising, made a lot longer by the fact that I slept with a man who was not Seth last night. That's why I'm feeling extremely frazzled and in desperate need of some time to myself.

'What?' I ask, dazed and not just from last night's hangover but from the residual shock of the party and the realisation that Seth doesn't just still care about me but loves me far more than I realised.

'Back at the apartment, when I woke you up on the sofa, before the party,' Seth reminds me. 'You said you needed to talk to me. So what was it about?'

It's not that I've forgotten that I was about to break up with Seth, it's that I haven't had the chance to actually do it. Not since he led me out of our apartment and straight into that party. But now I have that chance, it doesn't mean it's possible.

I mean, how am I supposed to break up with him now, after what just happened? Not only that, but having had a reminder of how much my family and friends love Seth during the party, how much my parents approve of him and how much my sister and my friends tell me 'I have a keeper there', it seems even harder for me to end it now. Everyone who was at that party thinks I'm the luckiest girl in the world to have Seth, the kind of man who loves me so much that he throws surprise parties to not only make me happy but to give me a dream proposal. I seem to be the only fool who didn't realise the extent of that love until it was too late. How could I get him so wrong? Seth is amazing, not just for throwing the party, but for how he made me feel when we started dating. I remember how he would send me text messages at work to make me smile. The way he would have a cup of coffee ready on my bedside table whenever he woke before me. I had started to dwell so much on the negatives that I'd forgotten all the positives and that's my fault, not his. Okay, so he hadn't been perfect recently, but neither had I.

I certainly haven't been perfect now, and that's all on me, not him.

'Erm,' I say, trying to buy time to answer his question, but as I look at Seth walking happily alongside me, relaxed by the several beers he's just consumed, I realise he has absolutely no idea that I was having second thoughts about us. In his head, he is the world's greatest boyfriend who has just pulled off something incredibly sweet and romantic for his partner. So how can I cause that same world to come crashing down by telling him what I did with another man last night while he was busy blowing up balloons and hanging party banners for me?

If only I'd known that he was planning such an amazing gesture for me, I would have felt very differently about things. I wouldn't have felt he was no longer interested in me or was putting work ahead of us. If that was the case, I certainly would not have fallen into Mateo's arms. But I did fall into them. But it's not Seth's fault, of course it isn't. My boyfriend is not responsible for my actions.

Damn it, I should have trusted the man I loved more than the man who persuaded me to do the one thing I never thought I'd do.

I'm pretty sure that if I was to check my phone now, there would be a message on there from Mateo, asking when he could see me again. But what answer can I give him?

I realise I can't do anything more until I tell Seth what I did behind his back. But I don't want to lose Seth. I love Seth so much, I realise.

'It's nothing,' I eventually say, feeling ashamed as the words leave my mouth – ashamed I can't tell him what I did behind his back – I am entirely incapable of saying the whole truth.

'Really?' Seth asks, not that he would have any reason to doubt me. He's most likely just making conversation. But I double down on the deception.

'Yeah, I can't even remember what it was now,' I reply. With that, whatever moment there was to confess my fling to Seth, whatever golden window of opportunity there might have been, slams shut, and I realise I'm going to have to carry the burden of my guilt for as long as I stay in a relationship with this kind, surprise-party-throwing man. The thing is, marriage is supposed to be forever. So considering what we've just done, am I going to have to take this secret to the grave? If so, that is a hell of a long time to live with my guilt.

'Sorry if I've been a little distant lately,' Seth adds as our apartment comes into view. 'It's just there's been a lot to organise with the surprise party and, of course, I was ring shopping. That was more stressful than I thought it would be, as well as time-consuming. I had no idea there were so many options when it came to diamonds but now I feel like I'm an expert. Seriously, ask me anything, I probably know it.'

Seth laughs as he waits for me to humour him and ask him something about diamonds. But I don't do that. Instead, I just rub my aching temples and wonder how I could fail to realise I already had the perfect man at home so did not need to go looking elsewhere. I should never have jumped to conclusions, but I did and now look at the mess I'm in. Not that Seth knows it. He's now whistling away as if he's the happiest man in the world, making me feel even guiltier.

I have to stop and hug him then, not just because it's a way to stop him seeing the tears in my eyes but because he deserves it. What a lovely thing he's done and it's all for me.

'Thank you,' I say, still dazed, but I shouldn't let all his hard work go today without recognition.

We make it back to our apartment and, unlike last night, I make it into my bed instead of passing out on the sofa. But while I was hoping Seth might just fall asleep and leave me to wallow in my remorse, I realise that's not the case when he starts trying to kiss my neck. Oh no, he's feeling frisky. Such a thing would have made me happy at any other time, but now? How can I go along with it when I'm feeling so wracked with guilt?

'I'm really tired,' I say softly. 'And I think I drank too much champagne at the party because my head is pounding. You don't mind if we just go to sleep, do you?'

Seth stops immediately and respects my request, because of course he does. He's perfect and I'm a fool for not seeing that.

'I hope you've had a great day?' Seth asks me as he snuggles in beside me, and I tell him that I have before he adds one last thing. 'I love you, Corinne, and I can't wait to spend the rest of my life trying to make you happy.'

As Seth closes his eyes beside me, I stare up at the ceiling and say that I love him too, because it's the truth. I do. I always have. I just got waylaid. I lost sight of everything I thought I knew, not just about Seth but about myself too. Now I need to try and make this right.

Once I'm sure that Seth is asleep, I dare to check my phone and, sure enough, there is a message on there from Mateo.

> *I can't stop thinking about last night. It was incredible. Please tell me you have left your boyfriend already so we can be together again soon xx*

The message churns my stomach, and I wish I could just ignore it. Then I realise that I could. What if I just don't reply to Mateo? Sure, he'd probably message again, but I could ignore that one too. It would be cowardly on my part, but what's the alternative? To tell him that I've changed my mind and don't want to leave my boyfriend? Would he accept that? It's unlikely given what we did last night, and based on how much he has already told me that he can't stop thinking about me, I fear that he would keep working to try and change my mind. I can't have that. I don't want to keep messaging him because Seth might see one of the texts and that would break his heart.

I tell myself that what I did with Mateo, whatever attraction I felt and whatever strange magnetic force drew me to him, was just an anomaly. A freak occurrence. A blip on my otherwise perfect record as a girlfriend. I was confused and mistakenly thought that Seth didn't love me anymore. I was also panicked that I was getting old and missing out on my opportunity to find the right guy who I would one day start a family with. And while it's a lame excuse, it's still true. I was very, very drunk when I fell into Mateo's bed last night. So when I consider all that, I realise that though it was still a mistake, I have some excuses for making it.

Next, I tell myself that Mateo was just an illusion and not the real thing. He got to swoop in and be the perfect hero while Seth seemed like the guy who was throwing me away, but in reality, I got Seth all wrong, which means I could easily have got Mateo wrong too. Sure, he seems amazing now, but that's only because we've had one drunken first date where everything was exciting. But I bet if we were to go beyond the first small hurdle and actually embark on a proper relationship, the magic would soon wear off and things wouldn't be so magical and exciting then. That's just how relationships work; they're fun at first but then they require more effort. Maybe Mateo would not be able to make that effort; I really don't know him well enough to be able to judge this. But having seen what he has done for me today, I know that Seth can take our relationship to the next level. Being in a couple is not all about trendy wine bars, clandestine coffee meetups and hot and steamy bedrooms, but splitting the bills, taking out the rubbish and putting up with one another's faults. It's going beyond surface-level attraction and having something deeper, more meaningful. I've done that with Seth but not with Mateo, and that's why I know that I want to stick with the man I'm in bed with now rather than run off and embark on something that might quickly fizzle out. To think I even considered Seth was doing the same thing to me, sneaking off and staying out late to spend time with someone else. How could I get this so wrong?

I cannot risk getting in touch with Mateo again. That's why I decide that I'm going to change my phone number so he can't contact me anymore. That wouldn't be enough on its own, not if I was to go to the gym and see Mateo there. So I realise I can't ever go back there again. I can't attend the fitness class where we first met or go for a drink in the gym café or set foot in any of the places we frequented together, like Angelos or Pablo's. I have to avoid anywhere where I could cross paths with Mateo. If I can manage to avoid him, maybe I can keep the secret of what we did too.

I delete all the texts from Mateo and put my phone down. I'll sort out getting a new number tomorrow. I can say I was getting hassled by too many sales calls or whatever excuse people might buy. Then I'll cancel my gym membership and hopefully that will be enough.

I feel bad for Mateo because he only treated me with respect, and the last time he saw me, he genuinely thought I was ready to be in a relationship with him. But it's clear what my biggest weakness is in life: I avoid difficult conversations. I do that because I don't want to upset the other person. I'm scared of upsetting Seth and the same goes for Mateo, so to avoid that, I am just keeping quiet.

It's crazy, but everyone who was at that party today thinks I'm winning at life and why wouldn't they? I imagine they also assume that the next steps for Seth and me, after the wedding, will be to buy a home and then, one day, have a baby. That would be the normal trajectory for a couple like us, a normal, standard couple, or at least that's what everyone thinks we are. But I know we are not. We are different now and I have caused that difference. Seth may not know there is a secret between us, but I know it and that means things are never going to be the same, whatever happens from here.

As I continue to stare up at the ceiling, I realise that this isn't likely to be the first sleepless night I endure over this. I bet that I'm now cursed to have many more nights just like this one, where I worry and fret over what I did and how crushed Seth would be if he ever found out. That is my punishment for my actions, and I'll have to live with them.

I haven't even become a parent yet and sleep deprivation is going to be my new best friend, but it's better than breaking Seth's heart.

As for Mateo, he's a confident, good-looking guy who could have his pick of any woman, so I'm sure he'll move on and forget about me.

Right?

EIGHTEEN

PRESENT DAY

How much caffeine can one person consume before it becomes life-threatening? That's the question I'm pondering while sipping my fifth coffee of the day as I attempt to stave off the consequences of yet another sleepless night.

It's been three days now since Mateo unexpectedly reappeared in my life and two days since he issued the deadline for me to tell Seth about the night we had together. That means it's now Wednesday, hump day, the halfway point of the week. For most people who work traditional jobs, that is good news because it means the weekend is on the horizon. Like everyone else I work with, I'd normally be excited at the prospect of the weekend myself, looking forward to a free couple of days to spend time with my husband and son. But not this week. This is one week that I never want to end and if I could be granted a wish, it would be for Saturday to never come. But I know it's futile. Saturday is approaching because the clock never stops ticking. I am running out of time to solve my dilemma and save my marriage.

I'm sitting at my desk and failing to concentrate on work once again. I'm also failing to be a good sister because Georgia has sent me a couple of messages asking me if she can call around to see me sometime this week, and I haven't replied to her yet. It's classic me, avoiding something awkward rather than facing it head-on, but if I can avoid having to see my sister in the short term, and listen to her gushing all about Mateo, then I will try and do it.

I'm hoping that my lack of a response will make her think that I am incredibly busy juggling my personal and professional life and she'll leave me alone for a while. But it's hard because we always exchange multiple messages. I also know that I can't avoid her forever, and even if I don't see her before Saturday, I will see her then, at the party, the one where Mateo will ruin my life if I haven't already done it myself before then. Unless I can come up with a way of not going to that party. I'd need a good excuse, a believable one, because it would be a big event to miss and it would disappoint a lot of people if I wasn't there. But other than feigning another illness, I can't see what else I can do. I'm afraid that even if I'm not there, Mateo could tell everybody and then I'd be a coward, as well as a liar, for staying away.

But while I'm not messaging my sister, there is someone I am messaging, and as I type out another text to Mateo, I am wondering if this might finally be the one that gets him to listen. That's because I've sent him several messages over the past few days, urging him to rethink his plan, though none of them have worked so far. But I can't give up.

Please, there's no reason to hurt Seth or Georgia or anybody. You're mad at me and I get that, so hurt me, but please, leave everybody else out of it.

Of course, I know that the best way for Mateo to hurt me is to leave my family in disarray, but I can't sit here and just allow him to do that without trying to stop him. But as he fails to respond to me once more, just like I failed to respond to him after I decided that I never wanted to see him again five years ago, I realise he has me exactly where he wants me. He holds all the power now, just like I guess he felt I held all the power when I changed my phone number and left the gym so he couldn't see me anymore. It's proving impossible to get rid of him now, but then again, I didn't make a totally clean job of getting rid of him the first time.

NINETEEN

FIVE YEARS AGO

The best way to forget about your worries can sometimes be to reach for a strong drink, and as I continue to enjoy a night of revelry with Seth and a group of our friends, I am managing to forget about a few of mine. It's been a couple of months since my night with Mateo and, in that time, I have managed to not see him or hear from him. Okay, so that's because I got a new phone number and quit the gym. Seth and I have grown so much closer again since I accepted his proposal. He's organised numerous date nights, made me feel more loved than I ever have before and even our sex life has perked up. What more could a girl want? Of course, there's also been a lot of wedding planning, something I was apprehensive to start on, but Seth has taken the lead on that, already coming up with lots of ideas for the various decisions we need to make before the big day itself. We haven't set a date yet, but it's only a matter of time. We're actually looking at a couple of potential venues next weekend. It's all moving so fast, and I should be loving it. And I am. But then I remember my secret and how none of this would be happening if I let it slip.

Right now, I certainly don't want another tequila shot, but

as my friends order another round, I guess I'm not going to get away with it that easily. Seth doesn't seem to mind that we're having another one though, and it's nice to see him so happy. He leans in to give me a kiss before our drinks are served.

'Next bar!' someone calls out over the loud music, and I grimace as more tequila goes down the hatch, and now we're all moving on.

I check the time as we leave and see that it is approaching midnight, but as no one in our group has kids yet or has to worry about babysitters or dealing with a little one while hungover, I guess the night is still young.

'Where are we going?' Seth asks as we follow the crowd.

'Pablo's!'

I stop dead in my tracks. I can't go in there. That was where I drank wine with Mateo before we went back to his apartment. I've consciously avoided anywhere I know he frequented, which means I cannot go to Pablo's now. I tried to steer my friends away from this area when we planned this night out, but they insisted on going out around here. I figured there were plenty of bars so the chances of going to the one bar I wanted to avoid seemed small. But the odds have just gone against me.

'Let's go somewhere else,' I try, but my friends already seem to have the plan. I see the wine bar up ahead, and I start to panic. Then I decide to abort.

'It's getting late. Maybe we should call it a night,' I say to Seth, hoping he's ready to leave too. But he doesn't look like he is because he appears shocked at my suggestion.

'What? No way! I'm having fun,' Seth cries, clearly drunk but happy. 'Aren't you?'

'Erm, yeah, but—'

'Come on, Corinne, we can dance in Pablo's!' one of my friends says, interlinking arms with me, and as Seth takes my other arm, I am swept through the doors of Pablo's before I can do anything else about it.

It's the weekend, so the place is understandably packed, but I'm instantly scanning the faces of everybody in here, fearing that Mateo is among the crowd. But there are too many people here and many of them are dancing, so it's hard to keep track. Add in the low lighting and I have no chance of knowing for sure if Mateo is in the same room as us. I just have to pray he is not. I tell myself the odds are unlikely.

'I'll get the drinks,' Seth declares, and he heads to the bar, leaving me with my friends. But two of them disappear off to the bathroom before two more head for the dancefloor and suddenly, I'm standing by myself in this place where I really do not want to be.

'He's not here,' I say, taking a deep breath, but it's impossible to relax. I can see the exact table over there where Mateo and I drank wine on that fateful night. Thankfully, he is not at that table now, but he could be anywhere else, watching me, approaching me, preparing to expose me.

But after another few minutes, I calm myself down and decide that he's not here. Then I look over to Seth at the bar, figuring I could go and help him with the drinks. Except when I spot him, I see who he is talking to.

Mateo.

I swear my heart actually stops beating when I see my boyfriend talking to the man I cheated on him with. My worst fears are true. Mateo is in here tonight, and now he is in conversation with Seth. It's so loud in here that I can't hear what is being said, but I'm not sure I dare to get any closer to try to pick up the conversation in case Mateo sees me. What if he has no idea who Seth is? It could just be a coincidence. They might have randomly got talking while waiting to be served by the bartenders. It could be an innocent interaction. But then I see something that turns my blood cold.

Mateo looks back over his shoulder and right at me before he delivers a devastating smile in my direction. It instantly tells me that not only does he know I am here, but he knows exactly who it is that he is talking to.

I decide I cannot stand by and potentially watch him tell Seth everything, so I rush forward, almost spilling the drinks of a couple who are moving in front of me at the same time. Then I squeeze my way to the front of the bar, eliciting a few tuts and groans from those waiting around me, before I reach Seth.

'Hey, there you are. Are you okay?' I ask him, figuring I'll be able to tell straight away if he has been given some bad news. Thankfully, Seth smiles.

'Yeah, all good,' my fiancé replies. 'I was just trying to get served when this kind gentleman offered to get our drinks for us.'

He gives Mateo a hearty slap on the back, as if the pair of them are old friends, and Mateo is still grinning widely as he looks at me.

'This is my fiancée,' Seth says proudly, and Mateo gives a nod of approval.

'Lucky guy. She's very beautiful,' he says to Seth but loud enough for me to hear too.

'Thank you,' Seth replies, thinking he's made a buddy at the bar, but I know he is very wrong. I need to get him away from Mateo as quickly as possible, so I nudge my way in between them. Then I look to my boyfriend.

'Everyone else has gone to the bathroom. Do you need to go?' I ask him, hoping he has a full bladder from all the drinks he's recently consumed. 'I can wait here for the drinks if you need to.'

'Yeah, maybe I will go, actually,' Seth says.

I'm grateful when he moves away from the bar, although not before thanking Mateo on his way past for the quicker service.

Now we're alone, so I waste no time turning to the man I have been avoiding for the past two months. But he speaks before I can.

'So you're still alive then,' Mateo says with a chuckle. 'I was worried you were dead. After all, I hadn't heard a word from you since that night. I also see that you're still with your boyfriend, despite what you told me while we were in bed together.'

'I'm sorry,' I start with, because I am. 'But things changed between me and Seth when I got home. It's complicated, but I realised I still loved him and didn't want to end things. I know I should have sent you a message, but I was scared of him finding out what we did. I don't usually behave like that, and I was worried, so I just panicked and cut contact. I apologise for that, but please, don't say anything to him about us. I beg you.'

Mateo seems surprised.

'Why would you think I would say anything?' he asks me. 'I'm not angry at you. Just disappointed.'

That almost feels worse, but I have no one to blame for this but myself.

'I'm sorry,' I say again before looking over my shoulder for Seth or any of my friends, but I can't see them.

'I wish you all the best,' Mateo says then as my drinks are served and he pays for them with a twenty-pound note.

'Wait,' I cry out as he walks away, because I at least want to thank him for the drinks, if not apologise one more time for what happened between us. But he's gone and my secret goes with him.

'Who was that? He's hot,' I hear one of my friends say in my ear as I spin around and realise I have company again.

'Oh, nobody,' I reply, and then I catch a glimpse of Mateo outside the bar, through the windows, walking away down the street. But as he goes, he turns and looks at me and there's something about the expression on his face that tells me this isn't over. While I hope it is the last time I ever see him, I realise I'm powerless to stop running into him again. I'm even more powerless to stop him if he actively chooses to try and find me or Seth in the future and blow things up between us. But at least he doesn't seem as if he wants to tell anyone what we did that night and maybe it will stay that way forever.

So I guess I don't have to worry about him anymore.

Despite wishing that was true, I spend the rest of the evening thinking about that look on his face and how ominous it seemed.

TWENTY

PRESENT DAY

I'm jittery on the drive home from work, thanks to all the caffeine I've had today. But I'm just as jittery as I stress about Mateo and what he might do next. I have until Saturday to do what he wants me to, but he could change his mind and move the deadline. It's not as if he hasn't changed his mind before. When I bumped into him that night five years ago in Pablo's, he seemed like he was at peace with how things had ended between us. He could have told Seth then, but didn't, so I thought I was in the clear. But now he's changed his mind and if he can do that once, he can do it again. I cannot trust anything that man says, and I'll have to bear that in mind over these next few anxiety-ridden days. I also don't know what prompted that change of attitude from him, which only makes him more unpredictable and therefore, frightening.

I get home but sigh when I see Georgia's car parked outside my house. I guess she has got bored of me ignoring her text messages and decided to come and speak to me in person. I take a deep breath before walking in, figuring I might as well get this next awkward conversation over with as quickly as possible. But when I see Georgia, she is standing in my kitchen, stirring a bubbling pot of sauce as if she owns the place.

'What's going on?' I ask her as I watch her cooking.

'Oh, hey sis!' she says, turning around, and I notice she is wearing one of my aprons. 'I'm making dinner for us. Seth is taking Freddie to Mum and Dad's for a sleepover, so we can have a nice evening catching up. Sound good?'

I'm surprised because this is the first I've heard about any of this, but that feeling only continues when Georgia keeps talking.

'I figured it was time for our first double date,' she goes on, but I frown because I'm not sure what she means. Me, Seth and Georgia doesn't sound like much of a double date to me. Then I hear the sound of a wine bottle being uncorked behind me, and as I spin around, my gasp would be audible were it not for the loud simmering pan.

'Hi, Corinne,' says Mateo with that devilish smile of his.

TWENTY-ONE

'Dinner is served,' says my sister as she places a hot bowl of spaghetti carbonara down in the centre of the table and, as she does, the two men seated at it both show their appreciation.

'Wow, that looks fantastic,' Seth says hungrily.

'I have to agree, mate,' Mateo adds, and the way he calls my husband his 'mate' is just another thing to ratchet up my discomfort. Fortunately, there is no way Seth could have recognised Mateo as that man from the bar that night years ago. He was far too drunk, plus it was only a passing interaction, not at all memorable for Seth.

Not like it was for me.

But that's where any luck ends.

Having just about concealed my surprise and dismay at seeing Mateo here to have dinner in my home, I am now doing my best to conceal my fury at how calm he is such a short time after making a threat to me. I already knew he was like this, but it really is as if he has two personalities. He has the side that he shows to most people. Then there's the part only I am privy to, the part that he hides so well from everyone else, but the part that really shines when he and I are alone together.

'I know I said it the other day when I was here, but you really do have a lovely home,' Mateo says as Georgia uses the spoon to put some pasta on her plate. 'You two are really blessed.'

Mateo looks at Seth first, then at me, and I can tell he's just waiting for me to go along with this act. He will get pleasure out of me playing my part, humouring him, pretending like we are all good friends here and it's lovely to make conversation around this table together. The problem is, I can't do anything else, so unfortunately, I have to give Mateo what he wants. For now, at least.

'Thank you,' I say before I take the spoon and put a little food onto my plate, although I don't take much because once again, my appetite evaporated the second I realised Mateo was near.

'Corinne is very house-proud,' Seth tells Mateo. 'She has put her personal touch on this place, and she's done a fantastic job. If it was left to me, it wouldn't be quite so nice.'

I appreciate my husband complimenting me on my interior design skills and the effort it took for me to really make this house a home, but I also feel like it's wasted on the person he is saying it to. Mateo doesn't care about any of this, not really; he's just feigning interest because he knows it's making me squirm.

'I hope it runs in the family,' Mateo jests then as he looks at my sister.

'Hey, everything will be fifty/fifty when we live together,' she says with a mouthful of food, a bad habit my sibling has had since childhood, yet no one ever seems to pull her up on it and I lost interest in doing so years ago.

'Fine by me,' Mateo replies with a grin, but I'm sure the grin doubles in size when he looks in my direction.

God, I wish I could pick up my plate and throw it at him. This smug, arrogant, cruel man who is playing with my family as if we are toys in a nursery. I'd love to bounce this plate off his head, hear him cry out in pain and see him covered in hot, sticky carbonara sauce that scalds his skin and causes him to leap up out of his seat. Yet such an act would require strong explanation, so as it is, I have to sit here and grimly keep nibbling my food while Mateo shoves mouthfuls of pasta into his.

'So Sunday is the big day, right?' Seth says, and my heart skips a beat as I wonder what he is referring to. It can't be Mateo's deadline on Saturday night, can it? Why does my husband think that Sunday will be a big day?

'Yep, Mateo officially moves in with me on Sunday morning,' Georgia says proudly, and I realise that's what my husband was talking about.

'Any tips for living with a Jones sister?' Mateo asks Seth cheekily. 'I mean, you've had plenty of practice so you must know a few of the traps that I'm better off not falling into.'

'Hey, there is nothing wrong with us, isn't that right, sis?' Georgia says, looking at me to keep the fun going. But I'm really not in the mood so I just shrug and look down at my plate again.

'I would love to help you, mate, but I think these two are quite different,' Seth replies, and now he's also using the 'M' word when talking with Mateo.

'Really? I'm not so sure,' Mateo replies, looking at Georgia first but then at me when no one else is watching him. 'I think they're pretty similar. Looks, personality. Double trouble.'

Seth and Georgia both laugh, but I do not because I know what he is hinting at. He's hinting that if a guy was to like one sister, they'd probably like the other one because it's true that Georgia and I are similar in appearance and personality. There are some differences between us, for sure, but Mateo is choosing to neglect them, as he knows that by suggesting we're the same, it's making me feel even more uncomfortable. He knows that I know he's been with both of us. But my unsettled feeling doesn't get any better when Mateo speaks again.

'Forgive me if I'm wrong, but you guys seem so happy

together,' Mateo says to both Seth and me. 'I mean, I've only met you both a couple of times but you each have this glow about you that just radiates happiness. So, what's your secret to a perfect relationship?'

'Oh, well, that's such a good question that I'll have to let my darling wife answer it,' Seth says as he looks at me with a smile. 'What do you think, Corinne? What's our secret?'

Of course, there is no secret because no couple in the world is absolutely perfect. But Mateo knows exactly where the flaw is in my relationship and now he's having fun poking at it while my husband and sister are none the wiser.

'Erm, I don't know,' I mumble while moving some pasta around on my plate with my fork.

'Come on, I'm dying to hear it,' Mateo maintains, and I'm not getting off the hook, so I better say something, anything, to stop this awkwardness building even more.

'Erm, I guess we just make a good team,' I say for lack of anything better to say, and Mateo nods as if taking that answer on board. But then he starts wagging his finger at Seth and me.

'No, I reckon it's something else. Something more important,' he tells us. 'I think the reason you two are so good together is because you are open and honest with one another. No secrets. That's it, isn't it?'

I grit my teeth and silently count to five, not wanting to tell him to get out because that will cause a scene, but wishing with every fibre of my being that this man would leave this table and leave my house by the time I stop counting. As it is, he continues to sit there, eating the food my sister cooked him, calling my husband his mate and toying with me by talking about how Seth and I have no secrets from one another.

'Has it always been plain sailing for you two or have there been any bumps along the way?' Mateo asks us then, and I know where he is going with this line of enquiry too.

'I'd say it's been pretty smooth sailing,' Seth replies, and I can tell he means that honestly, which only makes me feel worse.

'Really? That's interesting,' Mateo says, looking greatly amused as he stares at me. 'There must be something in the past. Don't tell me you actually are perfect?'

Thankfully, my sister interjects.

'Stop pestering them and let them eat their food,' she says with a laugh. 'How is the food by the way? Is everyone enjoying it? I could have put a bit more pepper in, but I forgot. Sorry.'

'Are you kidding? It's great,' Seth replies, and I smile, just grateful that we're talking about something else.

But Mateo won't let me off the hook that easily. He next says something that is really too much for me to handle.

'Tell me about Freddie? He's four, right? So that means you conceived him around five years ago. That must have been an exciting time for you. What was it like to start a family together?'

I drop my fork onto my plate, and it clatters loudly. It's still vibrating as I get out of my seat and leave the table.

'Are you okay?' Seth calls after me, and I mumble something in response but it's barely audible, and within seconds, I'm away from them all and locking myself in our downstairs bathroom.

I take several deep breaths then with both my fists clenched tightly, but it's not enough, and suddenly I lunge for the toilet and just about manage to lift the lid up in time before I'm sick into the bowl.

What's caused this sudden bout of nausea? I wish it was just my sister's cooking, but it's not. It's the fact that Mateo has just referred to the timeline of when my son was conceived, and there can only be one reason why he is doing that in my presence.

He's questioning who the father of my child might be.

TWENTY-TWO

FIVE YEARS AGO

My eyes sting and my throat burns and I'm praying to whichever God might listen to me to give me a break from this incessant wave of nausea. But perhaps my lack of religious faith throughout most of my life is now working against me because if there are any Gods out there who might be listening, they don't give me what I want.

I'm sick again and it's been this way all morning. In fact, this is the third morning in a row now and I'm fearing that what I initially thought was just a very bad hangover might be something much more serious. What if I'm ill? What if I'm dying? I guess I need to go to a doctor to find out, so when I get a temporary reprieve from the nausea, I grab my phone and complete the online booking form for my local GP, hoping that they will call me back with an available appointment today.

'Are you okay?'

I hear Seth's voice on the other side of the locked bathroom door, and I feel bad for shutting him out. But I don't want him to see me like this, and I certainly don't want him to see what I am regurgitating into the toilet bowl, so I had no choice but to keep him away. But he's concerned and I'm not surprised because over these past few days, I feel like I've spent more time in the bathroom than I have anywhere else.

'I think you should call the doctor,' Seth says then after I've failed to reply. 'Or I can do it for you. I really think you should see somebody about this.'

'Already on it,' I call back before taking a deep breath and hoping that the sickness is gone for now. Thankfully, I think it might be, so I slowly get to my feet before catching a glimpse of myself in the mirror. I'm not a pretty sight, but I wasn't expecting to be, not after what I've just been doing.

I quickly flush the toilet before rinsing some mouthwash and then, when I'm hopeful that my breath isn't totally foul, I unlock the door and step outside to see Seth.

'Oh, you look awful,' he says bluntly, in that honest way that many men possess.

'Thanks,' I mutter before I head for the bed and flop down onto it. I'm not going to go to work again today, not until I've resolved this health issue, and it's definitely for the best. Seth thinks so too.

'You get some rest,' he says to me as he tucks the duvet over me before checking I have a glass of water on the bedside table. 'I'm going to work but I want you to call me if you get worse. And let me know if the doctor can see you today.'

I nod wearily before closing my eyes. I hear Seth leave, though not before telling me he loves me. I mumble it back before he's gone, and now I'm left alone to wallow. This is almost as bad as actually being sick because all I have to do now is think about what might be wrong with me.

It's Tuesday now, which means it's three days since the night out with Seth and my friends. That was the night I bumped into Mateo in the wine bar, which was unpleasant but, ultimately, I came through it unscathed or at least my relationship with Seth did. So when I woke up the next morning, feeling sick and dehydrated, I just put it down to my overindulgences at the bar. I'd already drunk enough before I even saw Mateo and, at first, I thought this sickness was the shock. But the morning after was rough. So was the morning after that and this morning has been no better, and considering I've never had a hangover last more than forty-eight hours before, I really don't know what is going on here.

I must doze off at some point because I get woken by the sound of my phone ringing. It's the doctor's receptionist, asking me if I can make it in for an appointment just before midday. It's a relief to hear it, so I tell them I can and then I haul myself out of bed and try to get ready to face my doctor. I also text Seth to let him know that I am going to be seen shortly, so he's aware that I might have an update on my current health issues soon.

Please don't let it be bad news, I think as I take a shower, although part of me wonders if I might deserve it if it is, considering what I did behind Seth's back with Mateo. Does karma work that quickly? If it does, I guess I'm doomed and that's why I spend a lot longer in the shower than I anticipated. I'm sobbing, the water running over my face and merging with the tears running down my cheeks, and by the time I step out of the shower, I've convinced myself that I'm on my way to an appointment in which I am going to be told I only have a matter of weeks to live.

I manage to make it to my doctor's office without being sick on the way, which feels like an impressive feat considering I am nauseous almost the entire way there. I even had a little sick bucket beside me on the passenger seat as I drove. I carry it with me into the waiting room just in case.

I confirm my appointment with the receptionist before taking a seat and, while I wait, I receive a message from Seth to let me know he is thinking about me.

I'm sure you'll be okay, but call me if you need me and I'll be right there. I love you xx

Such a heartwarming text, but with my guilt and nausea swirling around inside me, it only makes me feel worse. Then I'm called in by my doctor.

'Hi, Corinne. Please, take a seat,' my friendly GP says, and I do as I'm told. 'What seems to be the problem?'

'I've been feeling sick for the past three days,' I explain glumly, the bowl resting on my lap. 'I thought it was a hangover from Saturday night, but it seems to be getting worse, and I've never been like this before. I'm not usually a sicky person.'

'I see,' the frowning doctor says, and I imagine he is frowning because he already knows I'm a dead woman walking and now he just needs to determine exactly how long I have left to walk. 'Is this sickness better or worse at any particular time of the day?'

'Erm...' I reply, thinking about it. 'It's definitely worse in the morning. It eases off at night. But I generally feel queasy for most of the day.'

'I see. Have you taken a pregnancy test?'

'A what?'

I look at my doctor as if he's just grown five new heads and several new arms. But he just looks back at me as if what he has suggested is a perfectly normal thing to say.

'Could it be possible that you are pregnant?' he enquires tentatively then, aware that my shock might mean pregnancy is the last thing I thought it could be. He would be right. That never crossed my mind. Dying of some awful disease I'd never heard of seemed more likely. But now he has put the idea in my head, something worse than nausea grips my body.

It's fear.

The fear of the unknown.

But it's not a question of whether I am pregnant or not – a

simple test will determine that. It's more a question of if I am pregnant, who is the father? That's because, as my doctor tells me I may be exhibiting symptoms of morning sickness, I realise it could be one of two men.

It could be Seth, my fiancé, the man I love and the man who is anxiously waiting for me to give him an update on my health after this appointment. He's also the man I have been sleeping with for the last few years, and I definitely slept with him the morning after he proposed.

Or it could be Mateo, my mistake, the man I went to bed with once and the man I was hoping I would never have to see or think about ever again.

'I think a test would be a good idea,' my doctor says with a kind smile, but he's simply referring to a pregnancy test.

But I already fear I know what the answer will be to that particular test. That's why, in what should be an incredibly happy moment for me, I'm feeling horrendously sick.

The only test I know I need to take now is a paternity test.

TWENTY-THREE

PRESENT DAY

'Are you okay? You look awful.'

It's a typical question from a sibling, one that shows both concern and then is immediately followed by a teasing analysis of my appearance. But I can't argue with my sister because she's right. I do look awful, that's just what happens when a person has been sick. But I knew I couldn't stay in the bathroom all night, so I had to come back out and show my face. Hopefully, it's not for long.

'I'm really not feeling well. I'm sorry but you're going to have to leave so I can go to bed,' I say to Georgia, hoping she will immediately tell Mateo that they are leaving. But it's wishful thinking when they're both barely halfway through their meals and most likely thinking that even if I'm ill, I could just excuse myself while they sit here and finish their food.

'What's wrong?' Mateo asks me, but I ignore him as Seth gets up and approaches me.

'What is it?' he asks me, concerned, just like he was at the restaurant on Sunday when we abruptly left the family meal before it even started. If either he or my sister could see the pattern emerging here and realised that I'm only ever ill when forced to spend time with Mateo, it could be a problem, but neither of them seems to have figured it out yet.

'I've just been sick,' I whisper to Seth, and he raises his eyebrows.

'Oh, okay,' he replies. 'Do you want to go and lie down?'

'Yeah,' I say, and I turn for the door. I pause when I hear what he says next.

'Corinne is just going to go and lie down, but you guys finish your meals and your drinks,' Seth says to Georgia and Mateo.

Wait, I thought they were going to leave?

'Only if you're sure,' Mateo says, pretending to be polite, but Seth assures him that he is.

As my husband retakes his seat, he notices that I'm still lingering nearby.

'It is okay if they stay and finish, right?' he asks me as if it never occurred to him that I would prefer our guests to be gone, even though I said precisely that when I came back from the bathroom. But now he's made it awkward, I can hardly stand here and explicitly tell my sister to get up and leave.

'We'll be quick,' Georgia says before taking another bite of her food, and I wonder if she is a little annoyed that I've spoiled the last two meals we have had together with my illness that still hasn't been explained.

'Yeah, we can just chat while you go and have a lie down,' Mateo says then with a smile, clearly wanting me to worry about what it might be that he chats about when I'm gone.

So now I have no choice.

I have to stay.

I retake my seat and take a sip of water as Seth again asks me if I'm okay, but I nod and glumly decide I'm going to have to wait this out until Georgia and Mateo have gone. At least by being here, I'll know everything that is discussed.

'So, Mateo, we don't know much about you yet,' Seth says then.

'What do you want to know?' Mateo replies coolly, as if he already has an answer prepared for everything – and I'm sure that he does.

'What was your story before you met Georgia?' Seth asks, and while I appreciate my polite husband is just making conversation, I really wish he wouldn't pry because it's surely playing into the game Mateo is already enjoying.

'My story? There isn't much to tell,' he replies before glancing in my direction.

'That's his usual answer to that question,' my sister adds. 'Any time I've tried to get him to open up about his past, he always keeps it a mystery.'

'Ahhh, you're one of those guys, are you?' Seth replies with a chuckle. 'Mysterious. Aloof. A few skeletons in the closet.'

My husband is only joking, but Mateo seems quite happy to play along with it, no doubt loving all the attention he is getting while I sit nearby and stress about what might be revealed.

'I guess you could say that,' Mateo replies. 'But isn't it better to have a bit of mystery? At least for a while. It makes things exciting, don't you think?'

He's looking at me again as he says that, but my unsuspecting partner has no idea why, so he just agrees.

'I guess so,' Seth replies. 'I wish I could be like that. I'm more of an open book, aren't I, darling?'

Seth takes my hand and smiles, so I smile back to keep up appearances.

'But don't worry, the truth always comes out in the end,' Mateo then says chillingly. 'At least that's what I've found.'

He's really loving this, but I've had enough and that's why I have a little outburst.

'Be mysterious all you like,' I say to Mateo. 'Just don't hurt my little sister or anybody else and we'll be okay.'

That surprising statement goes down like a lead balloon, and I see my sister's mouth visibly hang open as she processes what I just said to her boyfriend. She's probably wondering where that just came from, as is Seth. As for Mateo, if he is flustered by my sudden show of strength, he doesn't reveal it.

'Good to know,' he replies with a considerate nod. 'And great to hear that you care deeply about your sister. That makes two of us.'

Mateo has managed to turn my threat into an opportunity to say something sweet. But even though he has, Georgia and Seth still look uncomfortable, and then my sister decides she's had enough.

'You obviously need to get some rest, so we'll get going,' she says as she stands up. 'Come on, Mateo. Let's go.'

'Are you sure you're finished?' Seth asks nervously, not wanting to be considered a bad host, but my sister and her man are already on their way.

'I hope you're feeling better soon,' Mateo says to me as he passes, with a wry smile for effect, but I just wait for him to follow my sister out.

Seth then follows them, opening the front door for them as they put on their coats before they leave the house.

I hate that my sister is clearly annoyed at me. From her point of view, not only have I spoiled the meal, but I was a little rude to her boyfriend by warning him not to hurt her. But at least they're gone, and my secret remains safe, so I console myself with the knowledge that I've actually just protected my sister's feelings, even if she doesn't know it. I've done the same for my husband too, although again, he has no idea.

'What was all that about?' he asks me once he has closed the door.

'What?'

'Saying that to Mateo. Telling him not to hurt Georgia. It was a little unnecessary, don't you think?'

'No,' I reply with a shrug. 'She's my sister. I don't want her to get hurt.'

'Why would she get hurt? They seem really happy together.'

'Yeah, for now. But it's early days and anything could happen, so I just thought I'd mention it.'

'You didn't need to,' Seth accuses. 'Georgia certainly didn't appreciate it, and I'm not sure Mateo did either.'

This is the last thing I need, so I try and cut the conversation short.

'I'm not well. I need to go and rest,' I say as I head for the staircase, but Seth doesn't let it go.

'What's going on with you?' he asks me as I reach the first step.

'Nothing.'

'Yes, there is. You've not been yourself for the past few days, and I don't know what it is, but I've noticed it and I'm sure your sister has noticed it too.'

I stop as I realise I need to do something better than just walk away from my husband.

'I'm sorry. I've just been feeling under the weather. I think it's a sickness bug that has lingered. Hopefully, I'll be feeling better in a few days.'

'I hope so too,' Seth replies before he goes to tidy away all the plates from the meal we just 'enjoyed'.

I feel bad leaving all the cleaning up to him, but then again, I didn't decide to throw an impromptu dinner party this evening, so I carry on my way to the bedroom. Once in there, I lie down on the bed and think about what I just said.

'Hopefully, I'll be feeling better in a few days.'

It sounded hopeful and promising; I know it's anything but. It's only a few days until I reach the deadline for telling Seth about Mateo and me. The problem is, I can't speak the truth.

Maybe I should write it down instead. I've always found

that writing out my feelings is easier than expressing them verbally. I've done this in the past, usually for smaller things, like career anxieties or when I was a troubled teen worrying about whether my school crush liked me as much as I liked him. But I've also done it for more serious matters.

I've written about my mistake.

TWENTY-FOUR

FIVE YEARS AGO

I made a terrible mistake. I regret it so much. I love you and I don't want to hurt you, but I cannot live with this secret any longer. I have to tell you what I did. My guilty conscience won't give me any peace until I do. I'm so sorry, Seth. I'm so sorry for cheating on you.

I stop writing when a teardrop falls onto the piece of paper in front of me, and I put down my pen before reading over what I have just expressed on the page. It's honest, heartfelt and would be harrowing to read for the recipient if they were to ever gain access to it. But that's the thing. Despite writing this confessional letter to Seth, I don't think I have the courage to give it to him.

How do I know that?

Because I've written dozens of them so far, and yet, not one has landed in Seth's hands.

Despite my best intentions, I fear this is going to be another letter that goes onto the growing pile of letters that are currently locked away in a drawer in the spare bedroom. It's a lock that only I have the key to, and Seth has no reason to ever want to go in there or ask where the key might be. In that drawer is where I've been keeping all these attempts at my confessions, unable to throw them away because I keep fooling myself into thinking I will give them to Seth but unable to actually go ahead and do it because I know what it will mean. He'll be devastated and then he'll leave me. And I can't have that, not when I love him. But also not in my current situation.

I look away from the paper and down at my bump, the one that has been growing slowly but steadily over these past four months since I discovered that I was expecting a baby. The doctor was correct in his assumption. That strange nausea I was experiencing did turn out to be a form of morning sickness, and once I took a pregnancy test, the results were conclusive. I also know it is a little boy who is growing inside me and will be born less than half a year away from now. The only thing that remains a mystery is who is the father of my boy.

I pray it is Seth.

But I fear it could be Mateo.

When I've not been writing confessional letters or experiencing various pregnancy symptoms, I have been trying to ascertain who impregnated me. My loyal fiancé? Or my one-night fling? The problem is, while I can pinpoint the weekend I would have conceived, it doesn't help me because I was with both men at that time.

The shame burns brightly inside me as I mull over that fact, and whatever derogatory name a person might give me for doing such a thing with two different men in the same short space of time is no different to anything I have already called myself in these past four months. I'm totally ashamed of my behaviour, even if I did feel like I had my reasons at the time based on how I thought mine and Seth's relationship was going. But it doesn't change the facts. I did it and now there is a little life heading for this world who won't know his father unless I figure it out and tell him.

I'm tormented because if Seth is my baby's father, I could technically get away without telling him about my affair. We could just welcome our baby boy when he is born and then get on with life as a family. But if Mateo is the father, there is no way I could allow Seth to live a lie, thinking he is raising his own son when, really, he would be the son of another man. I would have to tell Seth the truth if the worst-case scenario came to pass, and then I guess I would have to track down Mateo and tell him too. But I don't want to do anything drastic unless I have to. However, despite what I want, the guilt I feel keeps gnawing away at me to confess the truth about my affair anyway, hence all these damn letters.

I decide I've written enough for one day and think about how all I have to do now is take this letter downstairs and hand it to Seth. He's currently reclining on the sofa watching an action movie, a big bowl of popcorn beside him. I could ruin his evening, and maybe even the rest of his life, by giving him this letter and watching him read it. It seems so unnecessary to do that, to destroy a perfectly good man, but the alternative feels just as bad too. That's why, despite giving it a lot of thought, I end up unlocking the drawer and putting this newest letter alongside the others. Then I lock it again and leave the room with that key safely on my keyring, among all my other ones, making it even harder for Seth to notice it and ask what it might be for. However, it's impossible to leave the guilty feeling that always carries itself with me every hour of the day.

As I move around my home, picking up laundry, tidying a few things in the bathroom, my torment and anguish come along for the ride. The life inside me grows bigger and stronger by the day, but my mental health is deteriorating just as quickly. Not that anybody would know it. Not Seth, not my parents, not my sister, or my work colleagues. Nobody knows because despite looking like I haven't slept for a long time and having a puffy face from many hours of crying, everybody just puts it down to my changing hormones. The fatigue, the sickness, the compulsive overeating; everyone just thinks it's the effects of pregnancy on my overworked body. But it's so much more than that. I have even contemplated running away to try and escape this living hell that I am trapped in. But where would I go and how would I support myself and my baby if I left my job and tried to start again? It would most likely be a disaster. I might want to flee, but I wouldn't be a good mother by bringing my son into an unstable life. My boy needs a loving home, a peaceful existence, not one fraught with uncertainty and potential disaster. All those negatives can be for me to suffer. So, for now at least, I stay and try to get on with my life, and Seth is carrying on as if everything is normal too, although his new normal is all about being excited to be a new father and the experiences and life lessons that will bring with it. Bless him, he's so excited to be called a daddy, and that's just one more dream of his that could be crushed if my mistake ever got out.

What about Mateo? If I was dreading bumping into him before, I'm certainly terrified of it now I am visibly pregnant. If he was to see my bump then he would inevitably have questions for me, awful questions like 'is that my baby you are carrying?' If I happened to be with Seth when I saw him, it could be disastrous. So I'm trying even harder to avoid him now than I was before. I'd already stopped going to the gym, but now I'm barely even going into town, afraid to browse the shops and supermarkets in case I see him in one of the aisles. As for the wine bar where I bumped into him last time, it's easy for me to avoid those kinds of establishments now because obviously, I'm staying well away from alcohol during my pregnancy. That means it's been easy to tell my friends that I'm not coming out at weekends, so other than going to work and coming home, I'm really not doing much. People are coming to me, family and friends alike, and as long as Mateo doesn't show his face, I'm okay, for now at least.

Seth has mostly been staying in too, not only to make sure I'm okay, but because he tells me he has turned a new leaf now. Impending fatherhood has made him reassess his lifestyle choices and he says he'd prefer to have a quiet night in than a late night out with his mates these days. That reduces the chances of him bumping into Mateo in a bar somewhere, although I did baulk at Seth's suggestion that he was going to join the gym and try and get in shape before succumbing to the inevitable 'dad bod' when baby is here. I did not want Seth anywhere near that gym, not when I know Mateo is a member and he could befriend him as easily as he befriended me. Thankfully, Seth decided that the money for a gym membership would be better spent being saved towards more practical things we need, like a pram or a crib.

But time is ticking, and while I'm aware of that every day with the gradual growth of my unborn child, I'm also aware of it when it comes to Seth and Mateo and how I can't just ignore the issue of paternity forever.

What will I do? Will I ever give Seth one of the letters? Will I ever bump into Mateo again somewhere unexpected? Will I be forced to start life as a mother single and alone? Do I even deserve to be a mother?

I don't know the answers to any of those questions.

Like everybody else in the world, I have no idea what the future holds.

Maybe it's better that way.

TWENTY-FIVE

PRESENT DAY

It's Thursday, two days before my Mateo-imposed deadline expires, and that's why I've decided to take action. I sent my tormentor a text, telling him to meet me at the park, because I need to show him something and, thankfully, he has agreed to come. Now I'm standing here waiting for him while armed with the thing I intend to reveal as soon as he arrives.

The thing hidden in my handbag is not quite as dramatic as a gun.

But it could be just as decisive.

I spot him from some distance away, that pacy, confident gait, the dark hair, the strong physique. All these traits that first attracted me to him are still on show as Mateo sees me too and makes his way over to where I am lurking. It feels like lurking because rather than standing out in the open expanse of this park, I am over by the trees, as if afraid to be seen by too many people. I suppose I am. I'm certainly afraid of being seen by anybody who knows me. But I'm confident that none of my family or friends are going to be in this park at this time on a midweek day. That's why I chose it as the meeting place.

As Mateo reaches me, I delve into my handbag and take out

the thing he needs to see, as I really don't want to waste any more time on this. If all goes well over the next few minutes, maybe this will be the last time I see Mateo. If he vanishes, the deadline vanishes along with him.

'Hello, Corinne,' Mateo says, but I remain silent as I pass him a piece of paper.

Mateo takes it and studies it for a moment before asking me the obvious question.

'What's this?'

'That is the result of a paternity test,' I tell him firmly. 'I had it taken when Freddie was born, and as you can see if you read it all properly, it confirms with ninety-nine point nine per cent accuracy that Seth is his father.'

I watch as Mateo does as I requested and reads the information on the paper properly before adding a little more context to it.

'I took the test secretly when Freddie was born using one of Seth's hairs. He has no idea about it, but I needed to know the results, and now you know them too.'

That's a very succinct way of summing up the immense relief I felt when I discovered that Seth was the dad and my situation hadn't just gone from bad to worse.

Mateo finishes reading the test results before looking up at me, perplexed.

'Why are you showing me this?' he asks, the paper in his hand fluttering slightly in the chilly breeze that blows through the park.

'In case this is why you are doing all of this,' I reply, doing my best to remain authoritative and not bow down to any pressure he might try and exert back onto me. 'In case the only reason you came back to try and ruin my life is because you think Freddie is your son. Because he's not, he is Seth's, so if you are wondering about him, you don't need to wonder anymore.'

Mateo just stares at me, so I feel the need to add one thing more and, hopefully, it is a thing that will cause him to stop treating me like I'm some villain who needs to be stopped.

'I would have found you and told you the truth,' I say. 'If Freddie was yours. I swear I would have done because you would have had the right to know, and I would have wanted my son to know his father too. But he's not yours, so that's why I never looked for you, and that's why it has been so upsetting for me to have you come back into my life when I have tried my best to move on from my mistake.'

I pause then and give Mateo the opportunity to respond.

'Your mistake...' is all he says before smiling and handing me back the test results.

I take the paper and put it back in my handbag, as if it's already been exposed to enough daylight and I can't have it out in the open for a second longer in case somebody sees it. My husband would be very curious to know why I had a paternity test done in private, which is why he can't know. Now I have shown this to Mateo, I can destroy the results. I only ever hung on to them just in case Mateo emerged one day and started asking questions, and when he brought up my son at dinner last night, I realised it was time to play my trump card. Or at least what I hoped was my trump card.

'Is that what you think this is all about?' Mateo asks me with a shake of the head. 'Freddie? You think I've come back to stake some kind of claim to him?'

My stomach sinks a little when I realise my efforts here today might have had no impact on Mateo.

'I wanted you to know,' I say, but Mateo just shrugs.

'Okay, now I know,' he replies. 'And maybe I am disappointed that he's not mine. Maybe I had thought about being his father. But it doesn't change anything. I still want you to tell Seth about us by Saturday night or I will do it for you.'

'Wait, why? There's no reason to break us up, not if Freddie isn't yours. You'd just be ruining a perfectly happy family, and for what? Pure spite? Jealousy? Because you can? Why would you do that when you don't need to?'

'I've already told you why I'm doing this,' Mateo replies calmly. 'I want you back.'

'You can't have me!' I cry, feeling like this meeting has gone wrong and now the deadline still looms large. 'I'm married to Seth, and I love him. What part of that don't you understand?'

'I understand it perfectly. But it doesn't mean things can't change, and I imagine they would do if Seth found out what you did with me while he was elsewhere. I imagine you wouldn't stay married for long then and if you are single again, who knows what could happen between us two. Maybe we could pick up where we left off.'

Oh my god. He's actually delusional if he's going to all this effort over our one-night stand. It meant nothing to me and I thought he knew that years ago, so it's time to make my feelings clear, if I haven't done so already.

'There is no world in which me and you are together again,' I say fiercely. 'Even if Seth leaves me, I'll never choose to be with you, and do you know why? It's because I hate you. I hate you for luring me into a mistake that has hung over me for the last five years. I'll always hate you, no matter what happens next.'

I'm hoping that making my hatred clear will be the deciding factor in getting Mateo to drop this nonsensical crusade against me and my family and leave us all alone. But will it work?

'Thanks for this meeting,' Mateo says with a smile. 'It's been nice to see you and you know I'll always come whenever you call. But if I don't see you before, I guess I'll see you at the party on Saturday night. And I'm sure I don't have to remind you, but just in case I do: you need to have told Seth about us before the party. Or I will do it there for you and, of course, it won't just be between the three of us. It will be in front of everyone.'

Mateo wishes me a good day then before departing. As I

watch him go, staring at his back and loathing his existence with every part of my soul, I wish I had brought a gun instead of the paternity test results. If I had, I could reach into my handbag and take it out before aiming it at his back and pulling the trigger. I'm not a violent person but that would solve a problem in an instant, although it would create another one too. But as it is, I can't hurt Mateo with a piece of paper, so I have no choice but to watch him walk away while thinking about the next time we are together.

He expects it to be at the party, and it probably will be, unless I come up with a solution before then. It would have to be something more permanent than what I tried here today. *Something that can rid me of him forever.*

I might not be able to get my hands on a gun before Saturday, but there might be something else I could do that could give me the same result.

It would be drastic, but it's either that or confess to Seth.

The problem is that either outcome is likely to end badly for me.

TWENTY-SIX

'How was your day?'

My husband's question is a normal one for a spouse to ask over dinner, and I look up from my meal to see Seth sitting opposite me eating his. Freddie is seated to the left of us, eating his own food, or should I say playing with his own food. But our son is being quiet, so we won't disturb him. Instead, I want to watch him because it's the little moments like these that I will miss if my family falls apart.

'It was fine,' I reply, preferring that response to the one in which I tell the truth and explain how I met Mateo in the park for a clandestine meeting during which the paternity of Freddie was discussed.

'Are you feeling better now?' Seth asks me then. 'I was worried about you all day. I didn't want you to be struggling in the office if you still felt a little off.'

Why does he have to be so sweet? He's been worried about me all day. Of course he has. From thinking he was the kind of partner who was too lazy to make an effort, he's proven me very wrong there. Sometimes, in my stupid moments, I think things would have been easier for me if I'd married a man who didn't care about me and acted selfishly and gave me a long list of reasons as to why I might leave him one day. But not Seth, which means that I am the bad one in this marriage. But I knew that already. He's been the perfect partner and I'm the one who has let him down. He may not know it yet, but I do, and the shame is just as strong.

'I'm feeling a bit better, yes,' I reply, and while Seth doesn't look like he quite believes that, he leaves it before going on to ask Freddie about his day.

Though he is only four, I imagine my son will be a better conversationalist than me this evening – and I'm not wrong. As Freddie launches into an excited story about something that happened to him and his best friend, Simon, at school, I stare at Seth and think about how I could just end my worrying by confessing my affair to him tonight. I would do it once Freddie was in bed, of course, making sure he was out of the way so the adults could have a serious conversation without him around to witness it. There would be tears, and there may be some shouting, so it wouldn't be fair for him to see that. If I do it tonight, if I put my marriage at risk to give Mateo what he clearly wants, I assume I won't be sleeping here this evening. Not after Seth kicks me out. I guess I'll go to Mum and Dad's and sleep in my old bedroom there, crying into my pillow until dawn before realising that Freddie will be waking up and looking for his mummy only to be told that she doesn't live with him anymore. That's assuming Seth wants us to separate.

But what if he doesn't?

The fact that my husband is some kind of modern-day saint, a fact that becomes more apparent to me with every year we spend together, means there might be a chance he could do the saintly thing and forgive me. Wouldn't that be incredible? How sweet would it be for me to tell Mateo that Seth knows and doesn't even care? I would love that. But of course I would.

Doesn't everybody love a fantasy that is unlikely to ever come true?

I know it's naïve of me to think that Seth won't be heartbroken by the fact I slept with another man during our relationship. Add on that it was the night before he threw me a surprise party and subsequent shock proposal and there's no way I come out of this positively. That's why, the more I think about what has happened this week, the more I wish I had given one of those confessional notes to Seth a long time ago. If I had done that, this could have been resolved then, whatever the outcome. It certainly would have taken all of the power out of Mateo's hands.

I hate the fact that my fear of the truth only makes that man stronger. If I had given Seth one of those letters years ago, which was the whole point of writing them, after all, I wouldn't be sitting here fretting about the outcome. I'd already know it. Either Seth and I would have parted ways years ago or he would have forgiven me because too much time hadn't passed. It would certainly have been better to have given him the truth before we got married. As it is, those letters never made it into his hands.

Not after what I did to them all.

TWENTY-SEVEN

FOUR YEARS AGO

'Ssssshhhh,' I whisper to my beautiful baby boy as his eyes close and his crying stops. I've just given him more milk to stave off his ravenous appetite for another couple of hours at least and now he looks like he's ready for a nap.

I keep walking around with him in my arms to give him comfort until I'm confident that he is asleep and then I carefully place him down into the Moses basket that my parents gifted us when he was born. The basket sits beside the sofa, the sofa I spend most of my day on during this initial stage of my maternity leave. If I'm not breastfeeding, changing nappies or singing lullabies, I am trying to take my own naps on the sofa, and it's just easier being down here than upstairs sometimes. Plus I have the TV down here and that helps with some of the longer hours that come from being at home all day without any other adults around.

Seth is upstairs now, getting some sleep after a long day at work, and I'm glad he's resting because I can't imagine going to an office feeling this sleep-deprived. At least I get to just be at home all day and bask in the warm glow of being a new parent. My poor man has only been a dad for a few weeks and he's already back to sitting in boring meetings and working towards insignificant deadlines. I say insignificant because now we have this little life to look after, everything else seems so unimportant.

Well, almost everything else.

It's usually at this time, when Freddie is fast asleep and I'm being still and quiet for fear of waking him, that my mind returns to Mateo. It does so, I guess, because that man is the only thing that could burst the blissful bubble I currently exist in. If I was worried about Seth finding out about my betrayal before I became a mother, I'm even more anxious about it now. I don't want my son to come from a broken home, so it's imperative that Seth and I don't split up. I also can't imagine having to be a parent all by myself; that strikes fear into me too, especially now I have seen exactly how much work is involved. That's why I have decided that instead of just trying to get some sleep while Freddie is asleep himself, I'm going to do something else. It's something potentially much more productive than getting some rest before the next round of feeds and nappies.

I'm going to destroy all of those confession letters.

Having recently, and very secretly, had a paternity test done that proves Seth is the father and not Mateo, I feel less of an urgent need to tell my husband about my one-night stand. Therefore, it's time for these letters to go because the only purpose they are serving now is increasing my anxiety that Seth might discover them one day.

I check on my son and make sure he is okay in his basket before I creep out of the room and slowly ascend the staircase. When I reach the top, I'm being as quiet up here as I just was downstairs around the baby, as I don't want Seth to hear me and wake up. The last thing I need is to be interrupted. It would be safer and easier to do this when Seth is at work; however, my sleep-deprived paranoia is urging me to get this over with tonight.

So I will.

I sneak into the spare bedroom and select the one key on my bunch of keys that will unlock this drawer. With the drawer open, I look down at the stack of papers inside. All these letters, all this writing, all these confessions. There is so much emotion in these pages. But they've got to go.

I pick up all of the letters, careful to check that I haven't missed one before closing the drawer. But I have to re-lock it because this drawer still contains one piece of paper that I am hanging on to. It's the test results proving who Freddie's real father is, and I will keep those just in case the worst happens and Mateo ever reappears in my life, trying to stake a claim to him. With the letters in hand and the test safely locked away, I go back downstairs. After making another check on Freddie and seeing that he is still snoring softly, I go into the kitchen and find what I need in a drawer there. Then I step outside in the cool night air, looking up at the dark sky and seeing a few stars shining overhead. I try to tell myself that the stars are a reminder of how small and insignificant we all are in this enormous expanse of a universe, but the truth is, what I am about to do here does not feel insignificant at all.

I walk down to the bottom of the garden before glancing back at the house and, specifically, the bedroom window upstairs. I want to make sure that Seth hasn't woken up and heard me go outside. If he has, he could be watching me now. But there's no movement at any of the windows. No curtains twitching or lights going on. I'm entirely unseen out here, which is just the way I need it to be. With that, I place the letters down on the small wooden table we have out here for use in the summer months before opening the thing I just took from the kitchen drawer. It's a box of matches, and as I light the first match, I stare at the flickering flame and think about how powerful fire can be.

It can destroy anything it touches and, in a second, it's going to touch these letters.

As I set the first piece of paper alight, I realise this signals a shift. This is the moment when I officially decide that I am never, ever going to tell Seth about Mateo. On the face of it, that could just seem like a cowardly decision. But I'm choosing to think of it as a sign that I am now putting all of my focus onto my family. These letters that are now burning are things that could wreck this valuable life I have here. The precious things behind me, from my sleeping baby to my sleeping husband to our lovely home, the house we bought once we knew we were going to be together forever and needed more space for our future child, are all so sacred. I want to keep all of this intact, so destroying these letters will increase the odds of me doing that.

Ten minutes later, as I watch the last letter burn, which is a moment that should come as a relief to me, a dangerous and dark thought occurs instead.

As a new mum, I will do anything to protect my child and the sanctity of the home in which he lives.

Anything.

That's why, as I watch the last glowing ember from the small fire I just made float away into the night sky, I tell myself that if Mateo ever comes back into my life and threatens what I have here, I will have no choice but to take drastic action.

I would stop at nothing to protect my family.

TWENTY-EIGHT

It's Saturday morning. The day of the deadline. The party is tonight. The party where Mateo will tell Seth about what we did unless I've done it first. I've spent all night lying in bed trying to think up ways to stop the party from happening. I've imagined it all, anything to stop all those people gathering and giving Mateo a big audience to play his game in front of. I thought about telling my family I've contracted a very infectious stomach bug and that means they'll all be struck down with it too, so they better stay in tonight and forget about partying. Maybe they'd believe me and cancel. Or maybe they'd see that story for the nonsense it is and go ahead anyway. I thought about hosting my own party instead and everyone but Mateo is invited, though of course, that would just be a huge red flag and give away the fact that I am trying to keep him away from my family. Lastly, just before dawn, I considered the most extreme excuse to get the party cancelled, which was to get myself involved in some kind of accident. Nothing too life-threatening, but it would have to be bad enough to at least warrant me going to the hospital. Maybe I could bump my car and say I have whiplash. The worry of it all might get my sister to postpone the party. But I quickly realised staging an accident was ridiculous, and dangerous, and also extremely unfair on all the people who love me and would be devastated at such a thing.

Therefore, I have no way of stopping the party.

That means I'm running out of hours.

So instead of rushing, why am I taking my time today?

'You look very handsome,' I say to Freddie as I comb his soft hair, and while this is usually a job that both of us want to get over with quickly because of how tricky it can often be, today is different. Sure, Freddie is still wriggling and wanting to get away from me and the comb so he can go and do something more fun. But I'm working slowly and diligently, really taking my time to experience and appreciate what I am doing. It's no different to how I've been with my son all morning, ever since he came into our bedroom to wake us up at 6 a.m.

While Seth groaned and rolled back over because he clearly wanted more sleep, I was already awake, so I made sure to leap out of bed and start playtime with Freddie as soon as possible. We went downstairs and I made him a big pile of pancakes for his breakfast, his favourite, before we spent the next three hours drawing, colouring and kicking a football around the garden. Seth appreciated the lie-in I gave him, but even he was amazed at how much time and attention I have been giving Freddie this morning because usually, like any parent, there are other things to get done and it's not always possible to devote every single second to attentive play. But I've mastered it today.

That's because I've had no choice.

As I finish combing Freddie's hair and give him a kiss on his head before he runs away, I am aware that this could be the last time I get to spend a Saturday morning with him. It may even be the last time I get to spend any meaningful amount of time with him. That's down to what I have in mind to do today.

Mateo might have a plan for how this Saturday is going to go, but he's not the only one.

I just don't know how it's going to end yet.

As Seth prepares to take Freddie to his football session at the local community centre, I accept that I have maxed out the time with my little boy this morning and it's now the part where I have to move on to the next bit of my day. That involves going to meet my sister to do some shopping after she invited me to join her this afternoon.

'Retail therapy and coffee' was how she sold it to me, not that I needed much persuading. That's because as important as it was to spend quality time with my son today, it's important to spend it with my sibling too. They are two people I will miss the most, other than my husband, if things go badly before the sun rises again tomorrow.

The thought has crossed my mind that I could confess to everything when I see my sister shortly, pre-empting what might happen at tonight's party and keeping things in my control rather than Mateo's. But realistically, how will I ever be able to look at my sister and tell her that I slept with the man she is excitedly preparing to move in with? No matter how much I'd love to deal with this problem myself rather than give Mateo all the power, I just don't think I can do it.

'Have a great afternoon,' Seth says to me as I come downstairs to see him standing beside Freddie, the little boy in his football boots and favourite team's shirt, a ball under his arm and a big smile on his face because he's excited to go and play.

'I love you so much,' I blurt out then to both of them, but while Freddie barely bats an eyelid, Seth seems slightly perturbed.

'Are you okay?' he asks me, querying my sudden show of emotion.

'Yes, I'm fine. I just wanted to say it,' I reply.

'I guess we better say it back then, hadn't we, Freddie?' Seth says, and he looks down at the little footballer beside him before giving him a nudge towards me.

'Love you, Mummy!' Freddie cries as he rushes towards me for a hug, and as he wraps his arms around my legs, Seth steps in and wraps his arms around my torso.

'And I love you as well,' Seth says. I had wanted a sweet moment like this before my family departed and I went to do what I have to do to, hopefully, keep us all intact, but it's suddenly too much and I feel on the verge of tears. Fortunately, neither Seth nor Freddie notices, as we stop hugging and they leave the house.

'Don't spend too much money!' Seth calls back before he gets in the car, a familiar warning that many a husband has given to their wives before a shopping spree ensues. But I know I won't spend much at all today. In fact, there's only one thing on my shopping list...

'Wow, shopaholic alert,' I say when I see how much my sister has got in her trolley. 'Are you moving house?'

I stare at the rapidly filling trolley and see pots and pans, cooking utensils and cutlery, as well as cushions and candles; and while my sibling has always liked to shop, this is taking things up a notch, even for her. But then she explains it.

'I want all new things for when Mateo moves in,' she tells me as she picks a set of coasters off a shelf and considers them before adding them to the trolley too.

Of course. Now it makes sense why she wanted to go shopping today. It's because Mateo is due to move in with her tomorrow, and this is her last chance to turn the home she has lived in by herself for years into a home that is more compatible for a couple. But while Georgia is shopping for her future with Mateo, I am aware that future most likely will never exist. I can't say anything though, not yet. I just have to keep up my act, although I'm not rendered totally useless and see an opportunity to have one more go at checking to see if there is any way that my sister might reconsider her plans with that man. If I can, it won't just help me but help her too. She deserves so much better than *him*.

'Are you sure about this?' I say as Georgia browses more homeware items. 'Settling down with a boyfriend might seem exciting and new, but it's not all it's cracked up to be. What happened to you saying that you'd always be free and single? That relationships were a burden? That you'd rather just travel and relax rather than get married and have kids?'

'Whoa, slow down there, sis. Nobody is talking about marriage and kids.'

'Not yet, but you do realise it's the next step, right? I mean, first you live together, which is a challenge in itself because you learn all about each other's bad habits and you see each other all day, not just when you show up looking your best on a date. But say you get through those years, marriage is the inevitable next step for a couple. And then Mateo might start wanting you to give him a child, and another one, and maybe even another. The next thing you know, you're drowning in nappies and sleep deprivation, having not seen your friends in months and barely even recognising the woman in the mirror anymore. Is that really you?'

Georgia realises this isn't just some whimsical chatter and that I'm actually trying to have a serious conversation here, so she stops shopping and looks at me, her overflowing trolley getting a momentary reprieve beside her.

'Are you jealous of me?' she suddenly asks.

'What?'

'I'm just wondering where all this is coming from. Why you can't just be happy for me and Mateo? Is it because you settled down too quickly and now you feel trapped?'

'I have no idea what you're talking about,' I reply, but Georgia nods her head as if I should do.

'You know exactly what I mean. I remember when you were dating Seth, back before you married. There were times when you were drunk, and you confessed to me that you weren't sure if he was the one. You remember those conversations, right?'

I do actually remember a couple of them, but like my sister said, we were drunk. However, I didn't realise Georgia remembered them all. What else might I have told her when I was drunk? No, there's no way I would have confessed to what I did with Mateo. I locked that secret away inside myself tightly and barring the letters I wrote and eventually burned, it has never escaped me since.

'This is different,' I fire back. 'It's normal to have doubts sometimes before settling down. But I love Seth and we're so lucky to have Freddie, so I don't regret a thing. But you are different to me. You had doubts about settling down with a man before you even met one, so is this really you? Or are you just panicking about being left behind and trying to get with somebody so you're not alone forever?'

'No, that's not what this is at all!' Georgia cries. 'I love Mateo and if I do end up getting married to him and having his babies then it's because it's what I want, not because I've panicked and rushed into anything. So just drop this please or I won't ask you to come shopping with me again.'

Georgia turns and pushes her heavy trolley away, and I'm left standing in the aisle feeling like I just failed in my final attempt to get my sister to leave that awful man. All I have achieved is realising that my sister really does care about Mateo, and this is far more than just a bit of fun with some guy she is dating. She thinks he is the one. But he's not, and while she doesn't know it, I do.

As Georgia disappears onto another aisle, I look down at the basket I'm carrying, the one that is so far empty because I haven't picked anything up off the shelves to buy yet. But it's time to change that fact, and when I see what I need, I step forward and pick it up. I examine it for a few seconds before deciding that it will do the job and drop it into my basket. Then I go to find a checkout.

It's time to buy this knife.

The knife I will use to kill my sister's boyfriend.

TWENTY-NINE

I stare at the knife lying on the passenger seat beside me. It's in a protective case that came with it, designed to be safe in case a child finds it, although even adults can have accidents. Then I look up through the windscreen at the home of the man I have come here to use the knife on.

I'm outside Mateo's apartment, an easy place to find because I've been here before, and even though it was years ago, I still remember it like it was yesterday. I knew Mateo was still living here based on how my sister described his apartment to me when she was talking about where he lived. The location matched the exact place I had been to before, although this is a place I wish I'd never set foot in, a place that has haunted me since I left it, and a place that holds a memory I wish I could erase.

Sadly, the memory isn't going to die.

But the man who lives here might be about to.

After saying goodbye to Georgia and getting in my car, I had assumed, and hoped, that I would lose my nerve on the drive over here and go home instead. I figured that was the most likely outcome as I considered what I was about to do. I have wracked my brains for an alternative solution, but I couldn't think of anything else to do to keep my secret safe other than what I am about to do right now. And while I expected to go into a stress-induced panic that would cause me to hit the brakes and turn around, that mental breakdown never occurred either, which most likely means I'm crazier and more desperate than I even realised.

Am I really about to do this?

There's no going back if I do.

Once it's done, it's done.

But he's left me no time. No time to make choices and consider options, because there are no options. Maybe I could have done something as drastic as hired a hitman to do this for me, if I'd had more time. But time is up. With that fact recognised, I pick up the knife, conceal it inside my jacket and then exit my vehicle, aware that while I don't possess the skills that a hitman might, the element of surprise should surely be on my side.

I have to hope that is enough.

I take several deep breaths before walking towards the front door to Mateo's apartment while looking around to see if there are any witnesses out on this street. Anybody who could say I was here after the fact. But it's quiet, which I expected it to be because this is not a busy area. I've also looked around for any cameras and can't see any, so luck is on my side so far. But I'll need plenty more of it before this is over with.

As I reach the door and look at the buttons for the several apartments in this block, I know which one I have to press to gain Mateo's attention. It's Number Five. As I put my fingers against it and hear a buzzing sound, I prepare to hear Mateo's voice through the intercom, enquiring about who his guest is. There's no video on this intercom, so the man inside will only be able to know who is here by the sound of my voice.

He'll get a surprise when he finds out that it's me.

But he'll get an even bigger one if he lets me inside.

But just before I hear Mateo respond, I get a flashback, one so sudden and jarring that it threatens to derail my whole plan.

I'm here, on this doorstep, and Mateo is with me too. He's smiling at me as he takes out a key to unlock this door. But just before he can open it, he stops and turns back to me, and I know what he is going to do. I close my eyes in anticipation one second before our lips touch...

That vivid memory of the kiss makes me feel sick, but there's no more time to process it or wallow in my regret because the buzzer is then answered.

'Hello?'

Mateo's voice through the intercom is clear, unlike the thoughts in my head, and I'm so distracted that I forget to answer him.

'Who's there?' he asks next as I snap back into the moment.

'It's me,' I say quietly, though I'm sure he can hear me through this device. 'Corinne.'

'What are you doing here?'

'I need to talk to you.'

There's a brief pause from the other end and I fear that Mateo might be having doubts about allowing me inside his home. If he is, what can I do then? The party is now only a couple of hours away and that means I'm almost out of time. I need him to let me inside.

'Come in,' he says before I hear an unlocking sound that tells me the front door has just been opened.

I push open the door before stepping into a small lobby area that I remember from before. Then I head up the staircase, the same one I ascended when I was on my way to Mateo's home the first time. If only I'd turned around and run out that night, things wouldn't be so bad. Sure, I'd have kissed him already but that's not as bad as sleeping with him, is it? There may have been more chance of Seth forgiving me. But I kept climbing these stairs until I reached the door with the Number Five on it – and that's exactly what I am doing again now.

When I reach it, the door opens, and I see Mateo standing there in a crisp white T-shirt and blue jeans. Looking casual, looking relaxed, not at all looking like a man who is ready to party this evening. That's what makes him so dangerous. Nobody would suspect a thing until it was too late. But as he looks at me, the woman who has a sharp weapon hidden on her, I'm hoping I appear just as harmless as he does.

'Welcome back,' Mateo says with a big grin, seemingly finding it amusing that I have returned to the scene of our infamous night together. Then he steps aside to allow me in, and I don't say a word as I enter his apartment and he closes the door behind me.

Should I just do it now? Get it over with? Take out this knife and stick it in him and then leave? It might make sense to do so because surely, the longer I leave it, the more chance there is of me talking myself out of this. But I've just missed my window of opportunity because Mateo's back is no longer turned and if I pulled the knife out now, he'd have a chance of dodging it or worse, taking it from me and using it to do me harm instead. So it remains hidden, for the time being, as Mateo gestures for me to take a seat on his sofa. But I choose to remain standing, prompting him to ask me a question.

'Have you told Seth yet?' Mateo wants to know, looking smug about the fact that either way, time is almost up.

'No,' I admit.

'Tonight will have to be the night then,' Mateo replies, and he takes a seat himself, spreading his arms out across the back of the sofa and looking relaxed in my presence. I'm a bag of nerves yet he's as cold as ice. Maybe I am out of my depth here. Maybe I should just leave. But I can't. If I walk out this door without doing this, there's nothing stopping Mateo from telling Seth about us – whether we go to the party or not.

'I'm sorry,' I say then, changing tack.

'What for?'

'For how I was with you earlier. For saying I would never be with you no matter what. You coming back into my life has reminded me why I was drawn to you in the first place. Why I went against my morals and did something out of character. It's because you gave me attention. Just like you're giving me now.'

Mateo chooses to stay quiet, no doubt intrigued about where I might be going with this, so I carry on.

'The truth is, nothing has changed,' I say, and I sit down beside Mateo as I speak. 'I'm still getting far more attention from you than I am from Seth. All these years later and you are still working harder to keep my interest than Seth has ever worked to keep mine.'

'He doesn't deserve you,' Mateo says, and I let that thought linger in the room for a moment before I carry on.

'Maybe I should have left him back then. After we slept together. I should have stuck to my plan, the one I told you about. How I was going to leave Seth and then we were going to be together. If I'd done it then, I could have avoided all these problems now. I could have been happier.'

I look at Mateo to see if he is believing what I am saying, and it looks like he is.

'Everything you have done for me. Everything you continue to do. At first, I thought you were threatening me, but I realise I was wrong about that. It just shows me how much you care. How far you are willing to go to try and get me back. And no matter how much I try to think of an example of when Seth has worked this hard for me, I cannot think of one.'

Mateo sits forward and places a hand on my leg. I force myself to let it rest there, not brushing it off because that would weaken everything I've just said.

'It's okay,' he says, looking at my eyes then at my lips. 'I understand. You're trapped with Seth at the moment, but it doesn't have to be that way forever. You can still be with me. We can have it all. We can be together.'

Mateo moves in for a kiss then, but I stand up.

'I'm so confused,' I say, sounding stressed. 'I just don't know what to do.'

I'm hoping Mateo will stand up too, and he does.

'You're not a bad person,' he says, coming closer again.

'I'm not?' I reply, standing still, looking vulnerable, weak, like prey, ready to be taken advantage of.

Just like the predator he is, Mateo swiftly moves in.

'No, you're not,' he tells me, his face inches from mine. 'Not at all.'

Then he closes his eyes and goes in for a kiss and, as he does that, I reach behind my back and pull out the knife that he still hasn't seen yet.

THIRTY

A loud buzzer cuts through the quiet of the apartment. I quickly hide the knife again behind my back as Mateo pulls away from me and opens his eyes.

He is thinking that someone has just interrupted our kiss.

He has no idea what they really interrupted.

We both hear the buzzer again, and I realise someone is outside, trying to get in. Then I realise that if they had been a few seconds later, I might have already stabbed Mateo by now and would be trapped in here with a dead body while somebody was buzzing to get in. The thought that I could just have been caught by whoever is outside is terrifying, but Mateo obviously doesn't know the danger he was in.

'Just ignore them,' he says before going in for a kiss again, but I pull back as the buzzer sounds once more.

'Who is it?' I ask him.

'I don't know,' he shrugs, and he steps towards me again, but I step back.

'Answer it,' I say.

'Why? It's probably just a delivery guy dropping off a parcel. They can leave it on the doorstep.'

'Check,' I insist, so Mateo reluctantly does.

'Hello?' he says into the intercom as I conceal the knife properly.

'Hey. It's me. Open up!'

I recognise my sister's voice and realise she is the one trying to get in. Mateo seems surprised too and looks to me as if unsure how to proceed.

'Don't let her in,' I whisper, terrified of her seeing me here.

'Hey, hurry up. What are you waiting for?' Georgia says again, her voice rattling around this apartment.

Mateo removes his finger from the buzzer, so she won't be able to hear what is said next.

'I have to let her in. What excuse could I have not to?' he says as I shake my head furiously.

'No. Get rid of her,' I beg him, but he looks calm.

'Maybe this is a good thing. It'll give us both the opportunity to tell her what is going on between us and we can let her know that we are going to be together. I can say that I have to break up with her and you'll shortly be breaking up with Seth too.'

'What? Are you crazy? You can't say that to her? She'll hate me!'

'I think she'd probably hate you whenever she found out,' Mateo replies casually. 'At least this way we get it over with and we don't have to sneak around behind her back.'

'No, please,' I try one more time, but Mateo doesn't listen. He just hits the button to unlock the front door and allow Georgia in.

As I realise my sister will now be coming up the stairs towards this apartment, I frantically look around for somewhere to hide. I cannot let her see me here. I cannot hurt my little sister. I love her too much to see her heartbroken.

'Help me hide!' I urge Mateo as I keep searching for a suitable place, but Mateo still seems like he wants Georgia to find us together because he's just standing by the door ready to let her in when she knocks on it. That's when I realise I have to say something extra to get him to help me, or this is all going to blow up in the next few seconds.

'I want to be with you, but I just need a little more time to process all of this,' I say. 'Please don't rush me. I don't want to make this harder for us both than it already is.'

I pray that Mateo will buy it.

He does.

'In the bedroom. Quickly,' he tells me as he leads me away from the door.

'Hide in the wardrobe,' he tells me once we're in the bedroom. 'I'll get rid of her as quickly as I can.'

I hear Georgia knock on the door and realise there is no time for any more discussion on this, so I open the wardrobe door and squeeze myself into my hiding space beside Mateo's clothes and shoes.

Georgia knocks again, and a few seconds later, I hear Mateo open the door to his apartment and my sister bursts in.

'Finally! I was beginning to think you didn't want to see me!' she cries in her typically boisterous fashion.

'I wasn't expecting you,' Mateo says as he closes the door.

I think about how all three of us are now confined in this small apartment, yet Georgia has no idea there is a third person present.

As I stand in the wardrobe, every muscle in my body tense and tight, I am not just angry at Mateo for allowing my sister inside but angry at myself for being in this position. I should never have come here. It was always going to end badly. Now I'm trapped, and until Georgia leaves, I can't go anywhere. But leaving without discovering me is not guaranteed, and if I am found in here, my entire life is going to implode. She'll react badly, of course she will. How would any sane person react if they found their sister hiding in their boyfriend's bedroom? It's got disaster written all over it. If it happened, I expect Mateo would just blurt out the truth because why wouldn't he? The situation would be irretrievable then and nothing I could do after leaving this apartment would make it better.

I have no choice.

I have to stay hidden.

'I thought I'd come and help you with your packing,' I hear Georgia say next before I hear something that makes me put a hand over my mouth, lest I should let out an anxious gasp.

My sister has entered the room.

As my sibling stands only a few feet away from where I hide behind the wardrobe door, I hear Mateo enter the room behind her.

'You don't seem to have got very far with the packing?' Georgia says. 'Have you even started?'

'It's all under control,' Mateo replies unconvincingly. Although I know he hasn't started packing because he knows he won't be moving in with my sister. Not when she finds out I got with her man before her.

'It doesn't look like it,' Georgia grumbles. 'Seriously, we need to make a start on this. You're supposed to be moving in tomorrow.'

'Honestly, it's fine,' Mateo tries. 'I've got it covered. I was just about to start, actually.'

'Great, well I'm here now, so I can help you and it'll speed things up,' Georgia replies, much to my horror. If she's going to help with packing, one of the first places she will turn to will be this wardrobe.

Fortunately, Mateo realises it's a bad thing too.

'No, seriously. I'm fine. I don't need any help,' he tries.

'I get it. You don't want to pack. It's a pretty boring job,' Georgia replies, and I get my hopes up that she might be about to leave. 'How about we do something a little more fun instead?'

My stomach sinks as I realise she is going to try and initiate something physical with him. She thinks the only reason Mateo is reluctant to pack is because it's a tedious task and she can now cheer him up with something else. What if Mateo doesn't resist her advances? What if I'm forced to listen to the pair of them as they get intimate with each other?

'I like the idea, but how about we save it for when I move in with you tomorrow?' Mateo says then.

'Really? You don't want to fool around with me?' my sis replies, sounding more than a little hurt at the rejection.

'There'll be plenty of time for that when we live together. But that won't happen if I haven't packed. So how about you go and do something fun, and I will do what I need to do here and I'll see you tonight.'

'Fine,' Georgia says, still sounding unhappy, but she leaves the room.

As I hear her and Mateo say their goodbyes by the front door, I prepare to leave my hiding place. Once I'm confident she has gone, I step out.

'The coast is clear,' Mateo says with a grin a moment later, as if that wasn't just one of the most excruciating experiences of his life.

But it was certainly one of mine, which is why I want to get out of here as quickly as possible. Although I can't do that until I am sure Georgia isn't nearby, so I go over to a window and look out to see if I can locate her down there. I can, and I watch her get into her car before she starts the engine and drives away. As she does, I'm grateful that I parked my car around the corner from here, so it's unlikely she has seen it. I did that because, based on what I was coming here to do to Mateo, I didn't want anybody on this street seeing my vehicle and telling the police it was parked outside around the time the murder may have occurred. But now, after the interruption and the extra time it has given me to come to my senses, there will be no murder here today. The knife is going to remain concealed, at least until I leave this apartment, which I am ready to do right this second.

'Where are you going? We need to talk,' Mateo says as I head for the door, but I don't slow down because I've been here way longer than I anticipated.

'I can't talk now. Not after my sister almost caught me here,' I say. 'I'll call you later.'

I leave the apartment before Mateo has a chance to discuss this anymore, and after rushing down the stairs, I pull open the front door and it's a relief to be out on the street.

I hurry back to my car and remove the knife from where it is tucked into my jeans behind my back, tossing it onto the passenger seat before getting inside and locking the doors. Then I put my hands on the steering wheel and rest my head against it too, sucking in air and trying to process what I almost did back there.

It doesn't take long for me to start crying, the shock of almost becoming a killer overwhelming me. If anybody walked past and saw a weeping woman in this vehicle, they'd probably think I was mad. But I don't care what they might think.

Maybe I am mad.

But I'm not a murderer.

Not yet, anyway.

THIRTY-ONE

'I don't want you to go, Mummy.'

The sweet words spoken by my son echo exactly how I feel in my mind as Freddie's babysitter arrives, as Seth and I are supposed to be leaving for the party shortly.

'I want to watch TV with you,' Freddie goes on, clinging to my arm as Seth makes small talk with the babysitter in the hallway.

I doubt I'm the first person to get mum-guilt from a child who doesn't want to be left with somebody else while I go out on a Saturday night, but of course, that's not the main reason I feel guilty. That would be because I realise that my reason for going out tonight could also be the reason why my family is not the same when I return home again.

'You love Lucy,' I say, referencing the babysitter's name, and I'm not lying because Freddie has told me before how much he likes her. 'You get to have pizza and watch whatever you want and stay up later than usual. You're going to have so much fun.'

'But I want you to be here too,' Freddie says sadly, and I wish I could give my boy what he wants and stay at home tonight, in this safe cocoon that I can pretend is impenetrable to Mateo. But I'd only be fooling myself if I thought that was the case because staying in tonight won't help me. I have to go to the party, and I know that because of what Mateo sent me earlier.

I hadn't been home for long, after returning from his apartment, and there had just been enough time for Seth to ask me how my shopping trip with my sister had gone before I received a message on my phone from Mateo.

I wish we hadn't been interrupted.

If I hadn't known it before, I knew it then. Giving that man false hope that there could be a future for us had been a terrible mistake. Sure, it had bought me a little bit of time, and yes, it had allowed me to get close enough to him to stab him with my knife, but what good was that when I hadn't made use of it? All I had done was to prove to myself that I'm not a killer, as well as make things worse because Mateo clearly now thought I wanted to be with him again.

I hadn't been sure what to send back to him in response, but it didn't matter because he had sent me a follow-up message a few minutes after that.

I appreciate you need time, but I can't just let this run on and on. That's why tonight is still the deadline to tell Seth. Tell him or I will do it at the party.

I'd instantly replied to Mateo then, begging for more time, telling him whatever he needed to hear to give me a reprieve and extend the deadline, or better still, cancel it altogether. But he refused to do that, and as Seth enters the room to say goodbye to Freddie, I realise my time is almost up.

'Have a lovely evening and make sure you behave for the

babysitter,' Seth tells Freddie as Lucy walks in behind him and says hi to me.

She's the daughter of a friend, eighteen and looking to make some extra cash by offering her services as a babysitter. As she's been known to our family for years, we were happy to give her the opportunity. She's great with Freddie, and he usually adores her, but for some reason tonight, he just wants me.

Maybe he can sense that something bad is on the horizon. Are kids capable of that? I read somewhere that animals can sense danger, and not just wild animals like lions and tigers, but even domestic pets such as cats and dogs. But are children the same? I have no idea and it's not as if I have the time to go and search the internet on the subject. All I know is that my son is being unusually clingy with me, so I have to assume he knows that me going to the party is going to end badly for us all. Whether it's intuition or a sixth sense, either way, my clever boy is right. But I have to go. I can't make an excuse not to attend this close to the party. I've already feigned enough illnesses for one week and I won't get away with another one. I also can't risk Seth going to the party alone because Mateo will just tell him then and I won't be there to explain myself. I have to go. But the main reason I will attend this party is because I am hoping I can convince Mateo not to go through with it.

There has to be a chance that he will stand down and not do this.

Maybe he has just been calling my bluff this entire time.

Now I'm going to call his.

'I love you,' I say to Freddie before giving him a big kiss and a hug, and while he protests again, he softens a little when Lucy reveals the chocolate bar she has brought him to have after he has had his dinner.

I'm not going to complain about my son having sugary snacks tonight; his diet is the least of my worries. I need to get to the party. As Seth and I leave, I just hope that Freddie's nutrition will still be something I have to manage when I get back. If not, I guess it means I've been kicked out of this house.

'Tonight should be fun,' Seth says to me as our taxi arrives on the street. My gentleman of a husband opens the door for me to get in first, and I take one last look back at my home.

I hope it is still my home by the time this evening is over.

THIRTY-TWO

My legs feel as shaky and uncertain as my son's did when he first learned to walk. That's the best way I can describe how it feels to put one foot in front of the other as I approach my sister's front door. But Seth is having no such problems, and he strides ahead to ring the bell, to let those inside know we are here. He seems keen to get inside, no doubt ready to pour himself a glass from that bottle of red wine he has tucked under his arm. By comparison, I'd be perfectly happy to stand out here all evening, away from the revellers inside, in the darkness, where no one can see my face. As it is, the front door opens and my face is bathed in the light from the bright hallway as I see my sister standing before us.

'Hello! Welcome!' Georgia says, throwing one hand up in the air triumphantly as if we are about to step into the world's most exclusive event. As well as the elaborate gesture, I see she is wearing a tightly fitting red dress and a pair of expensive-looking shoes. Her hair and make-up are on point, and she very much fits the part of the glamorous host. Not only does she look incredible, but she looks like she is already enjoying the beginnings of this party. This doesn't bode well for me because if my sister is in a euphoric mood, that only means there is further for her to fall if Mateo continues with his plan to bring everything crashing down.

'You're looking well,' Seth compliments my sister as they hug before he steps aside to allow me to enter first.

'Well, come on. Get inside. The champagne won't drink itself,' Georgia says, ushering me in and hurrying me along.

My feet feel like dead weights as I reluctantly raise them up and step over the threshold into my sister's home, and no sooner have I done that than I see my parents beyond my sibling. The pair of them are each holding a glass of champagne and looking at a photo on the wall. As I get nearer to it, I see that it is one of Georgia during her travelling days in India.

'I love this one,' I hear Dad say as he leans in for a closer look. 'Look how happy she is.'

Great. Another reminder of my sister's happiness, as if I needed it after seeing how joyous she was when I arrived. Why can't Georgia be in a bad mood or have a typically downbeat demeanour most of the time? That might make her suffering less, but Dad is right. She looks happy in that photo, she looks happy tonight, she looks happy all the time. Now she has Mateo, her happiness is off the scale.

'Hello, darling,' Mum says when she notices me lingering in the hallway behind her, and she turns to give me a hug before my father does the same.

'Are you ready for a fun-filled evening of partying?' Dad asks me, raising both his glass and his eyebrows with the clear intention that he is going to drink lots more champagne than he already has.

'Yeah,' I reply quietly before the resplendent Georgia approaches us.

'Everybody's here. Come on. Go and mingle. It's a party,' she tells us all before heading for the kitchen. As I can't see my husband anywhere, I presume he must have already gone in too.

My parents follow Georgia and then I have no choice but to walk behind them, and as I enter the kitchen, my aching heart feels like it sinks even lower in my chest. That's because there are a lot of people here and I know many of them. They're mostly Georgia's friends, but having been around my sister's mates for years, I recognise plenty of their faces, just like they will all know who I am. Several of them even give me a wave when they see me loitering in the doorway. I meekly wave back, feeling about as unsociable as I ever have in my life. This feels like a further nail in my coffin because the more people there are who know me at this party, the worse it will be if and when Mateo drops the big bombshell with my name all over it.

Where is he?

I scan the sea of champagne-sipping faces but can't spot him anywhere. I do spot Seth though, and as I predicted, he has been quick to open his wine and pour himself a glass. Now he's talking with my parents, probably small talk about something meaningless, a gentle opener into a slightly deeper conversation that might occur between them once the alcohol has lubricated their tongues a little more.

This is all so quaint. Simple. Nice. Suburban. Just as Georgia would have hoped and planned it. But while the party appears to have got off to a good start, I know there is a ticking timer that threatens to derail this entire thing. If Mateo makes a speech and mentions our affair, the pleasant, upbeat music I can hear drifting in from the other room will be replaced by stony silence followed by screams and sobs.

Then I see him.

He waltzes in carrying a large box of beers before he places them down on the kitchen counter. Then he rips open the box before taking out some bottles and handing them off to a couple of guys who I recognise as being among my sister's work friends. Then he grabs a couple more bottles before heading in my direction.

As I watch him approaching, I analyse everything I can about his body language to try and get a read on if he is really going to do what he threatened to do tonight. He's dressed smartly, wearing a short-sleeved black shirt that is a little tight and therefore accentuates his biceps somewhat. He completes the look with a smart pair of dark jeans and black shoes; his hair and stubble are trimmed neatly. He has made as much effort as Georgia has and as they each roam around this party, they very much look like the perfect couple – attractive, confident, happy. But I look beyond the clothing and try to stare into Mateo's eyes, where the secrets always hide. I notice he doesn't once look at me. As he gets closer, I realise he is not even acknowledging that I'm here. It's only when he goes to walk right past me that I can't take it any longer and feel the need to step in front of him and break his stride. Only then does he look into my eyes.

'Don't do this,' I say to him before he can walk away.

'Don't do what?'

I turn and see Seth has sidled up beside me and he's the one who has just asked the question of me.

'Erm, nothing,' I reply as Mateo smiles and holds out a beer bottle towards my husband.

'You want one?' he asks Seth.

'No, I'm sticking to wine tonight. But thank you,' he replies.

'What about you, Corinne?' Mateo asks then, holding the bottle towards me.

If I could get away with it, I'd knock it out of his hand and allow it to smash on the kitchen tiles because I'm angry that he is just treating me like any other guest here and pretending like he isn't holding my life in his hands. But all I can do is shake my head because now that Seth is with us, I'm rendered mute, unable to discuss what I so desperately need to discuss with him.

'Have you got any friends here, Mateo, or are they all Georgia's?' Seth asks as he looks around, and that is an interesting

question on my husband's part. Has Mateo brought anyone
from his side to witness the show this evening?

'I invited a few mates, but they couldn't get babysitters,'
Mateo replies with a shrug. 'You know how it is at our age.
Everyone has kids, don't they?'

'Not everyone,' I reply. 'You don't.'

It might be mean but I'm reminding him that Freddie is
Seth's, not his, and that whatever Mateo might do, it won't
change the fact that we have a child together.

'That is true,' Mateo says with another shrug.

'But it's just a matter of time, right?' Seth chips in then as he
slaps Mateo on the shoulder, insinuating that he and my sister
will most likely think about a family of their own one day if
things continue to go well between them.

'One thing at a time,' Mateo laughs before looking around.
'We'll talk soon, but for now, I better help Georgia make sure
everybody has got a drink. So if you would excuse me.'

Mateo goes to walk away, but suddenly turns back to say
one more thing.

'Enjoy the party.'

I grit my teeth as those words hit me while he just saunters
away and soon finds somebody who will take that bottle of beer
that he was unable to dispose of over here. I also think about
what he said about inviting his mates here, but they couldn't get
babysitters. Is that really true or was it a lie? Mateo always
seems to keep his personal life discreet, and while that air of
mystery is part of what initially attracted me to him, what is he
actually hiding there?

Could it be that he has no friends? No family? Why would
that be? Has he pushed them all away with his behaviour over
the years? Might I not be the only person he has made threats to
before? Are there other people who hate him just as much as I
do? Perhaps other people who have fallen afoul of his games
before? And if he has something to hide, could it stop him from

trying to ruin my life? There must be a reason for his urgency. I'm afraid of something, but what if he is too?

I wonder if there could be something in Mateo's past that I might be able to exploit, a thread I can pull on that he has left loose somewhere. Time is running out for me to counterstrike, but I am willing to try anything. I just need a way of delving into his secrets. But how can I do that if there is nobody here from his past?

As I keep watching Mateo, who is now chatting with one of my sister's best friends from school, I notice him take his phone from his pocket and glance at it. He does so a couple more times, which signals to me that there is somebody messaging him and diverting his attention away from the person he is talking to. I get confirmation of that when, after looking at his phone one more time, he seems to excuse himself from the conversation before leaving the kitchen.

'I'm just going to the bathroom,' I say to Seth before leaving the kitchen.

I walk into the hallway, trying to locate Mateo. I can't see him, but I do hear Georgia's voice coming from the lounge.

'What are you doing in here by yourself?'

I peep around the doorway and see that Georgia has just interrupted Mateo, who was in this room to use his phone in private. He instantly lowers it as my sister steps towards him, and before he can do anything, she swipes it out of his hand.

'I thought we said no phones tonight,' Georgia says to him. 'I left mine in the bedroom so I can be a good host this evening. Can't you do the same? My friends have been dying to meet you, but every time I look at you, you're doing more texting than talking. Who are you messaging anyway?'

'No one,' Mateo replies, taking his phone back off my sister.

'Okay, then you can put your phone down and come and chat to people,' Georgia says, testing him. I guess she doesn't have to be quite so demanding, although my sister is known for being that way, so it's hardly out of character for her. And it can appear rude if someone is on their phone during a conversation, so she has a point. But what will Mateo do?

'Fine,' he replies casually before putting his phone behind a cushion on the sofa. 'I'll leave it in here for a while. Let's go back to the party.'

'Thank you,' Georgia says before she gives Mateo a kiss. They turn to leave the lounge.

I quickly hide around a corner as they pass me and return to the kitchen, but I'm not planning on going in there. Not yet. I go into the lounge instead.

I reach behind the cushion to pick up Mateo's phone. I'm aware that without knowing his keycode, I won't be able to access his messages or anything like that, but I decide to take a look anyway, as whoever he has been texting might send something back that gives me a clue about something I could exploit.

I look at the phone, hoping that a new message will appear on screen that could be of use to me.

A minute later, I get what I want.

THIRTY-THREE

Tick tock. Time is running out for you.

Considering my circumstances, that message could have been meant for me, except it wasn't. It has arrived on Mateo's phone, so it was meant for him. But what could it be referring to? I know I'm running out of time tonight, but why would that be the case for Mateo too?

I now realise why he seemed distracted by his phone to the point that my sister wanted him to put it away so they could enjoy the evening together. Somebody is clearly pushing him into doing something, just like Mateo is pushing me into something too.

Why does he have a deadline?

And is it linked to mine?

I want to confront Mateo about this in the hopes that it might help me escape my predicament, but to do that, I need to leave this room and return to the kitchen where he and everybody else at this party are. What should I do about the phone? It might be a risk, but I decide to keep it with me, so I slip it into my pocket before leaving the lounge.

As I re-enter the kitchen, I look around for Mateo and I see him talking to my parents. Oh my, what could he be talking about with them? I hope the topic of the conversation is Georgia and not me, but I walk over to intervene and find out. As I do, Seth approaches me with two glasses of wine in hand.

'Hey, there you are. Did you get lost on the way back from the bathroom?' he asks me with a smile.

'Oh, erm, no. I was just...' My sentence trails off as I notice Mateo looking at me. He makes a point of checking his watch. Does that mean my time is almost up?

'I got you a drink,' Seth says, handing me one of the glasses of red wine, but while I take it, I keep my eyes on Mateo and watch him as he says something to my parents before making his way over to where Georgia stands chatting with a few friends. Then he does something that instantly turns my blood cold.

He taps a silver spoon against the side of his beer bottle, making a loud clinking noise that cuts through all the chatter in this kitchen and causes everyone to fall silent.

I know what that noise signals, just like everybody else in the room knows too.

It's a way for Mateo to capture everybody's attention and there's only one reason why he would want to do that.

He is preparing to make a speech.

I feel as if I'm frozen solid as I watch Mateo's mouth open, and his lips begin to move.

'First of all, Georgia and I would like to thank you all for coming here tonight,' Mateo begins as I do my best to discreetly but urgently get his attention. I'm subtly shaking my head so if he looks my way, he will hopefully realise that I am pleading with him not to do this. Because this must be it, the moment I have been fearing all week ever since Mateo gave me the deadline to tell Seth about us. This is the moment when he ruins my life in front of all these people who know me, most important of whom are my husband, my parents and my sister, the latter standing right alongside the man currently making the speech.

'It's clear to me that Georgia is very lucky to have so many good friends in attendance tonight,' Mateo goes on, still not looking in my direction and, therefore, still not showing any signs of shutting up. 'And of course, her lovely family are here this evening. Her parents are over there, enjoying the champagne, which is great to see.'

Everybody looks over at my mum and dad, and while my mother blushes slightly at the sudden bout of attention, my father loves the limelight and raises his glass to the sky.

'And I can't forget Georgia's beautiful sister, Corinne, and her husband, Seth. Thank you both for coming, guys.'

Only then does Mateo look at me. But, of course, now I am unable to shake my head at him or give any other signal to get him to be quiet. That's because all the guests are looking my way. Seth raises his glass towards the speaker, and I am left standing helplessly beside my husband, fearing that these are the last few seconds of being happily married before all hell breaks loose inside this kitchen.

'I'm aware that I am incredibly lucky to have met Georgia and for her to have considered me worthy of introducing to all her family and friends,' Mateo goes on, commanding the attention of the room effortlessly. 'It's a pleasure to call myself her boyfriend and I hope you are all happy that she is happy too.'

Everybody cheers then to show support for Mateo and Georgia, everybody but me, because I am just wishing I could turn invisible before the dreaded words land. Then Mateo speaks again, and I realise my time is up.

'However, there is something that I feel I must get off my chest before this party goes any further,' he says as my heart thuds against my insides. 'Something that I have to say and something that you all have to hear.'

Mateo looks at me as everyone else hangs on his next word,

no doubt curious as to what the big reveal might be. Then I have an idea. A sudden jolt of inspiration that might be enough to break Mateo's flow and interrupt what he is about to say.

I look down at the wine glass in my hand.

Then I let go of it and watch it as it falls to the floor.

The glass hits the tiles and shatters on impact, sending red wine spurting out in all directions as well as shooting several shards of glass across the smooth surface.

The noise causes a few people to jolt and gasp, but thankfully, one noise I do not hear is the sound of Mateo's voice. That's because my little stunt did the trick. I have managed to shut him up.

'Be careful,' I hear Seth say, both to me and to the other people standing closest to us because we are now surrounded by glass and not all of us are wearing footwear. It's often considered polite to remove your shoes when entering another person's home, but it's also considered dangerous when people are standing near broken glass without adequate protection on their feet.

'What happened?' I hear Georgia ask me, and when I look at her, I notice she seems annoyed at me, as if dropping the glass has just ruined whatever moment Mateo was trying to create. Of course, that's exactly what it's done and that was precisely my intention, but to my sister, I must just seem incredibly clumsy and annoying.

'I'm sorry. It just slipped from my hand,' I reply feebly as Seth and several other people form a sort of human barrier around the 'danger zone' of broken glass.

'Can you get the mop?' I hear Georgia ask Mateo.

I watch as he follows her order, moving away from the spot where he had planted his feet and begun his speech, now forced into doing something he obviously doesn't want to do. But as he goes, he glances in my direction and he's not stupid. He knows exactly why that glass fell to the floor and it certainly wasn't because it slipped. He knows I just silenced him by causing a distraction. This means I've won this particular battle. But the war is still very much far from over.

As everyone continues to be distracted by the mess I created and either tries to get something to help clean it up or advises others to be careful of the glass, I decide to follow Mateo out of the room. I find him in a small utility area where my sister keeps cleaning items like her mop, and before Mateo can leave again with the mop and bucket in hand, I corner him.

'I can't believe you were actually going to do it,' I say, mortified. 'You were really going to tell everybody about what we did.'

'I warned you,' Mateo replies, expressionless, seemingly unflustered by my party trick. But is he really? Remembering that message I saw on his phone, I am aware that there must be something troubling him, and even if it's not me, maybe it could help me.

'Why is time running out for you?' I ask him then as I reveal that I have his phone. 'Who sent you this message? Are you under pressure from somebody? Is that why you are doing this to me?'

Mateo is surprised to see that I have his mobile, and he quickly swipes it back.

'It's none of your business,' he replies.

'I think it is. Everything about you became my business the second you walked back into my life and threatened to ruin it. So tell me what is going on. Does this relate to me?'

Mateo's stance suddenly softens as he looks from his phone to my face.

'This isn't how I imagined it all going,' he concedes. 'I never wanted to threaten you. I was hoping that by seeing me, you would remember the spark that we once had, and it might ignite again. Yes, I only got with Georgia to get closer to you, but my initial intent was not to give you an ultimatum. I don't want you to hate me. I just...'

'Just what?'

'I want you to love me. Like I love you.'

I stare at Mateo and try to ascertain if he's being honest with me. But he seems genuine. This is certainly the most vulnerable I have seen him be with me, and as I look at the phone in his hands, I have to think part of it must be down to fearing the person who is giving him a deadline.

'I don't understand,' I reply. 'What are you talking about?'

Mateo takes a deep breath, and while we can hear the chatter from the party in the background, it remains just the two of us standing in this cramped utility room.

'I owe somebody money,' he says quietly. 'It's the person who sent me that message. They want the money by midnight or they're going to hurt me tomorrow. But I can't afford to pay them, so my plan is to leave town before then. I am going to leave tonight, after this party.'

I process that and realise that it explains why Mateo seemed so calm about ruining his relationship with Georgia by confessing what we did in the past. He was not going to stick around to witness the fallout, regardless. But something doesn't make sense.

'I don't understand. Why drag *me* into this? You say you love me, yet this is how you treat me?'

The fact he says he loves me is crazy by itself, regardless of anything else, because even though we have a history together, it was such a brief one. Falling in love from a one-night stand and pursuing that person years later is intense and extreme and would set alarm bells ringing even without other people being involved.

'I do love you,' Mateo insists. 'And everything I have done, from getting with Georgia to get closer to you, to wanting you to tell Seth and even to giving you the deadline, is all because of the way I feel about you.'

'It doesn't feel like it,' I cry, aware that Georgia could come in here at any moment to find out where the mop bucket is and catch us having this intense conversation.

'You don't understand,' Mateo says with frustration. 'I am planning to leave town, but I was hoping that I wouldn't be alone when I left. I was hoping that you would come with me. Will you?'

THIRTY-FOUR

I stare at the man who I've spent the last week hating and, suddenly, I realise I don't hate him anymore. Sure, I'll never forgive him for what he has put me through over this past week, but right now, as I look into his eyes, I don't see a man who wants to destroy my life just because he can. Instead, I see a man who is desperately searching for a little bit of happiness in his own life, a life that is seemingly under threat unless he flees town tonight. But he wanted to leave town with me?

'I can't leave. Even if I didn't love my husband, which I do, I have a son, and I would never leave him,' I tell Mateo. 'Surely you realise that?'

'I guess I panicked and got desperate,' comes the sorry response. 'I got desperate because I'm scared that the people I owe money to are going to kill me, so I know I have to run. But rather than run on my own, I thought it might be worth a shot at seeing if I could get you to run with me. You're the only thing that feels like it was worth something in the last several years of my life. Everything else was such a waste, so meaningless or stupid or reckless. But not you. You were different. You were the highlight.'

'You thought you could get me to run with you by threatening me?'

'I'm sorry. Like I said, I'm desperate and scared.'

'But you got with my sister before you got this deadline?' I ask, and Mateo nods to confirm. 'Wait, so that means you were planning on trying to get me back even before you had this deadline for your debt?'

Again, Mateo nods.

'I borrowed money from these people a couple of months ago. It was for a business I was trying to start up. Another failed business of mine...' Mateo's voice trails off before he regains his thought pattern. 'But yes, I was seeing Georgia by then and it was all because of you. I wanted to one day see you again, so I figured she was my best shot. If it didn't work out with you, maybe your sister was the next best thing, but even then, I knew it was you or nothing. That's why, rather than just leaving town last week when I got the deadline to repay my debt by tonight, I thought it was worth a shot at getting you back. I still love you and I have never stopped thinking about you since that one night we had together.'

Mateo does look utterly defeated as he admits all of this to me. Not only that, but he looks pathetic, not at all like the man who first attracted me and certainly not like the man who has made me feel powerless all week. Not only do I feel sorry for him now, but I actually see a way out of this for all of us. A way I might be able to help him, this man who loves me, but most importantly, a way in which I can keep my family, save my marriage and help my sister, all in one fell swoop.

'How much do you owe?' I ask Mateo as he stands listlessly before me, still holding the mop and bucket my sister sent him in here to fetch. All he does in response to that question is shake his head, so I'm forced to ask it again.

'*How much?*'

'Twenty thousand,' he eventually admits.

I raise my eyebrows at the large figure. However, as high as it is, it's also not a figure that feels entirely insurmountable, at least not to me anyway. I've always been employed and careful about what I spend and what I save, so my bank account has always looked healthier than that of other adults my age, those who maybe took time off for travel or simply spent what came in, I suppose.

'What if I told you I had enough money in my savings account to help you pay off your debt?' I say next. And Mateo looks surprised.

'Why would you want to do that?' he asks.

'I'd do it only if it meant you left town tonight and left me and my family alone for good,' I reply firmly as Mateo processes that information.

Now I'm the one making ultimatums, rather than him, although I can't say that it feels much better being on this side of it. There are no winners here, not really. Mateo might get his debt paid but he has to leave everything behind, including me and Georgia, such are the terms of our agreement. And while I might remove the problem of him being in my life, I will also be removing almost all of my savings from my bank account in the process. It's a business transaction, pure and simple, yet it's one where nobody wins, or at least Mateo and I don't win – and neither does Georgia. I guess the people he owes money to will win, but so be it. The most important thing is that the people I care about don't lose.

Seth, Freddie, Georgia, my parents. They won't have to be hurt, and if that's the case, I can live with that. The fact that none of them know how much I have saved away is a help – if they don't know the money existed, they won't miss it.

'I can transfer you the money you need tonight, but in exchange you do what you were going to do anyway,' I say firmly. 'You leave my sister, you leave town, and you never come back again. You allow me and my family to return to normal and our secret goes back to being buried again, just like it has been for these past five years. You forget about me and whatever feelings you have for me, and you move on with your life, just like I have moved on with mine. That's the deal and it's a one-time offer. You take it or leave it right now, this second. Or else you still have your debt, and you'll have to keep looking over your shoulder wherever you run to tonight.'

Mateo is thinking about it, but I don't have time for him to make a counteroffer, so I solidify my stance with even more finality.

'Either way, you don't get to have me, but at least my way, you don't have your debt anymore.'

The desperate man lets out a sigh, and as his shoulders sag, he starts to nod his head.

'Okay,' he says. 'I'll leave you alone.'

It looks like it is breaking Mateo's heart to admit that, but I have to be the strong one here because, unlike him, I have other people's feelings to consider besides my own. I also have to be proactive, so with that in mind, I tell him what will happen next.

'Give me your bank details and I will send you the money,' I say. 'Then you are going to leave my sister. I'd prefer it if you let her down gently, tell her that on second thoughts, you're not ready to settle down and you have decided to be single again. But if you're not brave enough to do that then I guess you just have to slip away from this party and leave and never come back. Either way, you'll break my sister's heart, but at least she'll let me in to help her pick up the pieces. At least this way, she won't hate me for the rest of her life, nor will Seth or anybody else I care about.'

Mateo takes all of that on board. Though I don't know which way he is going to end things with my sister, the polite way or the coward's way, he nods his head and then looks down at his phone. But before he can do anything with it...

'How can I trust that you will actually leave if we go through with this?' I ask him, aware he could lie in his response, so I'm going to have to try and figure out if he's telling the truth, which is a risky strategy but the only one I have.

'Because I'm a dead man if I don't,' he replies simply. 'The people I owe will never stop looking for me until they have their money, and without yours, I can't pay the debt back.'

That is good enough for me, so we carry on. As he accesses his mobile banking app, I do the same on my phone and suddenly, this tiny utility room in my sister's home has become a place where I have just spent twenty thousand pounds. This is money I was saving for future family holidays, such as expensive but memorable trips to Disneyland with Freddie as he got older, so he could meet Mickey and Minnie and let his imagination soar while surrounded by princes and princesses and castles and fireworks. Instead, this money is going on ensuring I get to be around him forever, to see my son grow up every day without losing half of him in a potential divorce. That might not seem quite as exciting as a trip to Disney's self-titled 'Happiest Place on Earth', but it is of vital importance to me, a mother and wife who will do anything to keep together the ones she loves the most.

'I'm sorry,' Mateo says once the transfer has been made. 'I'm sorry for not being able to forget about you. I'm sorry for using your sister to get back into your life. And I'm sorry for giving you an awful dilemma and making you hate me when all I ever wanted was to recreate what we had on our one night together.'

'It's too late for that,' I tell him unsympathetically. 'What's done is done. We've both made mistakes, and we have to live with them. Now I'm going to go back to the party and tell my husband that I'm tired, so we can leave. As for you, you're going to mop up the drink I spilt before you speak with Georgia. Then, by the time I wake up in the morning, I won't have to worry about this anymore. Okay?'

Mateo nods and, with that, I leave the room and walk back into the kitchen.

I see Seth standing in a similar place to where I left him, near to where I 'dropped' my wine glass. He is talking to my parents while everybody else seems to have just resumed the conversations they were having prior to Mateo's attempts at making his speech. I see Georgia talking to a few of her friends, and I know I'll have to say goodbye to her in a moment, but first, I need to extract my husband from this house.

'I'm feeling lightheaded. I think the wine went to my head,' I say before gesturing towards the spilt wine on the floor as if that's my reason for dropping it. 'I thought I was over whatever illness I had last week, but I don't think I am. Can we go home? I really feel like I need to get into bed.'

Seth looks disappointed but masks it well, possibly because my parents are standing with us, and he won't want to come across as uncaring in front of them. Especially not when my mum puts a hand on my shoulder and tells me she is sorry to hear that I'm still not feeling well, while my father puts down his glass of champagne and looks affected by my sense of unease too.

'Yeah, of course,' Seth says, reluctantly putting down his own drink, and I guess we're set to leave. But there's one more thing to do before we go.

'I'll just say goodbye to Georgia,' I tell him before I wander over to where my sister stands. As I go, I pass Mateo carrying the mop bucket, but I don't make eye contact with him, and I doubt he bothers to look at me either.

'Sorry to interrupt,' I say, intervening in my sister's conversation with her friends. 'But I'm really not feeling well, so Seth and I are going to leave. I'm sorry, sis. I hope you have a good night though.'

I feel awful because I know that my sister is not going to have a good night. Not when Mateo breaks up with her or even if he can't bring himself to do it formally, she'll figure it out tomorrow when he's not here to move in and she can't find him at his apartment either. My poor sibling's life is about to fall apart, and even though it's better for her in the long run to lose a guy like Mateo, who doesn't really care for her, it won't be easy at the time. She has no idea of the storm that is coming, which is why she doesn't seem too devastated that I'm leaving. Sure, she would like to have me around, but she has her mates here and she has plenty of alcohol, so she's going to have fun regardless.

'Oh, I'm sorry you're not feeling well, sis,' she says as she gives me a hug. 'I hope you're feeling better soon. I'll call you tomorrow, if my hangover's not too bad, that is.'

I just about manage to muster up a smile at her joke before I turn and walk away. I know I'll be back here soon, once Georgia has realised she is single again and needs a shoulder to cry on or just somebody to get drunk with and drown her sorrows with. At least things will be normal between us again. We'll go back to being best friends and I won't have to worry about keeping secrets from her and trying to keep her at a distance, which has been hard to do over this past week.

As Seth and I leave the room, giving a wave to my parents as we go, I have to glance at Mateo one more time. I can't resist it. When I do, I see a sorry sight. He's mopping up my mess and he looks very miserable about it. He looks even worse when he looks up and sees me watching him. But before our look can linger any longer, I turn my head. With that, I leave the room and leave my sister's house.

I'm aware that I'm also leaving Mateo behind. He will return to my past, where he belongs. As for Seth, he will be my future. I hope the rest of our marriage is plain sailing and as drama-free as possible. I don't need anything else to happen to know that I love him dearly and want nothing more than to be with him until my dying day. I'm also excited for the two of us to continue being permanent fixtures in Freddie's life with no risk of separation and custody hearings. I just want the three of us to spend as much time together as a family with absolutely nothing getting in the way of that.

It's cost me a lot to keep it this way, but I know that when I get home and lay my head on my pillow, I'll sleep a lot better than I have done for the past several nights.

I'll sleep better knowing that I'm not going to lose my family anytime soon.

THIRTY-FIVE

My first thought when I wake up is that Mateo is still a problem that needs to be dealt with. Maybe I had a nightmare about him or maybe it's just the fact that I've had seven days of sheer stress from worrying about him that means it has become a habit now. Whatever it is, it takes me a few moments to remember that I resolved my problem last night and I don't have to worry about him anymore. But of course, remembering that, as pleasant as it is, subsequently means remembering what I had to do to make it happen.

What's it like to wake up having spent twenty thousand pounds the night before? It doesn't feel great, but it sure feels a lot better than waking up with my family hating me.

As I rub my eyes and figure out that I probably only got a maximum of two hours' sleep last night due to all the stress at the party, it's at least a relief to see my husband sleeping soundly beside me. There's no way we would have shared a bed last night if the truth had come out, that's for sure. I'd have been in a separate bedroom, or worse, in a different place entirely. Then I would have had to spend today apologising to Seth and telling him that the one night I spent with Mateo meant nothing, which would be the truth, but how would I ever truly convince him of that?

I shiver at the thought of how my life could look right now if I hadn't seen a way of making the Mateo problem disappear. But just because it has, it doesn't mean that I feel good about myself or what I have had to do to accomplish it. It pains me to think about all that money that has gone from my account, money that should have been used to create fabulous family memories and give Freddie experiences that he would cherish for a lifetime. Not to mention the memories that Seth and I could have looked back on in our old age and felt proud that we were able to create for our child. Instead, that money is with Mateo, who will be sending it to some shady character to pay off his debt, and I have no idea what the money will be spent on after that. Unfortunately, I doubt it will be for anything positive. The funds may even end up in the hands of the police one day, but hopefully they've been laundered enough by then to remove all trace of having originated from my bank account.

Paying off debts. Money laundering. Keeping even more secrets from my loved ones.

This is not a world I belong in, yet here I am, right in the middle of it.

Who even am I anymore?

That's a question I won't bother trying to answer today because I've got enough to wrap my head around. But with Mateo gone, I console myself with the thought that Seth will never know about the substantial amount of money I transferred to Mateo at last night's party. That's because I never told him about how much I had been squirrelling away in my personal bank account over the years.

I've always been a fairly private person when it comes to money, never one to be seen as extravagant as I accrued excess funds as I got older or never one to get too down on myself if money was ever tight in my younger years. I just kept my head down and got on with things, regardless. I guess I got that trait from my parents because neither Mum nor Dad ever made a big deal about their finances either. If I asked for something as a child, I either got a 'yes' and we bought it or I got a 'no' and after a little tantrum on my part, we all moved on. They taught me that material things were to be earned and looked after and money was only ever spent on something you really cherished. I guess my parents could tell when I really wanted something when I was younger because it meant a lot to me or when I just wanted something for the sake of it. That's how I've tried to approach it with my own child, figuring out Freddie's motivations and deciding whether to splurge on a toy he wants because he has a specific reason to have it or refusing it because he's just being an impulsive toddler. But my ways with money go beyond my son and extend to my behaviour with my husband.

There's a big reason why I have never told Seth that I had been saving a reasonable percentage of my wage for several years in my own bank account, separate to our joint. It's because I've always known that he covets having a big home one day, one of those spacious, four- or five-bedroom detached houses with a big garage and sprawling garden; the kind of property that makes people say 'Wow, this is nice' when they see it for the first time.

As for me, I couldn't care less about having a big house because to me, it just means a bigger burden. More mortgage to pay and more years to pay it, which usually means retiring later in life and having fewer holidays along the way. No, thank you. I love our house, our modest home, which we bought after leaving our rented apartment, and this place is perfect for our family of three. While nobody might ever stop by here and say 'Wow, this house is incredible', those same people will likely be paying off their mortgages many years after mine has already been completed, and for me, I prefer more freedom over more furniture. So that's why I kept that money quiet, as Seth would start house hunting if he'd known about it. I only wanted him to find out about it when I suggested Disneyland in a year or two and floated the idea of us giving Freddie the summer holiday of a lifetime. As it is, Seth will never know about it. Nor will Freddie ever know just how close he came to meeting Mickey Mouse.

That last thought makes me incredibly sad, so I get out of bed in the hopes of distracting myself. I leave Seth asleep in his room and go to check on my son, peeping around his bedroom door and seeing that he is fast asleep too. It is still early, and I'll be exhausted all day, but at least I have some peace and quiet to start today as I go downstairs and make myself some breakfast.

As I make myself some tea and toast, it seems peace and quiet only exists for me in my outer world because my inner world is still in turmoil. My next thought is of Georgia and what is happening between her and Mateo. I've already checked my phone and not seen any messages from her or anybody I knew at that party, so I have to assume Mateo did not break up with her last night. Perhaps, unsurprisingly, he has chosen the option to just leave town without actually telling her they are over, which is obviously the easier way of doing things for him. Instead of a very awkward face-to-face conversation, he will just disappear, leaving Georgia to slowly figure out that he is not coming back. I hate him for choosing that way, but what can I do? I just have to bide my time and wait for Georgia to make contact, and then I'll have to act as clueless as everybody else as to where Mateo might have gone and what reasons he might have had for doing a runner.

I spend the next hour nibbling my toast and sipping my tea, both of which go cold long before I finish them. But I'm not hungry or thirsty, just anxious, both because of the financial loss and the loss that my poor sister will be having to process soon.

As much as I wanted some peace and quiet, it's actually a relief when I hear Freddie get up.

After he has managed to wake up Seth by bounding into the bedroom and triumphantly declaring that he is awake, he rushes down the stairs to find me. I smile at my son's energetic entrance before making him his breakfast, and when a still-sleepy Seth joins us, I make sure he is looked after too by putting some extra bread into the toaster. But he wants to check on me as well, which is understandable considering we left the party early last night due to me being unwell.

'Are you okay?' he enquires, looking worried.

'I'm fine,' I reply. 'Much better after a good night's sleep.'

A good night's sleep is the opposite of what I had, but Seth doesn't know any better and he doesn't look as worried now.

'At least I don't have a hangover this morning,' he says then, looking on the bright side of having to leave the party early. 'What shall we do today?'

'The park!' Freddie cries, eager to play on the swings and roundabouts, and Seth laughs before turning to me.

'I guess we're going to the park then,' he says, wrapping a hand around my waist and giving me a kiss. 'The weather looks nice, so we could take a picnic too. Make a day of it. What do you think?'

I'd love to say yes, but I'm also aware that at any moment, Georgia might get in touch, in tears because Mateo is not moving in with her today as he was supposed to be doing. When that call comes, I should be ready to go to my sister and offer my support. But when will that call come? An hour from now? Three hours? Six? Tonight? I don't know, so I can't really ruin a day with my family waiting on it.

'The park sounds good,' I say, figuring I'll just act as if everything is normal until I hear otherwise. If the call comes while I am at the park, I'll just leave my boys there.

Until then, I'll try to carry on as normal.

. . .

As it turns out, I'm right about the call coming while we're at the park. My phone rings as I'm making a pretty pathetic attempt at trying to catch the frisbee that my husband has just thrown in my direction. As the frisbee lands tamely on the grass, well away from my outstretched arm, I stop as I fear that the time has come.

Taking my phone from my pocket, I see the caller ID, though it's not Georgia. It's Dad. Maybe this call is about something else other than my sister's relationship. At least I think that until I answer the call.

'Hey, me and your mother are on our way over to your sister's,' Dad says.

I can hear a bit of background noise, so I assume he is driving and speaking to me through his car's hands-free technology.

'She's asked for us all to come over, so can you meet us there too?'

'What's it about?' I ask, playing dumb because it's all I can do in the circumstances.

'It's something to do with Mateo,' Dad replies. 'I'm not sure what exactly, but Georgia just says she needs us there, so we're on our way. Can you get there?'

'Yeah, I can,' I reply as Seth jogs over and picks up the frisbee before mouthing to me to ask who is on the call.

I hang up and look at my husband and my son.

I'm going to have to disappoint both of them now by telling them I have to leave. But I imagine on the disappointment scale, it will be nothing compared to how my poor sister is feeling now she has realised her relationship is over.

'I have to go to Georgia's. Something's come up,' I say to Seth. 'Family stuff. Are you okay here with Freddie? I'll come back and get you if I'm quick, but you might have to walk home. Is that all right?'

'Sure,' Seth replies

I look at Freddie, and he seems happy chasing his ball around, so I decide to just go rather than risk him getting upset by me saying goodbye.

As I reach the car, I am wishing I didn't have to do this.

I'd much rather be driving somewhere where reaching my destination wouldn't result in drama, heartache and maybe even a few tears. As it is, that is exactly what I am going to be walking into, so I decide to just get it over with and drive as fast as the speed limit allows towards my sister's place.

Parking and getting out of the car, I tell myself to be the best sister I can be now. Supportive, provide a listening ear, make as many cups of tea or pour as many glasses of wine as Georgia needs. Whatever it takes to make the rest of today easier for her.

I knock on the door and Dad answers.

'Thanks for coming so quickly,' he says before I follow him in.

'What's this about?' I ask as he leads me into the kitchen, the same room we all partied in last night before I left abruptly, twenty thousand pounds lighter than when I arrived.

Before Dad can answer, I stop walking and that's because my legs stop working.

The reason they do is the same reason why my jaw hangs open and my stomach churns.

I expected to come here to console my sister over losing Mateo.

Instead, I find that very man standing in her kitchen, smiling at me.

THIRTY-SIX

'Are you okay, sis?' Georgia asks me as I continue to stare at the man I thought I had seen the back of. That man who is leaning casually against the kitchen counter with a big smile on his face.

Mateo is as pleased to see me as I am surprised to see him.

What the hell is going on? Why is he still here? Why hasn't he left town like we agreed he would?

Why is he still in my life, threatening to ruin everything?

'Yeah, you look a little pale,' Mateo says. 'I heard you left the party early last night because you didn't feel well, but we hoped you'd be feeling better by now.'

I hear the words coming out of Mateo's mouth, but I still can't summon up the strength to speak. Not to anybody in this kitchen. Not to Mum, or Dad, or my sister. Instead, I feel like I am actually unwell now, not like the other times when I was faking illness, but actually really, really ill. How else is my body supposed to react to this shocking appearance of the man I gave twenty thousand pounds to disappear?

Am I seeing things? Is this a hallucination? Am I still asleep? Did I not actually get out of bed earlier and make breakfast and go to the park with my family and drive over here and walk into this craziness?

'Darling?'

My mum's concerned word snaps me out of it as I realise this is real and I better sort myself out before I give myself away.

'Sorry. I'm just a little frazzled from rushing over here so quickly,' I say, which is my best attempt at explaining my strange demeanour. 'I was worried there was bad news or something.'

'Bad news? No, not at all,' Georgia says, looking as surprised as I just did when I walked in. 'Why would there be any bad news?'

'I don't know,' I reply feebly as Mateo looks amused over there by the counter.

'Yeah, there's no bad news,' he says. 'Instead, it's good news, but I've been waiting for you all to get here so I can tell you together. Shall I go for it, G?'

Mateo looks to my sister, as if what he is about to say is something they have both discussed and now they have both decided they are ready to share it with us.

'Yeah, go for it,' Georgia replies with a smile, and with that, Mateo does as they wish.

'I'd like to thank you all for welcoming me into your family,' he says, looking at my mother, then my father, then finally, at me. 'I really appreciate how amazing you have all been towards me since you met me, so I want to do something kind in return.'

'You don't have to do that,' Dad replies with a dismissive wave of the hand. 'We're just happy that Georgia is happy. It's about time she met a good guy and now she has, that's all me and your mother could have hoped for.'

He smiles at Mum then, who also smiles, and the pair of them look so happy it makes me feel sick. They've probably already discussed what they will wear to Georgia and Mateo's future wedding, such is the palpable sense of joy coming from the pair. But there's no joy to be had where I'm standing and it only gets worse when Mateo reveals his grand plan.

'I appreciate that, but still, I'd like to do something as a gesture, to show you how grateful I am. With that in mind, I have booked a hotel out in the countryside, for us all. It has excellent spa facilities. I figured we could make a weekend of it, all of us, and Seth and Freddie, of course.'

Mateo beams as he adds that last part, as if aware that including my husband and son in this will only confuse and frustrate me even more.

'You don't need to do that,' Mum says. 'Seriously, as lovely as that sounds, it's not something we would expect.'

'I know that, Mum, but it's something Mateo would like to do, so please, let him do it,' Georgia replies as she sidles up to her man, and he puts his arm around her as they snuggle up together.

This is not what is supposed to be happening. He is not supposed to still be here and he is certainly not supposed to be inviting us to go on a spa weekend.

'How much will this cost?' Dad asks then, ever the pragmatist, because he's not one to get too swept away in fantasies about lounging around in bathrobes by a jacuzzi in some fancy hotel without first knowing the price tag associated with such a thing.

'Don't worry about that. I'm paying for it all,' Mateo says with a shrug. 'All you guys have to do is turn up ready for a relaxing time.'

While Mum and Dad look at each other, impressed upon hearing that, all I can do is worry about one very concerning thing.

'How can you afford this?' I ask, fearing that the answer to that question lies in the rather large amount of money I sent to Mateo yesterday.

'That's a very personal question,' Georgia replies, looking a bit shocked. 'Seriously, sis. If Mateo wants to pay for something nice for all the family, what does it matter?'

It matters a lot, way more than my sister could ever know. But what can I say? I can't push Mateo on this until the two of us are alone again, although I have no idea when that might be. It shouldn't even have to happen because I thought our final conversation had already occurred. But it clearly hasn't and until we speak privately again, I'm left reeling at whatever game Mateo has decided to play next.

'We were thinking of going next weekend,' Mateo says. 'Georgia thinks you guys might all be free then, so if you are, I can make the booking and we'll be set. Sound good?'

'Next weekend would be lovely,' Mum replies, and Dad seems happy enough with that too.

'Does next weekend work for you, Corinne?' Mateo asks me then, an angelic look on his face as if he isn't really the devil in disguise, tormenting me at every turn.

'I don't know. I'd have to check with Seth,' I reply before I decide that I have to get out of here now, before I totally lose my cool and say something I'll regret. Something like *'Hey, Mateo. Why the hell haven't you left town already and, just as importantly, what have you done with my twenty thousand pounds?'* Instead, all I can say is that I need to get home to Seth and Freddie, and before anyone else can say anything, I turn and leave.

As I get into my car, I know that I am in no fit state to drive. In my current condition, which is one of extreme shock and despair, I'm certain that I'll crash if I attempt to drive home now. That's why I end up sitting in the driver's seat and staring at the wheel, trying to make some sense of all this.

I must end up sitting there far longer than I realise because I suddenly hear a knocking on the window beside me, and when I look up, I see my sister staring at me in confusion.

I lower my window as Georgia leans in.

'What are you doing?' she asks me. 'We thought you left half an hour ago.'

I look through the windscreen and see Mum and Dad leaving her place, followed by Mateo.

'Erm,' I reply, trying to think of a reasonable excuse as to why I have been sitting outside for thirty minutes. 'I just took a phone call. Something about work.'

'On a Sunday?' Georgia asks sceptically, but it's the best I've got so it's all she's going to get.

As our parents get into their car and drive away, I notice Mateo is getting into his.

'Where is he going?' I ask Georgia as I keep watching him.

'Back to his apartment. He has a few more things to finish packing, then he will officially be moving in with me by tonight.'

She seems so happy as she says that, but while I can read her mind, it's a good thing she can't read mine.

As I watch Mateo drive away, I have already decided that I am going to follow him. This is my chance to find out what he is doing.

Maybe it's a good thing I don't have the knife with me this time.

That's because as I start my engine and my sister steps back to allow me to leave, I am feeling extreme anger towards the man in the car I am about to follow.

I'm not going to let him win.

It's time I got my revenge.

THIRTY-SEVEN

I don't know if Mateo was aware that I had been following him all the way back to his apartment, ever since he left my sister's. But I am certain he sees me now as I leave my car and storm towards his, and he's barely been able to make it out before I confront him.

'What are you doing? You were supposed to have left town last night!' I cry, aware that a street is not the best place to have this conversation, but I don't care.

'Why are you here, Corinne?' Mateo replies calmly, not looking ruffled at all, so I guess he did spot me in his rear-view mirror tailing him all the way back here.

'You know why I'm here! I gave you that money so you could pay your debt and leave me and my family alone. This wasn't part of the deal! You're not supposed to still be here!'

'How about we go inside and have this conversation in there? I could pour us a drink. You look like you could use one. You seem a little wound up.'

'Don't patronise me!' I snap, pointing a finger at the cause of all my misery. 'You know exactly why I am like this. It's because you lied to me. You said you would leave if I gave you that money. I kept my end of the bargain, so why haven't you kept yours? What the hell is all this about taking my family to a spa next weekend?'

'The spa is a good idea, don't you think?' Mateo asks me, and then he does something that really causes me to see red. *He laughs.*

'Answer me,' I cry, putting both my hands on his shoulders and feeling like I want to push him over. I'm pretty sure I possess the strength to do so, given how angry I am. If Mateo is worried about being shoved to the ground, he doesn't show it.

'Seriously, Corinne. You really need to relax. You're going to burst a blood vessel if you're not careful.'

It might be sensible advice, but I don't listen to it, though I do remove my hands from his shoulders and take a small step back.

'What have you done with my money?' I demand to know, fearful that I have squandered my life savings on absolutely nothing. 'Are you using it to pay for the spa next weekend? Was your debt even real?'

'Yes, it was real,' Mateo replies, and it sounds somewhat positive, because it seems he hasn't lied to me about everything. 'I just exaggerated it somewhat.'

'Excuse me?'

'I told you the debt was twenty thousand pounds, but it wasn't. It was only ten, but thanks to your generous donation, I have now paid it off, thank you very much.'

'Wait, what? Why would you tell me it was more?'

'Isn't it obvious? So you would give me more, of course.'

Mateo doubled the size of his debt just to extract more money from me?

'What have you done with the extra ten thousand?' I cry. 'Where is that money now?'

'It's in my bank account, the one you happily transferred it into.'

'I only did that because you told me you needed that much. But you lied!'

'And you've never told a lie in your life?' Mateo replies casually. 'Is that what you're trying to say? You've never told a fib?'

'Stop trying to turn this back on me! You know why I gave you that money. I never thought I'd see you again. So why are you still here?'

'It's a free country, isn't it?' Mateo replies before laughing. 'Well, it's not for you. You paid a lot of money and what do you have to show for it?'

My anger is starting to turn to panic because I'm realising something awful. I'm realising that Mateo has just played a game that he has won and I have spectacularly lost.

'What was all of this about? Did you do this just to get my money?' I ask him, anxiety coursing through every vein in my body.

'Let's just say that all of this hasn't simply been about me trying to win you back,' he replies. 'You didn't actually believe what I said about being in love with you, did you?'

Oh my god. This is as bad as it gets. I thought the nightmare was over. But it's not even started.

'You've been lying to me about everything?' I ask pathetically, and Mateo is happy to agree on that.

'At first, I thought about not even bothering trying to get close to Georgia and just coming to you and asking for money in exchange for keeping our secret quiet,' Mateo tells me. 'But there was a risk you would refuse to pay, especially if you didn't think I was serious, so I felt it better to show you just how serious I really was. I decided to increase the stakes, and I knew that once you saw me with your sister and how I was embedded within your family, your fear would be far more tangible.'

I cannot believe what I am hearing.

'I wanted to get you to the point where you were most afraid, which is why I allowed things to go right up until the deadline. When I started to make that speech at the party, I just knew you'd do anything at that point to shut me up and get rid of me. Dropping the wine glass was a nice touch, I must admit.'

'What if I hadn't done that? Would you have just told everybody?'

'Not quite,' Mateo replies. 'I wanted to keep that particular ace up my sleeve for as long as possible, so I would have made some speech about how wonderful Georgia was. It would have all been to make you sweat a little more.'

'How did you know I would find out that you had a deadline too? How did you know I would offer money to make you go away? You were running out of time as much as I was.'

'I will admit that it was getting a little close, and I was about to come right out and ask you for the money in exchange for my silence,' Mateo admits. 'But then I saw something interesting. It was just after your sister had told me to leave my phone in the lounge at the party. I didn't want to do that because I knew I was receiving messages about my debt. No sooner had I left it than I went back to retrieve it. But when I did, I caught you looking at it.'

I can't believe Mateo saw me pick up his phone. I was so engrossed in reading the message on the screen that I hadn't noticed him appear in the doorway.

'I left the room then, figuring that if you were snooping at my phone, then you were starting to get desperate,' Mateo goes on. 'I also knew there was a chance you might see one of the messages, which you did, and therefore, if you were inclined to get rid of me, you might want to help me. But even if you hadn't, I was eventually going to give you the lifeline of paying me money to disappear. Another hour or so at that party, when you were really squirming, I would have suggested it. As it turned out, you were so desperate that you offered first.'

'So all of this was simply a perfect plan to take whatever savings I had?' I ask regretfully. 'You did it all to make some money? Is that it? You're a conman? A grifter? Have you done this to other women before?'

Mateo scoffs.

'You think I make a habit out of sleeping with women who are already in relationships?' he asks me, shaking his head. 'I'm afraid not. You are unique, Corinne. That's why I realised you might be the only one who could help me pay off my debt.'

'I don't understand.'

'It's simple. I needed somebody who was so desperate that they would do anything for me, like give me thousands of pounds, for instance. You were the only person who fit that bill. So that's why I came back into your life.'

'How did you know I had savings?' I cry, wondering how someone like me, who is so private with their financial affairs, could have been exploited like this.

'At first, I figured you'd be good for a couple of thousand pounds,' Mateo explains. 'That would be better than nothing. Then when I had the idea to get with your sister, she said something interesting during one of our dates while we were getting to know each other. I asked her if she had any siblings, and when she mentioned you, I asked if you were similar or different to her. Georgia said you were very different and one example of that was how you were with money. While Georgia said that she liked to spend her money as fast as it came in, she told me that you had a lot of money saved away that not even your husband knew about.'

What? How could my sister have possibly known that?

Mateo reads my horrified expression and smiles.

'I guess you don't remember telling her that. That makes sense because Georgia said you told her while you were really drunk one night. I guess you forgot about it, but your sister remembered and when she mentioned it to me, I realised I could take you for a lot more money than just a measly two thousand pounds. And guess what, I was right. Of course,

Georgia had no idea she was helping me; she was just gossiping about you.'

This is all too much. Not only has my sister's boyfriend defrauded me of my savings, but my sister inadvertently helped him to do it by discussing me and my frugal ways. Then I think about how the last time I was here, outside Mateo's apartment, I had a knife, and I planned to use it. At the time, it seemed like a terrible idea, and I was glad I hadn't gone through with it. Right now, I really, really wish I had that knife with me because I'm fairly certain it would be getting used today. This man still has no idea how he almost pushed me to the point of trying to kill him. Instead, he continues to tell me things I don't know.

'I'm not going anywhere, Corinne. Not now my debt is paid, and I have a spare ten thousand pounds that I can use for fun things. I plan on further ingratiating myself with your family with the spa weekend, and after that, I feel like taking your sister on a very lovely and expensive holiday. The Caribbean, perhaps. I hear that's a nice part of the world. I also hear it can be the perfect place to make a proposal.'

Mateo winks at me as my blood turns cold. Did he just hint that he's thinking of asking Georgia to marry him?

'That's right,' Mateo says, grinning because he's winning. 'I'm going to be in your life for a very long time, Corinne, and the best part of it is there's not a damn thing you can do about it. Well, not unless you want to tell your husband that you cheated on him with me, while also telling your sister that you paid her partner twenty thousand pounds to disappear.'

Mateo goes to enter his apartment, leaving me standing out here on the street in stunned silence. But then he stops and turns back, and still grinning, delivers the devastating final blow.

'No, actually, I'm wrong. The best part of all this is that you have funded everything that happens next,' he tells me. 'The spa weekend. The Caribbean holiday. A ring. Maybe even some of the wedding plans. Thanks to you and your hard-earned money, not only am I debt-free now, but I'm also wealthy enough to make your sister fall in love with me even more.'

Only then does Mateo leave, going inside his apartment, and I'm grateful for that because now he can no longer say anything else to make me feel worse. But he's said enough and I'm perfectly clear on my situation as it stands.

I wiped out all my savings to get rid of him and now I have no way of getting that money back.

Worse than that, I have no way of getting rid of Mateo.

THIRTY-EIGHT

I've been reeling all day from Mateo's deception and I'm not silly enough to think that people haven't noticed. Seth can sense something is wrong with me, as can everybody I work with, because I've been irritable and distant for the past five days.

How could I have been anything but?

I have wiped out my life savings so that the man who holds my worst secret can now spend lots of money on my sister and it will most likely end in a marriage proposal – and he will be in my life forever. If I heard about such a story in one of those gossip magazines where people share their craziest real-life stories, I would have been critical of the woman at the centre of it. I never thought those kinds of stories were real, but now it's happening to me. Although I certainly won't be sharing my story in any magazine. If I was desperate for the secret of my one-night stand with Mateo to never see the light of day, I'm even more desperate to keep what has happened since then under wraps.

I've made things worse and I'm struggling to see how I'm going to be able to hold everything together. My career. My marriage. My entire life. It all feels like it's unravelling, and Mateo is the one tugging the strings.

As it is a Friday, I've been able to work from home today, so at least I haven't had to slog through a day in the office trying to pretend like all the money I worked incredibly hard for hasn't just been frittered on my sister's boyfriend. But because I'm at home, Seth figured I could help out with something that needs doing, namely all our packing for this upcoming weekend's getaway. That's right, tomorrow I'm supposed to join the rest of my family in attending the luxury countryside hotel and spa that Mateo has paid for us all to enjoy. He's disguised my money as his own and I'll have to sit there and listen to everybody thank him and tell him how wonderful he is for spending it all on them. That's my punishment for the mistake I made all those years ago.

I desperately wanted to get out of the trip as soon as I heard it was happening, but not wasting any time, I discovered Mateo had already created a WhatsApp group for the weekend, adding all family members to it, including Seth. Therefore, my husband was already seeing all the messages in the group about the plans, making it harder for me to come up with a good reason why we should do something else this weekend. It freaks me out that Mateo has Seth's number now, obviously procured from my sister, but I have to hope he won't be sending my husband anything too explosive before I've had a chance to resolve this situation once and for all.

This weekend has to happen, if only because this is when I will end it for good.

The thing is, I haven't done any of the packing yet, even when Seth has assumed I'd have time while working from home. Now he's arriving home with Freddie in tow and he's going to wonder why I've made no effort to prepare for what he thinks is going to be a brilliant weekend of pampering and relaxing. What can I say? That I haven't packed because it's my money that has actually paid for the hotel and spa? Of course not. Seth will be the one packing then and it wouldn't be for a weekend away, it would be because he's leaving me and he'd be taking Freddie with him.

'How's your day been?' Seth asks as he enters the spare bedroom that becomes my makeshift office every Friday.

'Busy,' I lie. 'I've had back-to-back online meetings all day.'

'Oh no, that's not what you need on a Friday,' Seth replies as he leans over my chair and gives me a hug. 'We're okay. Freddie is having a snack downstairs, and I can make dinner. Have you had a chance to start the packing?'

'No, like I said, I've been too busy,' I say, continuing my lie. I'm almost hoping Seth decides that this weekend away is not coming at the right time for us and suggests cancelling our attendance, but I know that's not going to happen, as he's been so excited about it.

'Don't worry, I can do the packing now,' he says cheerily, leaving the room to presumably go and get started on it.

I think about calling after him and then trying to come up with some excuse as to why we shouldn't go, but I can't think of a good reason other than the truth and I can't give him that. So I just stay in this spare bedroom, staring at my laptop screen, and even though it's gone well past five o'clock now, I'm still sitting here as if I'm working late. Eventually, I have to leave and when I do, I find Seth in our bedroom with a couple of small suitcases open on the bed.

'Do you want to check my work?' he asks with a smile, knowing I have a habit of never fully trusting him when it comes to packing and ultimately doing it myself.

'No, it's okay,' I reply as I slump down on the end of the bed while he continues to pack beside me.

'I cannot get over what a nice guy Mateo is,' Seth says as he folds a pair of his swim shorts and adds them to his case. 'Paying to take us all away this weekend. I mean, I love your family but I'm not sure I'd be willing to spend a small fortune on them.'

Seth chuckles to himself as he throws in a pair of socks before asking a question.

'How much do you think this weekend has cost him? I went on the hotel's website earlier and tried to price it up, but it's tough to get a proper idea of it. It must be at least a thousand pounds though, don't you think? Or could it be more?'

I try to pretend like I'm not listening, but Seth carries on talking anyway.

'The guy must be loaded. Imagine having the spare cash lying around to just drop hundreds of pounds on taking the in-laws away. Either that or he's mad.'

Seth laughs again, clearly amused at the thought of Mateo being so eager to impress us all that he is paying a fortune to do so. As much as my husband likes my family, he's never done anything like this. But of course, it's all just an illusion. Mateo isn't the charitable gentleman everyone else thinks he is. It's my money he is lavishing us all with.

'Can we go in the pool as soon as we get there?' Freddie cries as he runs into the room, his favourite pair of swim shorts in hand.

'Hopefully,' Seth replies before he leaves our cases and walks over to Freddie. 'Here, let's go and get your things packed. Do you want to take some toys for the pool?'

'Yeah!' Freddie cries as he turns and rushes out of the room, no doubt on his way to find said toys. Seth goes to follow him, but just before he does, he turns back to me.

'I think I've pretty much packed everything you'll need, but if you just want to do a quick check,' he suggests before he goes, leaving me sitting beside my case.

I reluctantly have a look through it, impressed to see that Seth has actually done a good job of packing for me – pretty much everything I could need this weekend is in there. But there is something missing from my case, something I wouldn't usually pack but something that I have been thinking about taking all day as I have sat stewing at the desk in the spare bedroom.

I walk over to my wardrobe and open the doors before reaching up to the top shelf and pulling a couple of baskets of my shoes out. It's up here – well out of Freddie's reach, hidden behind all these shoes that Seth would never touch – where I find what I am looking for.

I take it down and then return to my case before burying it at the bottom, underneath all my clothes so that Seth won't see it should he take one last look at my packing. He won't know what else has gone into this suitcase, but I know it's there and it will provide me some comfort over this weekend to know that I have it with me.

I zip up my suitcase and then lower it to the ground, placing it by the door so that it's ready to be carried to the car tomorrow morning when we leave for the hotel.

My suitcase, full of all sorts of essential items for a weekend away.

My clothes.

My toiletries.

And my knife.

THIRTY-NINE

'Wow, look at this place.'

Seth might be in awe of the destination we have just reached as he drives us closer towards it, but I did not need him to voice it out loud, as I can see how incredible it is for myself.

The lush green lawns that surround either side of our car. The sprawling woodland that spreads beyond them. The wooden bridge over the tumbling river in the distance to our left. The large water fountain straight ahead of us that forces my husband to gently steer us around it. The sound of our tyres crunching over the gravel driveway. And last but not least, the huge, whitewashed building we are just parking outside of now, the one with countless windows and doors. While I know it is a hotel, it could also pass for a lavish French villa, the kind you see in movies where the characters arrive in the south of France at the home of some mysterious millionaire. We're not in France now, we're actually only a couple of hours' drive away from our hometown, yet it feels like we have been transported into another world. This is a world of luxury and decadence, where we can put our feet up and rest while others will run around after us, fetching us food and drink and making sure the water temperature is just right in the pool or jacuzzi.

Another glass of champagne? Coming right up.

More cake? Sure, plenty where that came from.

Are there enough bubbles in the hot tub for you? Let me take care of that.

I know we have all of that to come, but it begins with the staff taking care of our luggage and no sooner have we got out of the car, a couple of employees in immaculate white uniforms are on hand to carry our cases inside.

I spot Mum and Dad's car parked nearby, as well as Georgia's, so I guess we're the last ones to arrive. That's only because I did my best to delay us for as long as possible, finding any excuse I could to hold off getting in the car. I had to 'check' something in my suitcase. Then I had to make sure something was 'turned off' in the kitchen. After that, I had to go for one last 'toilet stop'. It was all just time-wasting on my part, but it couldn't go on forever. Now we are here, I've only delayed the inevitable.

It's time to begin this weekend away that Mateo has paid for, via my bank account.

After checking in and being given a vast amount of information about this hotel and its facilities by the smiley man behind the reception desk, we are led to our room by yet another employee who seemingly can't do enough for us.

'I know the room you're staying in,' the staff member says as we step out of the elevator on the third floor and start walking down a long corridor. 'It has fantastic views of the outdoor pool and the countryside beyond it.'

As we reach our room, he swipes an electronic keycard at the door before pushing our luggage inside on the trolley he wheeled them up here on. Then Seth, Freddie and I follow him in to see what he has correctly assured us is a fabulous room.

'This is amazing,' Seth says as he gets a look at the view, while Freddie runs around and explores the large bathroom complete with sunken bath and walk-in shower. Meanwhile, I just stare at the king-size bed and the crisp linen sheets and think about Mateo booking this room with my own money. He's clearly spared no expense and why would he? The more he spends, the more he knows it will anger me.

'So, what do you think? Nice, right?'

I spin around and see Georgia entering the room, a big smile on her face. She is followed by Mateo, who is also grinning because of course he is.

'Nice? It's incredible!' Seth cries as Georgia hugs me and thanks me for coming. As for my husband, there's only one person he wants to thank.

'Seriously, Mateo, we really appreciate this. Thank you so much,' Seth says as he shakes Mateo's hand.

'I don't want to hear another word about it,' Mateo says with a dismissive shrug, as if shelling out so much money on other people is all in a day's work for this charitable man. 'All I want you guys to do is get your swimwear on and come and join us by the pool. The sun is shining, and the water looks lovely, so we'll see you down there!'

'Mum and Dad are already in the hot tub,' Georgia says with a laugh before she and Mateo leave, allowing Seth to give a small tip to the employee who brought our bags up here before we start unpacking our swimwear.

'Hurry up!' Freddie cries as he finds his shorts and grabs his goggles before running for the door. He's ready to head downstairs to the changing rooms, as is Seth, so just like when we left home earlier today, I'm the only one holding everybody up.

'What's wrong?' Seth asks me when he notices I'm not in as much of a rush as everybody else to dive into the water outside.

'Do you not think this is a bit...'

'What?'

'Flash?'

'It's amazing!'

'Yeah, I know, but is it us? Five-star hotels. Having staff members carry our bags around for us. Spas and saunas and whatever else they have here. It feels a bit... pretentious.'

'You'd rather go home?'

I obviously would, but I can't say it.

'Look, I know it is a bit flash, but Mateo is trying to impress us and it's working, so let's just give him what he wants and have a good time. What's that famous saying? Don't look a gift horse in the mouth? If Mateo wants to spend money on us, who are we to turn it down?'

With that, Seth heads for the door, where an impatient Freddie is already waiting. They head out into the corridor, and I am forced to grab my swimming costume and follow them out.

I get changed in what are possibly the nicest changing rooms I've ever used before finding Seth and Freddie as they leave the men's rooms. We pass the indoor pool, which is quiet because nobody wants to be inside on a beautiful day like this, before we step outside into the warm sunshine. No sooner have we done that than I spot my parents relaxing in the hot tub, and their faces are so red that I guess they've been in there a while. Beyond them, I see Georgia reclining on a sun lounger, a cocktail in one hand and a paperback in the other; she is watching Mateo swimming lengths in the huge outdoor pool. His toned arms are cutting through the water effortlessly as he performs the front crawl while his strong legs are propelling him along the pool, and he easily fulfils a couple of laps while we're still busy finding somewhere to put our towels down.

'There he is!' my father says when he sees Freddie. He leaves the hot tub to come and pick up his grandson. Then he carries him to the pool before jumping in, and as they both come up for air, Freddie is laughing hysterically.

Seth goes to join them while Georgia leaves her lounger and walks up to me, her bare feet padding across the clean patio.

'Let's join Mum in the hot tub,' she suggests, so we climb into the bubbling water. I experience none of the relaxing feelings that one would normally have by doing such a thing though.

'I could get used to this life,' Mum says with a chuckle as she basks in the warm sunshine that hits her face while the rest of her body is warmed by the hot water.

'I already have,' Georgia replies slightly smugly. 'And it's only going to get better. Mateo is taking me to the Dominican Republic next month.'

'Oh my, you lucky girl. I've always wanted to go to the Caribbean!' Mum cries, a mixture of both envy and excitement in her voice.

Meanwhile, it feels like this water has suddenly got even hotter as I process the fact that Mateo has clearly gone ahead and booked the holiday he was taunting me about after I confronted him outside his apartment last weekend. If he's done that, maybe he's also done the other thing he was taunting me about.

Maybe he's already bought a ring, to propose to my sister.

As I hear Mateo suggest getting a couple of beers to Seth and my father, and as Georgia tells my mother she simply has to try the cocktail she just had because it's to die for, I realise this has to end tonight.

I cannot allow this man to get away with what he is doing any longer, and that's why I'm now thinking about the knife I packed in my suitcase. I'm also thinking about how all this sprawling land that surrounds the hotel might make a good place to hide a body.

I still don't know for sure if I'm capable of murder, but I do know one thing.

Mateo is not leaving this hotel alive.

FORTY

'Dinner is served.'

The smiling waiter opens the door to the private function room that Mateo has hired inside the hotel for this evening, which allows us to get a glimpse of the large dining table that is set for seven people.

'This is dining in style,' Dad declares as he and Mum step into the room and approach the table, placing their glasses of champagne down before taking their seats.

Freddie runs in and takes the chair beside his grandmother while Seth ambles in with his beer in hand, at least the fourth one I've seen him have since we got here. As such, he has a silly grin on his face that tells me he is tipsy, but just like my parents, he's making the most of this weekend of hotel living.

Next into the private dining room is Georgia, and after a day spent lounging around in her bikini by the pool, she is now wearing a flowing white dress that accentuates the slight suntan she gained by having so much skin on show earlier. As my sister takes a seat, that just leaves two of us who haven't entered the dining room.

Me.

And Mateo.

'After you,' Mateo says to me, playing the part of the perfect gentleman, just like he's been playing a part in front of my family all day. But I don't play along. Instead, I stay where I am and rather than entering the dining room and sitting down, I reach into my handbag and take out a small, folded piece of paper. Then I hand it to Mateo. Only after that do I join my family at the table.

As I take a seat beside Seth, I glance back at Mateo to see that he is looking at the note I just gave him. I see his eyes scan the words written on the paper before he folds it up and puts it in his pocket, and then takes his seat, no one but me having seen that he was given a note to read at all.

Now we're all seated, the waiter brings in our starters, chosen for us by Mateo who has paid for the hotel's set menu, and of course, paid for it all with my money. But as a plate of bruschetta is placed down in front of me, I'm not thinking about how hungry I am. I'm just thinking about how I hope Mateo follows the instructions on the note.

We need to talk. Meet me at 10 p.m. at the bridge over the river.

That's what the note says. But will he do what I have told him to?

I'll have to get through this meal before I find out, so I pick up my knife and fork and start eating.

'This is delicious,' Mum says and everyone agrees. Begrudgingly, I have to agree too because it really is tasty, but I just think it rather than voice that opinion because I don't want to give Mateo the pleasure. I'm sure he's enjoying me mentally calculating the cost of every bite of this meal, wondering how much of my money he has blown on this dining experience tonight. But it's fine if that's what he thinks I'm thinking about. I'd rather that than him know what is really on my mind. It involves our meeting at the bridge later, the bridge that runs over the full, tumbling river that runs through the pretty grounds of this hotel. If Mateo is there when I have told him to be, it won't matter how much of my money he has spent impressing my family. All that will matter is I am alone with him.

'I'd like to make a toast,' Mateo suddenly says as he raises his champagne glass just after we have all finished our starters. 'To family.'

I could almost be sick, such is my disdain for what Mateo has just toasted. I also feel like reminding him that he is not part of our family, nor will he ever be if I do what I am planning to do to him later tonight. I tell myself that I don't have long left of having to pretend like everything is okay, so I just raise my glass and toast with everybody else.

The main course is salmon and, as much as it pains me to think it, I enjoy every mouthful of it. I've also decided that because I have paid for all this, I might as well do my best to enjoy it, because I've got nothing else to lose at this point. That also involves drinking the champagne on offer, which has the added benefit of giving me the extra confidence I'll need to do what I need to do later tonight. However, one glass too many and it might impair my ability, and I decide to moderate my intake.

There are several occasions during the meal where I look at Mateo and notice him looking right back at me, but that's the extent of our communication at this table. He only speaks to chat with everybody else, while I only talk to tell Freddie to stop doing something he shouldn't as he wriggles in his seat beside me. I don't think anybody notices that Mateo and I don't say a word to each other, either because they're all too busy talking themselves or too busy enjoying all the luxury food and drink.

By the time dessert is served, I'm feeling full, so I decide not to eat my cheesecake because I need to stay sharp, and all these extra calories would only make me feel sluggish. Mateo tucks in, and Seth does too, gratefully eating my dessert after I have declined it. Seth then once again thanks Mateo for what he has done for us all this weekend.

'Seriously, the pleasure is all mine,' Mateo replies with a wistful smile. 'I like to see people having a good time, so if you're all happy, I am happy.'

It's so cringe-inducing that I want to throw a piece of cutlery at him, and if it was to do some damage, even better. But that would be very unacceptable of me in this environment, not to mention a terrible example to set my child. So I just finish my champagne and smile when I see the waiter coming to clear away our empty plates. That means this meal is almost over. As I check the time, I see that it is just past nine o'clock. That means there is less than an hour until I am due to meet Mateo at the bridge.

Will he show up?

I have to trust that he will.

Before that, I have to put Freddie to bed, so I give Seth a nudge to remind him that we have parenting duties to complete, because my husband looks like he could happily forget that and sit down here in the hotel drinking with Mateo all night.

'Have a good night, everyone,' I say as I lead my very tired son out of the room.

'Thank you so much for the meal,' Seth says to Mateo before shaking his hand. 'I'll have to take you out for something to eat soon, although I can't promise it will be as nice as this was.'

'Sounds good,' Mateo smiles back, playing at being a buddy with my husband because it's just one more thing he can do to irritate me.

The three of us head upstairs before getting Freddie into his pyjamas and settling him down on the small bed in our family room. But he only has eyes for the big bed his parents are going to be sharing.

'Can I come in with you?' he asks me, wanting to snuggle in between his mum and dad tonight. Normally, considering we are away from home, I'd give in and allow him to do just that if it would mean a good night's sleep for all of us. But not tonight. Tonight is different. Tonight, I already know I am not going to be getting any sleep.

'No, you're sleeping here tonight,' I say before tucking Freddie into the smaller bed while I hear Seth brushing his teeth in the bathroom.

As I turn off the lights and Freddie settles down, Seth joins me on the bed. He has brushed his teeth but I still detect a whiff of alcohol on his breath. He's overindulged this evening, but I don't mind because that just means he'll probably fall asleep faster. Although, it might not be fast enough because as I check the time, I see that it is quarter to ten. I need to leave so I can get to the bridge in time, and I need to go now.

'I think I had too much to drink,' I whisper to Seth as Freddie snores softly from the other side of the room. 'I could do with a little bit of fresh air. I'll be back soon.'

'Shall I wait up for you?' Seth asks as I head for the door while he lounges on our luxurious bed.

'No, don't worry. Just go to sleep. I'll be quiet when I come back in.'

With that, I leave the room and head to the elevator, making my way down and outside to where I hope Mateo will be waiting for me by the bridge.

My husband doesn't know the real reason I have left our room at this hour to go outside.

Just like he doesn't know that I unpacked the knife and hid it on myself while he was busy in the bathroom.

FORTY-ONE

While the hotel is bright and welcoming, the grounds that surround it are dark and uninviting as I leave behind the warmth and comfort of the building and walk out into the wilderness. I'm on my way to the bridge. Aside from a couple of spotlights in the hotel car park, there isn't much in the way of light to guide me towards my destination. Although it's better this way because if I can't see where I'm going, it means nobody else is going to be able to see what happens when I get there.

I walk quickly and carefully. If I take too long to get back to the room, Seth might still be awake and get suspicious. Hopefully, he's asleep now, just like Freddie is, and I would hope most of the other guests in this hotel are snoozing too. The fewer people there are awake, the less chance I have of being seen.

I left the hotel via a side door rather than via the main entrance and I have also avoided walking through the car park, opting for the darkness that surrounds it. That's in the hope that I avoid any cameras outside the hotel, as I'd prefer not to be seen going out at this time of night. What happens next is between me and Mateo and nobody else.

My shoes brush over the soft blades of grass beneath my feet until I hear the rushing of the river up ahead. That tells me that the bridge must be near, and then I see the silhouette of it through the gloom, although I don't see anything else.

As I arrive, I am definitely the only one here.

Where is Mateo? Is he coming? Or has he ignored the note I gave him?

I realise that I didn't contemplate that he might not show. But if he knows it would mess with me, why wouldn't he stay away? He is a master at having things his own way, so has he just scored another victory over me by not meeting my request to join me here? Is he still sitting in the hotel bar now with my sister and parents, sipping more champagne and toasting to the future? If he is, I have no use for the knife.

Could it be more than that? Could Mateo have deduced that my request for a late-night rendezvous would be my attempt at hurting him? Surely he doesn't consider me capable of murder? Unless he realises he might have pushed me too far this time and figures it's safer to never be alone with me again...

I'm just considering giving up and walking back to the bright lights of the hotel in the distance when I hear something that makes me reach into my coat pocket and grip the handle of the knife tightly.

It's the same sound I heard when I was making my way here.

It's the sound of shoes moving over grass.

I step onto the bridge, my feet now resting on the wooden slats that sit above the water, and I wait for Mateo to join me here. As he does, he steps onto the opposite end of the bridge, and we stare at each other for a moment before he speaks.

'I wonder. What could make you prefer to stand out here on this cold bridge rather than in your luxurious room with your family?' he asks me. 'It's obvious that you are desperate to get me alone. The only question that remains after that is, why?'

'Walk away,' I say firmly. 'Leave this hotel tonight and never see my sister or any of my other family members again. If you do that, I will accept that you won, I lost. And you can do whatever you want to do with the rest of the money I gave you. Just leave us all behind tonight and this can be over.'

It's very dark but I can still see that Mateo is smiling at that suggestion, which doesn't bode well. For either of us.

'Over? I consider this is over already,' he replies, his voice as cool as the chilly night air. 'Your defeat is absolute and now all that is left to do is revel in my victory for many years to come. That is exactly what I intend to do, and while you might think that it's what I'm already doing to you, believe me when I say that I haven't even started yet.'

He's not doing what I want him to.

He's not backing down.

He's leaving me with no other choice.

'As soon as we're finished at this hotel, I'm going to go on that trip to the Caribbean with Georgia,' Mateo goes on. 'By the time we get back from that particular holiday, paid for by you, thank you very much, then the only thing you'll be doing is listening to your sister talk about how I proposed to her with a diamond ring at sunset on the beach. Then you'll have to hear all about her wedding planning. Don't worry, you'll be chief bridesmaid, I'm sure.'

He's deadly serious. He is going to marry Georgia and use her to torment me for the rest of my life. That's why I don't regret what I am about to do.

As I start to walk across the bridge towards Mateo, I grip the handle of the knife in my coat pocket tighter and tighter until I'm fairly certain I might be drawing blood on the palm of my hand. But it's the blood I'm about to draw from the man standing in front of me that is my primary focus.

'What are you doing, Corinne?' Mateo asks me.

I ignore his question, choosing instead to make my intent very clear by removing the knife from my coat pocket and rushing towards him with the edge of the blade aimed directly at his torso.

'Die,' I say urgently as I lunge towards him. But my blade penetrates nothing but air as Mateo swiftly steps to the side before he lunges at me himself, pushing me off balance.

As I fall to the deck, the knife clatters across the wooden panels beside me. Mateo instantly swoops down and picks up my weapon – and it is now his. Now I fear I am about to become the victim. Rather than raise the knife above his head to plunge it down into me, though, Mateo simply holds it at arm's length and laughs.

'What did you think you were going to do with this?' he asks me as if mocking an insolent child. 'Did you think you could take the easy way out? Did you think you could just get rid of me like you thought you got rid of me once before?'

It feels like this nightmare is never going to end. As I lie at Mateo's feet in the darkness, I am trying to muster up my last reserve of strength to fight back against this man.

Before I can do that, somebody grabs the knife from Mateo. I can't see who it is.

Before Mateo can say another word, they stick the knife into his stomach, causing my enemy's eyes to widen with fear as he realises what has just happened.

Mateo drops to his knees and looks into my eyes for several awful beats. Then he collapses to the deck beside me. In seconds, *Mateo is dead.*

I should be happy but all I can do is look up in horror at the person who just killed Mateo for me.

'Seth,' I gasp as I stare at my husband, who still holds the bloody knife in his hand.

FORTY-TWO

As Seth checks to confirm that Mateo is definitely dead, I continue to stare at the man I married and wonder how he could possibly have just done what he did.

I thought he was back in our hotel room, sleeping in the bed.

I did not expect to see him here on this bridge.

And I certainly did not expect to see him kill the man I hated so much.

'Are you okay?' Seth asks me as he reaches down and, despite the lack of light out here, I can see that he is searching my body for any signs of injury. But I am not injured, I'm just in shock. He attempts to help me to my feet, once he has made sure I haven't been harmed, and he's certainly going to have to help me because my legs are extremely unsteady after what I just witnessed.

Only once I am back to my feet do I find the strength to speak again.

'What are you doing here?' I ask Seth as he continues to support me, his priority apparently me rather than the dead body beside us.

'I'm making sure you are safe,' he replies firmly, no glimmer of remorse or fear in his voice, which makes me think he is not as scared as I am, nor does he seem to regret what he just did.

'I don't understand. How did you—'

'Know you were in danger?' he cuts in, finishing my sentence. 'I could tell something was wrong when you left the room.'

'Where's Freddie?' I ask, worried that he's been left on his own in the hotel room.

'I woke him and took him to your parents' room. He's having a sleepover there tonight instead. I told your mum and dad that you were tired and needed a good night's sleep, so they were happy to have him in their room with them. Don't worry, he's okay.'

It's a relief to hear my son is fine, though it's about the only thing in my life that I can be relaxed about at present. Mateo's body lies here next to us on this dark bridge. The sound of the river running underneath us has none of the calming effects that the sound of water usually has.

'I still don't understand,' I say. 'How did you know I was down here? With Mateo?'

'After I left Freddie with your parents, I went downstairs and looked for you. I couldn't find you, but I did see Mateo leave the hotel. When I saw him coming down here in the dark, I realised something was going on. So I followed him.'

I'm terrified about what my husband may have heard or detected from mine and Mateo's conversation. Or if he knows why it even occurred, but the fact he intervened when things got dangerous suggests he saw enough.

'It was him, wasn't it?' Seth says then, surprising me.

'What do you mean?' I ask nervously and, for a second, even though it must be impossible, I swear the water stops running under the bridge and everything falls silent.

'He's the one you cheated on me with,' Seth replies as all the air leaves my lungs and I stare at my husband in total shock.

I want to say something. My instincts make me want to deny it. It just feels natural for a wife to tell her husband that no, she has never done anything to hurt him before. Protect your spouse's feelings at all costs. But I can't do it and the reason for that is because Seth somehow, shockingly, seems to have already known my deepest, darkest secret.

'Yes, I knew,' Seth confirms, breaking the still silence.

'How?' is the only word I can manage to muster as my husband puts his palms down on one of the handrails of the bridge, leaning his weight against it while also looking like he has been carrying the weight of what he knows for a long time.

'I found one of your letters,' he admits, blowing my mind.

The confessional letters. The ones I burned. The ones I thought were gone forever.

He found one of them?

'It was inside that desk we used to have in the spare bedroom,' he tells me. 'You remember the one? We got rid of it last year, so I dismantled it and took it to the recycling centre. It was while I was taking it apart that I found a letter. It must have been in one of the drawers. I guess it had fallen down the back.'

To my horror, I realise that could have been possible. I used to store all those letters in a drawer in that desk. They were kept under lock and key. They only came out when I removed them all and took them into the garden to set them alight. But one piece of paper must have inadvertently slipped into the back of the desk, a lone letter that became a ticking time bomb, only I never knew it existed. That's why it didn't seem like a big deal when Seth suggested we get rid of that desk that we rarely used, so I left him to deal with it while I was busy with Freddie one day. But it was while conducting that seemingly mundane household task of removing an item of unwanted furniture that he discovered the secret I have been hiding for years.

'I don't know what to say,' I admit, feeling awful. It dawns on me that if I had confided in my husband sooner, or if Seth had done the same to me, Mateo might not have died.

'You don't need to say anything,' Seth replies. 'The letter said it all.'

I have no way of knowing exactly which letter it was that he found, and to me, they were all a blur of regret and remorse. I could ask Seth to try and recite it word for word so I can pinpoint exactly which letter it was and how bad my mental state was at the time I penned it, but that would be cruel, for both of us. Instead, I ask the more pertinent question.

'If you knew what I did, why didn't you say anything to me?' is all I can ask next.

Seth looks at me and in the darkness I notice the glint in his eyes that tells me there are tears in there.

'I could tell from what you had written that you were incredibly guilty about what you had done. It came across in your words on the page just how ashamed you were of your actions and also how despondent you were about the future. You obviously wanted to tell me, but you were afraid it would mean the end for us. I can see why you would be afraid of that, so I understand why you couldn't find the courage to talk to me about it. It was clear from the letter that it was just a one-time thing, rather than a full-blown affair, so I figured it was just a one-off mistake that was never to be repeated.'

I think about how incredibly understanding and accepting this is from my husband's point of view. Rather than get angry or jealous, which would have been the typical way for a man to react when faced with the knowledge of another man being with his wife, he chose to see things from my side instead.

'I chose to try and forgive and forget,' Seth goes on. 'It was easier considering we were already married by the time I discovered the letter, and of course, we had our son by then too. The three of us make a great family. I knew I'd lose a lot more than I'd gain if I left you, so I forced myself to forgive and I was happy I was able to do so because we have a good life together, don't we? So I don't regret forgiving you and I guess I've mostly done a good job of it. A good job of keeping that one big question out of my mind.'

'The big question?' I ask, and Seth nods.

'The question of who you cheated on me with.'

The answer to that is the person lying dead by our feet, but Seth explains his thought process.

'That was the only thing I didn't know. Who was the mystery man you slept with? You never named him in that letter, and I tried to think about the men you came into contact with in your life, from friends to work colleagues, but I never really nailed down one particular suspect. In the end, I realised that if I was going to forgive you, which I really wanted to do, it was healthier for me to stop trying to figure out who the guy was and just move on with life.'

It breaks my heart to imagine my husband spending sleepless nights beside me trying to predict who I slept with behind his back. Countless hours of him doubting every man who was in my life, and second-guessing if every interaction I had with another guy was as simple as it seemed on the surface or if there was more going on underneath.

'Then we met Mateo and I saw the change in you instantly,' Seth says grimly. 'The way you wanted to leave that restaurant so fast when we first met him. How you suddenly felt ill all the time when he was around us. The look on your face when you came home and saw him in our house. I didn't want it to be true but the more I thought about it, the more it made sense. There's only one reason you've been acting weird around your sister's boyfriend this whole time. It's because he was the guy you slept with.'

I can't believe that Seth had figured it all out while I was so busy trying everything I could to keep it secret. I was prepared to kill to protect that secret, yet he'd already worked it out.

'I noticed the change in you and figured you were under a lot of pressure and stress,' Seth goes on. 'Then, when you said you were leaving the room tonight, I knew it had something to do with Mateo. At first, I feared the two of you might be trying to rekindle what you once had. But when I saw you bring out the knife, I knew what you were trying to do. You wanted him gone and I can only think you wanted that because he was threatening or tormenting you in some way.'

I stare at my husband, my understanding, selfless and ultimately correct husband, and realise he was always far stronger and wiser than I ever gave him credit for. All this time, I tried to keep the truth from him because I feared he wouldn't be able to handle it. I worried he would react to it in stereotypical male fashion, getting angry and bitter and aloof, or worse, getting upset and devastated and never being able to trust another person again. Yet he was far more capable of not only processing what I did but, in the end, forgiving me and helping me get rid of the problem entirely. Except it's not resolved, not when Mateo's body is lying here for somebody to discover it when the sun comes up tomorrow morning.

'What do we do next?' I say, unable to imagine what our lives might be like as a couple now that murder has entered our marriage.

'You mean with the body?' Seth asks me as he looks down at the corpse.

'I mean with everything,' I reply as the water continues to run underneath us, an auditory reminder that while some things can change drastically in an instant, other things always stay the same.

Is it really possible to get away with what we've just done?

Or as bad as things have been, are they about to get even worse?

FORTY-THREE

How do you sleep after you have just watched your husband murder your sister's boyfriend? The answer is that you don't. All you can do is hope that nobody ever finds the body.

The sun has risen and, with it, the dawning of the first day of the rest of my life, a life that will now have to be spent not only dealing with the guilt of what I've done, but looking over my shoulder for fear of the truth ever coming out. Some might say I've been living this way for a while, considering how long I have spent trying to keep my one-night stand with Mateo a secret. But this is different and it feels like I've exchanged one problem for an even bigger one. Back then, the worst that could happen was that my marriage would end and my family would break apart. Now, the worst that could happen is Seth and I spend the rest of our lives in prison and little Freddie spends his life wondering why he had the bad luck of having the worst two parents in the world.

That can't happen. I can't go to prison, and neither can the man lying in this bed beside me. We both have to do whatever we can to ensure ours and Freddie's futures are positive. It won't be easy, though one thing does feel a little easier than the last time I had a dark secret to keep.

I'm no longer doing it alone.

'I guess you were awake all night like I was,' Seth says as he rolls over on his pillow and looks at me with the same weary expression that I must be showing him.

'I didn't even get five minutes' sleep,' I reply glumly.

'It'll get better,' Seth tells me, putting a reassuring hand on my bare left shoulder that is poking above the top of the duvet. 'It'll just take time, but it will get easier. We just need to get through the next twenty-four hours. If we can do that, we stand a good chance.'

'How do you know it'll get better?' I ask, assuming my husband has never killed a man before.

'I'm just trying to stay positive,' he replies, which tells me he doesn't actually know if things will get better and is simply hoping they do because the alternative doesn't bear thinking about.

I see that he's trying his best to be brave for me, but despite wanting to be the same for him, I have a moment of weakness and break down, tears flowing down my cheeks as Seth pulls me in for a hug. The two of us lie like that in the bed for several minutes until we eventually separate, and I realise I have to pull myself together. He's right, these next twenty-four hours are crucial, and I can't ruin everything by crying. It's time to stay strong. Mateo might be gone now, but this is far from over.

I watch Seth get out of bed and wander into the bathroom before I hear the shower go on. We both showered when we got back to this room last night, doing our best to wash off whatever dirt, blood and DNA might have been on us after our crime. But another one can't hurt, and I'll be using that same shower again as soon as he is finished with it. For now, I take a few more moments to compose myself, grateful, because my mind is extremely cluttered and chaotic, though our room is not. That's because Freddie is not here. He's in my mum and dad's room, where he spent the evening, and as any parents will know, there is a big difference between waking up with kids around and waking up without them. Instead of having to entertain my son, or tell him to stop doing something he shouldn't be doing, or simply listening to him making a lot of noise, I can use the peace and quiet from his absence to compose my thoughts and get myself ready for what is sure to be a very testing day for everybody.

But then something happens to send me into a spiral.

Seth is still in the shower when I hear a knock at the door. I lie in the bed, frozen in fear. I am afraid the bad day has begun early. Is that the police at the door? Have they found Mateo's body already and realised who the culprits are? Have they come to arrest us and drag us out of this hotel in handcuffs?

I'm going to have to answer the door because I doubt Seth has heard it amid the running water in the bathroom, so I reluctantly lower my legs down until my bare feet are on the carpet. Then I very slowly and very anxiously walk to the hotel room door, wondering if these are the very last steps I'll ever take as a free woman. Once I'm at the door, all that is left to do is open it and face my fate.

'Dad?' I say when I see who it is waiting for me on the other side. It's a huge relief to not see a uniform and handcuffs, though it's still bad news due to the expression on my father's face. He looks tense and tired and, somehow, I have a feeling it's not just because he has had his grandson in his bedroom for the night.

'Have you seen Mateo?' Dad asks me, looking past me into the bedroom, as if he is hoping he might be lurking in here.

'Mateo?' is all I can say in reply.

'Yeah, we're looking for him everywhere, but we can't find him. Have you seen him?'

'No.'

Dad frowns but accepts my answer because why wouldn't he? He's hardly going to suspect me and Seth of having something to do with him going missing.

'Georgia thinks he didn't come back to the room last night,' Dad explains. 'When she woke up this morning, she couldn't see any sign that he had returned. She hoped he might have got up early and was using the gym or pool, or maybe just getting an early breakfast, but she hasn't been able to find him anywhere. So she came and knocked on our door and asked us to help find him. Despite looking everywhere, I can't seem to find him either.'

I heard everything Dad just said, as well as hearing the shower go off in the bathroom. But I don't say anything in response.

'Hello? Did you get that?' Dad asks, waving a hand in front of my face, causing me to snap out of it.

'Erm, yeah. Sorry, just waking up,' I say, realising I can blame my nervousness on the fact the sun has only just come up. 'What time is it?'

'Early, but your sister is really worried now, so we're going to have another look around the hotel for Mateo. Can you and Seth help?'

Joining the hunt for the man we killed? That might just be the most torturous thing my husband and I ever have to do. But what can we say? *No, we're okay, thanks, we'll just chill out in our room while the rest of you worry about where that man might be.*

'Of course,' I say. 'Just give me a few minutes to get dressed and I'll come downstairs. I'll bring Seth too.'

'Thanks,' Dad replies, the tension clear in his hunched shoulders. 'And don't worry about Freddie. He's watching TV with your mother in our room. He slept fine.'

'Thanks,' I say, glad my son is okay, although I knew he would be because my parents always take good care of him.

As Dad leaves to keep searching the hotel for Mateo, I close the door just as Seth walks out of the bathroom with a towel around his waist. But despite the hot shower he just had, he hardly looks refreshed.

'Georgia knows he didn't come back to the room last night,' I tell him. 'She's got my dad looking everywhere for him and he wants us to help look too. I told him we would help because I didn't know what else to do.'

I'm trying not to panic but it's impossible, although Seth seems calmer.

'That's okay,' Seth says, nodding as if he might even mean it. 'We need to act normally, so that would mean we would help your family look for him. We have to do this for Georgia. She's just worried about her boyfriend, and we have to be worried about him too. We can't let anybody know that we know more than they do.'

I know Seth is right. We have to keep up appearances. I'm going to have to be the supportive sister, helping Georgia as she worries why Mateo might not have come back to their room last night.

It's not going to be easy.

But, in my life, what is?

It was me or him. One of us had to go.

Mateo came out on the losing side.

But there's still time for the same thing to happen to me.

FORTY-FOUR

Just hold yourself together, Corinne. You have to. If not for you, do it for your son.

Through a large glass window, I'm watching Freddie playing a game of chase with my husband, the pair of them running around on the sun-drenched hotel patio outside. I'm aware that their game is not going to help my sister locate her missing boyfriend, but it doesn't matter about that because there are people here who are much more adept at searching, so I look away from my family and back to them.

They are sitting opposite me on one of the sofas inside this grand reception area, and their appearance here is turning more than a few heads. Hotel guests are gawking and gossiping about what might be happening, casting curious glances towards us before reluctantly being on their way because they can't just walk over and ask us outright what the problem seems to be. They'll have to make do with hearing about it on the news shortly. I'm sure when they do, they'll be quick to tell their friends that they were staying at the same hotel where a man went missing and the police were called. It'll be exciting to them. Less so for me. That's because it's never as fun when you're at the centre of the news story.

'You say you fell asleep while your boyfriend was out of the room?' The first of two police officers who arrived here twenty minutes ago says to my sister, who is seated beside me. The second officer who accompanied him is out now taking a walk around the hotel grounds, which makes me extremely anxious, not that I can afford to show it. Our parents are on the sofa to our left and we are all gathered here because Georgia insisted on calling the police after another fruitless hour in her search for Mateo.

'Yes, I've already told you this,' Georgia says, both her tone of voice and body language tense. 'I'd drunk quite a lot of champagne yesterday, so I fell asleep without intending to as soon as I got back to the room. I presumed Mateo would return to the room sometime after a couple more drinks in the bar and that I would wake up next to him this morning. But that didn't happen. He never came back.'

'You're absolutely sure he never returned to your room last night?' the officer asks again.

'Yes, she's sure. She wouldn't be so worried if he had,' my father laments then, defending his daughter from the questions from the policeman who is clearly not at the stage of taking this too seriously yet. It's clear from my parents' pained expressions that they are just as worried as Georgia is and that is why they are putting pressure on the police for them to find where Mateo could be.

'He may have simply left the hotel last night,' the officer says next, not sounding nearly as concerned. 'Did the two of you have a disagreement at all?'

'No, we did not!' Georgia cries, snapping back at the man in uniform. 'Everything was fine between us. More than fine. We've just moved in together and we were having a great weekend, weren't we?'

Georgia looks to me then to back up her story, and as I feel the police officer's eyes turn on me, I realise I'm not just going to be able to sit here and ride out this awkward situation in silence.

'Erm, yeah. You two seemed very happy,' I reply, which is the best I've got under the circumstances.

'Seemed?' the police officer says, picking up on that one word I used. 'Why would you say that? Was there something to make you think all might not be well?'

The officer stares at me and I feel like he already knows my secret and is just toying with me. But he can't do. No one but Seth knows it. Not yet, anyway.

'No, that's not what I meant,' I try again. 'They were happy yesterday evening. They are happy. It's very strange that Mateo is not here, but hopefully he did just leave the hotel like you suggested. He might have a good reason for it.'

'Like what?' the officer asks, and now I'm wondering why I'm the one being asked so many questions when it was my sister who called him in the first place.

'I don't know. Maybe he's planning a surprise or something,' I say, which is a lame attempt at giving Mateo an excuse to have abandoned us all, but I had to say something.

'Was he known for surprises?' comes the next question, though that is more to all of us rather than just directed at me.

'Well, he did pay for this whole weekend,' Mum replies, gesturing around at the hotel we sit inside of. 'That was certainly a surprise to us.'

'Really? That can't have been cheap,' the officer muses.

'He's very generous,' Georgia adds. 'And very kind, which means there is no way he would have just left here without telling me that he was going somewhere. He loves me. He cares about me. He wouldn't just abandon me, so that's why I think something bad must have happened to him.'

The officer thinks on that as I do my best not to squirm in my seat.

'My colleague is conducting a search of the hotel grounds, just in case we find anything of interest,' he says. 'I'll go and join him in a moment, and then we'll come back and let you know if we have found anything. If not, due to the fact Mateo is a grown man and may have willingly left here of his own accord, this won't become a missing person's case for several days yet. I'm sure he'll have turned up well before then.'

'He didn't leave here of his own accord!' Georgia cries. 'I've had the hotel staff check the CCTV footage and there's no sign of him leaving via the car park or going out of the main exit gate at the bottom of the track. The last footage is of him walking through reception just before ten o'clock last night. But he didn't leave through the gates in a car or on foot, so he must still be on the grounds somewhere!'

'Georgia, try and stay calm,' Dad says as he reaches out and puts a reassuring hand on her shoulder, trying to keep her relaxed in the presence of the police. I realise it would look good if I did something similar. I take Georgia's left hand and give it a squeeze before telling her quietly that everything is going to be okay. Then I look at the policeman to see if he is buying my show of sisterly support.

'I understand your concern,' the officer says with a sigh. 'If you could excuse me for a little while, I'll go and find my colleague.'

With that, the officer stands and leaves and as I watch him go to find his fellow man in uniform, I think about how there are now two policemen searching for Mateo instead of just one. That means the odds of finding him have just doubled. I watch the officer pass Seth out on the patio, and I see my husband pause from playing with Freddie to watch him go by as well. He's probably thinking the same thing as I am.

They're going to find something.

When they do, this will get even more real.

For now, all we can do is act as clueless as everybody else. I sit and listen to my parents tell Georgia that everything is going to be all right, while I spot several hotel employees talking urgently over behind the reception desk. They are probably worried about any negative publicity that might stem from this, which is a legitimate concern for them, but I wish that was all I had to worry about.

Eventually, I can't take seeing Georgia's tears any longer and excuse myself to get some fresh air, joining Seth and Freddie on the patio. As the mid-morning sun bears down on me, I approach my husband and lower my voice.

'Do you think we should leave before they find anything?' I ask him as I look out and see the two officers wandering towards the bridge where Mateo was stabbed to death several hours earlier. 'We could tell my family that we need to get Freddie home and then we could go. I can't stay here. It's too hard.'

'No, we have to stay,' Seth tells me as Freddie runs past us, excitedly chasing his own shadow. 'We have to support your sister. Leaving might only make us seem suspicious and draw unnecessary attention.'

That sounds right and the sensible thing to do, but it's certainly not as easy to do as getting in the car and driving away from here. I'd love to be on the way home now, and while I would still worry incessantly when we got there, it would be nice to put some distance between ourselves and the scene of the crime. As it is, we have to stay and when Seth suggests we go back inside the hotel and rejoin my family, I ultimately have to go along with it.

We sit with my parents and Georgia for half an hour, waiting for the police officers to come back, and when we finally see them approaching, I hope they are about to tell us that they didn't discover anything of note, so they will return to the police station now and be in touch should anything come up in the next few days. After that, I guess we could all go home.

But that's not what happens.

As both officers reach the sofas where we sit, I can tell from the pensive expressions on their faces that it's not going to be the better news that I was hoping for.

'We've just requested that a couple of our colleagues join us,' the first officer says while the second officer looks at my emotional sister.

'Why?' Georgia asks in between sobs.

'We've found something.'

FORTY-FIVE

'Do you recognise this item as belonging to your boyfriend?' a police officer asks my sister as we all stand behind her, looking on at the discovery on the ground.

'Yes,' Georgia says, nodding solemnly. 'What does it mean?'

'We're not sure. It could just be that he dropped it by accident or maybe he left it here on purpose. We'll have to take a look at it and see if there is anything on there that might help us determine where he might be now.'

'Why would he leave it here on purpose?' Georgia cries as she watches a police officer wearing a glove pick up Mateo's mobile phone from the woodland floor and drop it into an evidence bag. 'He wouldn't do that. It makes no sense. And he wouldn't have accidentally dropped it either because why would he be wandering around out here in the woods? Somebody must have attacked him!'

As Georgia lets her deepest worries be known, I watch the phone being carried away, while Seth does the same thing. Then, once it's out of sight, I look around at all the tall trees that surround us down here on the outskirts of the hotel grounds and think about how the police found that phone a lot quicker than we thought they would.

I knew we should have hidden it better.

That's what I want to say to my husband, a sort of 'I told you so', albeit one laced with far more danger and consequence than the typical exchange between a married couple. But I can't say it, not in the company of the police or anybody else, for that matter, so I'll have to save that particular comment for when we get home. Until then, I have to continue to stand with my family members and try to stay calm. It's getting harder by the second and even more so now that Freddie is becoming aware that something is wrong here.

It was easy at first to keep him occupied with a little play-time, but the longer this goes on and the more police arrive here, not to mention the more Georgia starts to panic, the harder it is to protect my son from worrying himself. He knows Mateo is missing even though he was locked away in my parents' hotel room all night, because my sister asked him if he had seen him this morning. Then he himself asked why the police were here, but apart from that, he doesn't really understand why it might be a serious problem. He's four, so he doesn't appreciate why an adult suddenly vanishing in the night could be cause for concern, at least not unless it involved one of his parents. I know if I vanished, then Freddie would be bawling his eyes out because he's used to seeing me every day, but Mateo? He can handle not seeing him for a little while. But my sister can't, and it seems the police can't either because now they have found his phone lying on the ground, they are taking this a lot more seriously.

'It will take some time to check the phone, so I suggest you all go home and we will be in touch if we have any news,' another officer says to us all then, which is met with instant objection from my sister.

'I'm not going home until I know what has happened to

him!' Georgia cries. While I understand her angst, I can see Freddie getting scared now as he witnesses his auntie having a meltdown.

'We might have to take Freddie home,' I whisper to my parents. 'I don't want him getting scared.'

'That's a good idea,' Mum replies, much to my relief because it seems I have just got our pass out of here. Of course, I want to protect my son by removing him from this scene of so many police officers and my distressed sibling, but I also want to leave for my own wellbeing too. This time, Seth doesn't object to the idea of getting in our car and getting away from the hotel, so we prepare to leave.

'I'll go and get the bags,' he says, heading back to the hotel, while I approach my sister to give her a hug.

'Everything is going to be okay,' I say, wishing I could mean it, for all our sakes.

'Will it?' Georgia replies meekly, feeling much weaker than the last time I hugged her, so I guess the discovery of the phone has a grave impact on her. It would do the same to me if Seth was missing and the police found his mobile lying in the woods. I'd fear that he had been attacked and was now dead, so it's understandable that Georgia is so concerned. The problem is, the thing she is fearing has actually already happened. Mateo was attacked and he is dead. The only thing she doesn't know yet is that the person hugging her was there when it happened.

'Come on, let's go,' I say to Freddie after he has given my parents and sister a hug. He reluctantly follows me back to the hotel, holding my hand while looking around at the police officers he sees in various parts of the grounds.

I decide to wait by the car for Seth and, thankfully, it doesn't take him long to pack our things back into their cases and check out of the hotel before joining us by his vehicle.

As he throws the bags in the back of the car, I get myself and Freddie seated inside and it's a relief when Seth gets behind the wheel and starts the engine. It's even more of a relief when he drives us away and I see the hotel shrinking in size in the rear-view mirror.

'Will everything be okay?' Freddie asks innocently from the back seat.

I turn back to look at my precious boy, who in turn is looking at me for some words of comfort.

'Yes, everything will be fine,' I reply because what else am I supposed to say to him? I can't tell him that his parents are currently petrified about being arrested and charged with Mateo's murder, so I have to pretend like everything is okay. Fortunately, he's so young that he still believes every word that comes from his mother's mouth, so he falls quiet and stares out of the window as we reach the main road. He'll be happy enough watching the world go by until we get home, though there will be no such peace on this journey for the two adults in the front of the car.

'How are you doing?' I ask Seth quietly as he focuses on driving, but I already know the answer to that question based on how tightly he appears to be squeezing the steering wheel.

'I'm good,' he replies, keeping his eyes on the road as if driving perfectly can make up for what he did wrong last night. 'You?'

I decide not to answer that one. If I can't be honest then it's better to just stay quiet rather than lie again.

I decide to copy what my son is doing and stare out of the window, hoping to find some comfort in all the countryside that is whizzing past on the other side of it. But there is no comfort for me there either. Despite looking at the tranquillity of nature, I am fretting about the potential of modern technology revealing what happened last night. Now I wish we had just called the police, as soon as Mateo had died, and explained to them that he had attacked me, that Seth had stepped in to save me. Maybe they would have accepted that and we could be free of all this worry. But it's far too late for that now.

The police have Mateo's phone, which means they will soon be checking his messages. That means my freedom rests entirely on the answer to a couple of questions.

Did I delete every single message on there between Mateo and me?

Or did I accidentally miss one?

FORTY-SIX

What does it feel like waiting for the police to knock down your door and rush into your home to arrest you? I've felt better, that's for sure. Although at least I don't have to go to work while I feel like this. That's because I've requested a few days off so I can be available to support my sister as she continues to worry about Mateo's whereabouts. Not having to be in the office means I can worry about my freedom in a more private environment.

'Can I get you another drink? Or something to eat?' I ask Georgia as I continue to worry about her health and general state of mind. She's currently in my house after telling me that she needed a break from staring at the walls of her home and wondering if Mateo would ever appear. It's been two days since we all left the hotel and, in that time, there has been no news beyond the phone being found. That means it's three days since I have slept properly, but I'm not the only one, so it's easier to hide my exhaustion when everyone else is in the same boat. Seth's not sleeping, Georgia isn't, nor are my parents. Everyone has worries of their own, but as yet, nothing has happened to alleviate any of them.

My sister has failed to answer my question about any food or drink, so I decide to answer it for her.

'I'll make you a cup of coffee,' I say as I go to leave my lounge where we are currently holed up, before Georgia suddenly speaks.

'Do you have any wine in the house?' she asks me, indicating that she wants something stronger than caffeine.

'Is that a good idea?' I reply, hinting that it is not, and we should all stick to something that keeps us sober.

'Probably not, but I'm going mad here and coffee isn't cutting it anymore,' Georgia tells me, rubbing one of her bleary eyes. 'So if you have some wine, please pour me a glass and bring the bottle in because I'm going to need more.'

I could argue with my sister that getting drunk won't help her mood, or simply lie and say that I don't have any wine in the house. But I feel so bad for her, so guilty that mine and Seth's actions have put her in this holding pattern of hell, that I just stay quiet and go to fetch the bottle I know is chilling in the fridge.

While I've been impressed at how long my sister has resisted drowning her fears with alcohol, I am just as impressed that Seth and I have done the same. That's because, after getting home from the hotel the other day and putting the TV on for Freddie in the playroom, the pair of us had a serious conversation in the kitchen about how we had to proceed over these coming days.

'We can't do anything that seems out of character or anything that might make us more likely to have a mental breakdown and confess,' Seth had told me. 'We're going to be anxious and sleep-deprived anyway, so alcohol will only make things worse. I know the easy thing to do would be to try and drink to forget, but we can't do that. We have to appear worried for Georgia, but nothing more. Understand?'

I had agreed and, so far, Seth and I had not drunk a drop of anything but water or coffee since, ensuring our minds were anxiety-ridden but clear beyond that. But now Georgia wants some wine and as I'm holding the bottle in my hands, it's very tempting to just give in and have one glass, just to try and take the edge off things. I won't get drunk, but I think one glass would help. It might give me a minor mood boost and I sure could use that. Besides, Seth isn't here. He's at work, so he doesn't have to know. With my mind made up, I take two glasses from the cupboard and then rejoin my sister back in the lounge.

'Thank you,' Georgia says after I have poured and handed her a glass. I sip my wine slowly, as if I'm afraid of what it might do to me, whereas Georgia glugs hers and will soon require a refill.

'Maybe he has just left me,' she says then. 'Maybe he got bored of me or realised he was making a mistake. I always worried I was punching above my weight with him. He was so gorgeous and kind and I was afraid it was too good to be true. I guess it was.'

My sister is needing me to tell her that this is not the case, and that Mateo didn't decide to just leave her. But that would then mean I am suggesting something terrible happened to him instead, and is that any better? Which would she prefer? To think that her dream man left her because he was attacked? Or that he left her because he decided he could do better? In my unsure state, I'm unable to determine the answer to that, so I just take another drink and see if the wine makes things any clearer.

Five minutes later and one glass down, the answer is no, it does not.

Inevitably, Georgia picks up the bottle and pours us both another drink and as the alcohol keeps working overtime to calm our biggest fears, she speaks again.

'He better pray he was actually attacked,' she says, almost

laughing. 'Because if he has just decided to leave me, he's going to be a lot worse off when I get my hands on him.'

I know my sister is only trying to make herself feel better by making a joke, but unsurprisingly, it doesn't work, and as her attempt at humour falls flat, she starts to cry again. As she weeps harder than I have seen her do at any point over these past few days, I get confirmation that the wine was a terrible idea, although it's far too late for that. I'm about to put my glass down and try to comfort her when I hear a knock at the door.

'It's probably Mum and Dad,' I say as I get up to answer it, leaving Georgia on the sofa with a tissue. Although I expect she's more likely to comfort herself with her wine glass than anything else.

I take a deep breath as I approach the door, preparing myself for another difficult conversation with my parents as I sadly let them know that Georgia is still in a bad way and there is still no more news from the police. Then I open the door and realise I'm going to be having a very different conversation than expected.

'Hi, Corinne Adams?' a man in a brown suit asks me.

I nod my head while wishing I could shake it.

'May we come inside?' comes the next question.

Now I furrow my brow before I look past him and see another man in a suit, albeit a younger guy who looks far less assured than his colleague.

'Sorry, who are you?' I ask, aware that they obviously already know who I am because they just said my name.

'I'm Detective Aspinall and this is my partner, Detective Burns,' Aspinall replies. 'We just have a few questions for you.'

Questions for me? That can't be good.

I immediately go to reach out for the side of the doorframe so I can support myself because I suddenly feel very weak. Then I realise I can't grab it because I'm still holding my glass of wine. I thought I'd put it down just before I came to answer the door, but I realise that I didn't, and I worry about how the sight of it might give these detectives a very bad impression. If they have come here to accuse me of having something to do with Matteo's disappearance, how does it look that I seem to be enjoying a tipple? A woman with wine hardly looks worried. I knew it was a mistake to open that damn bottle. But it's too late now, just like it's too late to stop these men coming into my house.

There is nothing else I can think of to say except, 'Sure. Come in.'

I allow them inside my home while resisting the urge to run out of my open door, choosing instead to close it because I know I wouldn't get far if I did run. Then I show the detectives into the lounge, where they find Georgia sitting on the sofa.

'What is it? What's happened?' she cries as she stops wiping her eyes with the tissue I gave her and looks to the two men with hope.

'You must be Georgia,' Aspinall says sadly. 'I'm afraid we haven't found him yet.'

'Then why are you here? Have you been trying to find me? I haven't had any missed calls,' Georgia says before checking her phone just to make sure she is correct.

'We're here to speak to your sister,' Aspinall replies before turning to me.

'Corinne? Why?' Georgia cries, and that is indeed a very good question.

'We found something of interest on Mateo's phone,' Detective Burns says, and now I'm wishing he had just stayed mute because it sounds like one of my worst nightmares has just come true. My biggest fear is that the police find Mateo's body. But my next biggest is that they find a message on his phone from me that makes it obvious there was a problem between the two of us.

'It appears that Mateo was messaging somebody he owed

money to,' Aspinall explains as my heart thunders inside my fluttering chest. 'There are several messages back and forth in which a debt is discussed, as well as a timeline for that debt to be paid.'

'What?' Georgia cries, confused. 'That doesn't make any sense. Mateo didn't owe anybody any money.'

'It's possible that he kept it quiet from you,' Burns says in a slightly condescending way, as if to suggest a secret between a boyfriend and girlfriend requires no great stretch of the imagination.

'The texts were dated as recently as last week,' Aspinall goes on as my sister and I listen with bated breath. 'It's not clear from the message if Mateo paid his debt or not, so it's possible that his disappearance is connected to the person he owed money to.'

'Can you find this person?' Georgia asks next. 'If they've hurt Mateo then you have to find them.'

'We're looking into it,' Aspinall replies. 'And we are looking into the possibility that this person has contributed to Mateo's disappearance. But without any evidence so far, it's impossible to know for sure.'

I am still holding the glass of wine, unable or unwilling to put it down now, and I almost wish I could steal a sneaky sip of it because my nerves are really jangling. That's because the detectives haven't got to the real reason they are here yet. Then my sister goes and reminds them of that.

'I don't understand something,' Georgia says. 'You said that you were here to speak to my sister. Why would you need to tell her this? Why wouldn't you just tell me?'

The whole world seems to stop spinning as I wait to hear the answer to that.

'It's because we're not here to discuss Mateo's debt and the person he owed money to,' Aspinall replies as he and his colleague turn away from Georgia and look at me. 'Rather, we're here to discuss why Corinne paid Mateo twenty thousand pounds shortly before he disappeared.'

That's when it feels like my heart sinks into my stomach and the world is suddenly deprived of all oxygen.

I'm in the crosshairs of the police.

The question is – can I get out of them?

FORTY-SEVEN

A good question demands a good answer and that's what I better give now or I'm going to be suspect number one in Mateo's disappearance. Judging by the way the two detectives are glaring at me, I might already be at the top of that particular list.

However, I wasn't previously appearing anywhere on my sister's list of suspects, which is why she is staring at me in horror, waiting to hear what I have to say for myself. I'm taking my time to respond, not because I don't know how to but because I have to be very careful how I do it.

It's no good just to tell them my story.

I have to make them believe it.

'What are you talking about?' Georgia asks the detectives. 'Corinne didn't give Mateo twenty thousand pounds. That's ridiculous, isn't it, sis?'

I take a deep breath.

'Sis?' Georgia says again.

Then I start talking, hoping the wine doesn't make me forget what I have carefully been rehearsing in front of the mirror before bed the past few nights.

'Mateo came to me and my husband, Seth, and told us that he was having trouble paying back some money he owed,' I begin carefully. 'He wondered if we might be able to help him.'

'What?' Georgia cries, but I push on while I still have the nerve to lie to two detectives.

'He said he didn't want to ask you or our parents because he was embarrassed,' I say, looking at my sister. 'He didn't want to do anything that might give a bad impression. That's why he came to us. I guess he thought there was slightly less shame asking Seth and me.'

'Did he tell you why he owed this money or who he owed it to?' Aspinall asks me, but I shake my head.

'No, Seth did ask Mateo but he just said it was better if we didn't know the details. He said it was safer that way.'

'So what happened? You just handed over a spare twenty thousand pounds that you had lying around?' Detective Burns asks me, scepticism seeping through his sentence. 'As easy as that?'

'No, it wasn't as easy as that,' I snap back, not appreciating the detective's tone, but I have to remember it is his job to question things and never just take everything at face value. He's a trained professional, so I better be just as professional in dealing with him, which means getting frustrated isn't in my best interests.

I take another deep breath.

'I had enough in my savings, but I obviously wouldn't have just given him the money unless I felt it was going to help him,' I say. 'And I wanted to help him because I could see how much my sister liked him. I didn't want anything bad to happen to him because if it did, it would impact my sister too.'

'So you sent him the money and kept it quiet from the rest of your family?' Aspinall asks, and I nod my head.

'I can't believe you didn't tell me about this!' Georgia cries. 'Why would you keep this from me?'

'Like I said, Mateo was embarrassed about it,' I reply. 'I guess he was worried you might leave him if you found out he was the kind of guy who got into debt with bad people.'

'It might make sense that you didn't tell your family members about this at the time,' Burns says then. 'But it doesn't make sense that you would keep this from them or, more importantly, from us when Mateo went missing. So why have you done that? Why did you not tell anyone about this money, when it could be connected to his disappearance?'

'I should have done,' I admit, shaking my head. 'And I was going to if this went on any longer. It's just that Mateo swore me to secrecy about the money. He really didn't want anybody else to know about it. He was so ashamed.'

Will the detectives buy that?

'You don't see how his disappearance could be connected to this money?' Aspinall asks me, which is a worry because it has been his partner who seems to mistrust me more so far. 'You should have told us about this instantly.'

'I know that now and I'm really sorry,' I say. 'But I was also scared.'

'Scared?' Georgia asks. 'Of what?'

'I figured the people Mateo owed money to were bad people,' I admit. 'Then, when he went missing, I was terrified that something might happen to me or Seth if we were linked to it. I've been so afraid of telling you in case those people try and hurt us. We have a young son to look after, so I can't risk anything happening to us.'

I hate having to use my son to add credibility to my lie, but every card has to be played here if I am to win this awful game.

'You should never have got involved in this,' Georgia tells me then, understanding my concern. 'I can see why you wanted to help him, but you didn't have to do it for me. You should have said no. He could have got the money from somewhere else.'

'I'm not sure he could have,' I say sadly before forcing a

frown onto my face and looking at the detectives. 'Wait, I don't understand. If I gave Mateo the money to pay his debt, why would he go missing? If he paid it off then he would be okay, wouldn't he?'

Aspinall and Burns share a look as if they are deciding whether or not to share some extra information they may have.

'What is it? What else do you know?' Georgia asks. 'You have to tell us, please.'

'There is something,' Aspinall admits with a sigh. 'According to Mateo's bank accounts, he only withdrew ten thousand of the twenty thousand pounds you gave him.'

'What does that mean?' I ask, still perfecting my confused frown.

'Well, if he told you he owed twenty thousand but only withdrew half of that amount, it would appear that he only paid half of his debt,' Aspinall suggests. 'Which might explain why he has gone missing now. If he still owed somebody ten thousand pounds, that person might have had enough of waiting for it and taken action, especially when they realised he could afford to stay at a luxury hotel at the weekend.'

'Why wouldn't he pay it all if you had given him the money?' Georgia asks me, as if I could answer that.

'I don't know,' I reply, shaking my head. 'He assured me his debt was for twenty thousand pounds, and I obviously wouldn't have given him the money if he wasn't actually going to use it on clearing that debt.'

'Did you not think it was suspicious that he was lavishing your family with gifts shortly before he went missing?' Detective Burns asks me. 'Didn't you wonder if he might have been using the money you gave him to wine and dine your little sister, as well as everyone else in your family, including yourself?'

Burns really is testing me, I realise. But I cannot afford to crack, so I go on the offensive.

'No, I had no idea what he was doing with the money. I

thought he had paid the debt and that was it. I certainly didn't think he was using the money to fund the hotel stay. Why would I? Mateo promised us that he would repay what we had given him. I presumed the hotel stay was a gesture from him to say thank you for helping him. It was obviously disguised as a family getaway, but Seth and I knew he had invited us because we had saved him. I didn't think anything else was going on.'

I'm extremely cautious because I know that giving Mateo such a substantial amount of money could give me a motive to hurt him if, for example, I felt he was frittering the money on something other than the debt. But without concrete evidence of that, I should be okay. Right?

'We'll need you to come and make a formal statement about this at the station,' Aspinall tells me. 'And we may have a few more questions for you at a later date.'

'Of course,' I say, having already figured that, which means I am prepared for it.

'We'll also need to speak to your husband,' Burn adds. 'To corroborate his story with yours.'

'Sure,' I reply, aware that the next few days are going to be absolutely critical for the pair of us.

'You need to find this person who Mateo owed money to,' Georgia cries then. 'They must have hurt him, so you have to find them. Stop wasting time on my sister and her husband and go and find them!'

I appreciate Georgia deflecting the blame for this away from the two people who actually caused Mateo to go missing, even though she doesn't realise she is doing that. But as the detectives leave my house, I know this isn't over yet.

Seth and I will have to hold our nerve for a little longer.

If we can do that, everything might just be okay.

But if not, everything will be over.

EPILOGUE

I've often wondered what the food tasted like in prison.

I can't imagine that it would be nice or leave me wanting more. I expect I'd go back to my cell hungry and disappointed but accepting that by losing my freedom, I also have to lose the ability to eat delicious meals. Fortunately, the meal I am eating right now in this restaurant is the exact opposite of that.

'This is so good,' Seth says as he takes a bite out of his salmon.

I am in agreement as I do the same with mine. This fish is perfectly cooked, and the salad and roast potatoes that accompany it only make the meal even better.

This food is so tasty that I wish Freddie was here to taste it too, although it might go underappreciated by him, which is why he is staying at my parents' house tonight. He's having a sleepover there, which means a child-free evening for Seth and me. We intend to enjoy it, especially after what the pair of us have been through recently.

We're not just here to sample good food though. We're here to celebrate, which is why we both raise our champagne glasses and clink them together before drinking.

'To plans,' Seth says after he has drunk. 'May they always work out as well as this one did.'

I would smile at those words if it wasn't for the circumstances. My sister has had to endure a difficult time, and I wish that hadn't been so. But she is strong and she is getting stronger every day, so I have no doubt she will eventually get over what happened and move on with her life. I regret that someone had to lose their life in all this, especially someone my sister cared about, but Mateo instigated it and if he was still alive, it might mean that I was dead now.

If I could smile, I would, because my husband was certainly right.

Our plan did work out.

It worked out to perfection.

As we continue to salivate over the sumptuous salmon, I think about how that plan began when I took Mateo's phone from his pocket while he lay dead on the deck of the bridge. Using his facial ID to unlock his device, I was able to delete all the messages on there between the two of us. I was sure to leave the messages between him and the person he owed money to, because I knew they would be convenient for the police to see when the phone was eventually discovered, as it would help establish a possible motive for Mateo suddenly vanishing.

After that was done, we buried the phone in the woods near to the hotel, hoping that it would never be found. The phone being buried a good distance from where its owner had died, in the vast grounds of the hotel, reduced the chances of them searching for Mateo back at the river. However, something we definitely didn't want anybody to find was the knife that Mateo was stabbed with, so Seth washed that knife in the river, removing Mateo's blood from it, before we threw it into the water and watched it wash away. I'm guessing it won't be found at all.

It's not the only thing that hasn't been found.

Once we have finished our food, and the bottle of champagne has been finished, Seth and I get up and decide to go for a short walk. It will help to burn off a few of the countless calories we have just consumed, but the light exercise will also serve another purpose. An important one. One that is the main reason we are here this evening.

As the two of us step outside into the fresh air, it's nice to see the sunset just beyond the tops of the trees that surround us. It feels good to be outside, walking away, free to do as we please. It feels even better when we both know we could have easily lost the right to do this if things had gone differently with those detectives.

Though I went to the police station and was formally interviewed about the money I sent to Mateo, as well as repeating my reasons for not mentioning it earlier when he went missing, I was not charged on suspicion of anything. Neither was Seth after he had attended the station to talk about the same thing. The detective bought our stories, and while it was nerve-wracking at the time, in hindsight, why wouldn't they? We're just a normal married couple with a child who have never been in trouble with the law before, so what could we have done to be involved in someone's disappearance? It's far more plausible, at least from the police's perspective, that the shady person who Mateo owed money to decided to take revenge on him over any unpaid funds.

I keep walking, hand in hand with my husband, until the two of us stop at a place that has become very familiar. A place neither one of us is ever likely to forget about for as long as both shall live. It's the bridge upon which Mateo and I fought for control of the knife before Seth stepped in and stabbed him right in front of me.

We're back here again, after finishing our meal in the hotel restaurant, and we are here because we are making sure our secret is still very much contained. From our current vantage point on the bridge, it appears like it is because we see no blood and no body.

When Seth stabbed Mateo, I didn't see much blood at the time; it was dark, his clothing must have obscured and collected most of it. As for the body, it was heading away from here as soon as it went into the river and the current took over, taking it away far more effortlessly than we could have done.

'It's weird to be back here,' Seth says, and I nod as we both listen to the sound of the water running beneath our feet.

Mateo is still classed as missing, but how determined the police are to find a man who was obviously involved with some nefarious people is a matter for debate. Even Georgia has accepted that Mateo must not have been honest with her and was therefore merely presenting a character he wanted her to like when he was around her. My sister, as well as my parents, accept that while it seemed Mateo was perfect when he was wining and dining us all here not so long ago, he was clearly not really like that and it has brought everything he ever said or did into question. It makes it easier for them to move on without him. As for me, I guess I'll never really move on from what happened with Mateo, simply because of what my husband had to do to get rid of him for me.

'We shouldn't come back here again,' I say to Seth as we both lean on the edge of the bridge. 'It was good to do this once, just to check. But let's not return again. We need to focus on the future. On Freddie. On ourselves. We can't keep living in the past. I've spent long enough doing that to know it never leads to a good place.'

'Okay,' Seth replies, putting an arm around me. 'That sounds good to me.'

The two of us stand there for a few more moments before we decide we've had enough and walk away, leaving the bridge behind. We leave the river that runs underneath it behind too. In doing so, we also leave behind the memory of the body that fell from this bridge into the water and washed away downriver, evading the police search. It means what happened to that man shall remain an unsolved mystery, at least to everyone but my husband and me.

Mateo brought me to this hotel to torment me.

Now I'm leaving him here.

Forever.

A LETTER FROM DANIEL

Dear reader,

I want to say a huge thank you for choosing to read *The Ex Who Came Back*. If you did enjoy it and would like to keep up to date with all my latest Bookouture releases, please sign up at the following link. Your email address will never be shared and you can unsubscribe at any time.

www.bookouture.com/daniel-hurst

I hope you loved *The Ex Who Came Back*, and if you did, I would be very grateful if you could write an honest review. I'd love to hear what you think!

You can read my free short story, 'The Killer Wife', by signing up to my Bookouture mailing list.

You can also visit my website, where you can download a free psychological thriller called *Just One Second* and join my personal weekly newsletter, where you can hear all about my future writing as well as my adventures with my wife, Harriet, and daughter, Penny!

Thank you,

Daniel

KEEP IN TOUCH WITH DANIEL

Get in touch with me directly at my email address
daniel@danielhurstbooks.com. I reply to every message!

www.danielhurstbooks.com

facebook.com/danielhurstbooks

instagram.com/danielhurstbooks

PUBLISHING TEAM

Turning a manuscript into a book requires the efforts of many people. The publishing team at Bookouture would like to acknowledge everyone who contributed to this publication.

Audio
Alba Proko
Sinead O'Connor
Melissa Tran

Commercial
Lauren Morrissette
Hannah Richmond
Imogen Allport

Cover design
Lisa Horton

Data and analysis
Mark Alder
Mohamed Bussuri

Editorial
Natasha Harding
Charlotte Hegley

RAISING READERS
Books Build Bright Futures

Dear Reader,

We'd love your attention for one more page to tell you about the crisis in children's reading, and what we can all do.

Studies have shown that reading for fun is the **single biggest predictor of a child's future life chances** – more than family circumstance, parents' educational background or income. It improves academic results, mental health, wealth, communication skills, ambition and happiness.

The number of children reading for fun is in rapid decline. Young people have a lot of competition for their time, and a worryingly high number do not have a single book at home.

Hachette works extensively with schools, libraries and literacy charities, but here are some ways we can all raise more readers:

- Reading to children for just 10 minutes a day makes a difference
- Don't give up if children aren't regular readers – there will be books for them!

- Visit bookshops and libraries to get recommendations
- Encourage them to listen to audiobooks
- Support school libraries
- Give books as gifts

There's a lot more information about how to encourage children to read on our websites: **www.RaisingReaders.co.uk** and **www.JoinRaisingReaders.com**.

Thank you for reading.

hachette
UK

Printed in Dunstable, United Kingdom